FRIGID

IT WAS A THIRTEEN YEAR WAIT.

The original version of *The Girl Who Kept Winter*, titled *Tuyet Den* in Vietnamese, was published in Vietnam in 2007. Its sequel *Frigid,* originally titled *Liet Than*, was not published until 2020. That makes it the only series in Vietnamese literature in which the timeline in real life is longer than that of the novel.

I could not be more appreciative that after thirteen long years, the love and support for the book is still going strong, and it has given me the motivation to continue writing.

I want to dedicate *Liet Than* to the first generation of *Tuyet Den* readers, who had to wait thirteen years for the sequel.

I also want to thank the team below, who didn't make
The Girl Who Kept Winter readers wait as long:

TRANSLATORS:

Cam

Chu Manh Toan

Lai Ngan Tam

Phan Tu Tuan Cuong

Nguyen P Ngoc Ha

Tran Thanh Thien An

Linh Nguyen

Huong Chau

ILLUSTRATOR:

Niayu

And most importantly, our kick-ass editor:

Ashley Sowers

FRIGID

GIAO CHI

Copyright © 2021 Giao Chi
All Rights Reserved
ISBN-13: 978-1-7359642-2-5

TABLE OF CONTENTS

Chapter 1: A Disastrous Beauty :........................1
Chapter 2: Unmatched Strength:.......................17
Chapter 3: Lingering Memories: 37
Chapter 4: The Gentle Man: 53
Chapter 5: Newcomers:..............................73
Chapter 6: The People at Your Side: 89
Chapter 7: The Eyes Looked, but the Heart Saw:.......105
Chapter 8: A Desperate Desire: 121
Chapter 9: For the One He Loves:....................135
Chapter 10: Precious Little Brother: 151
Chapter 11: A Fragment of the Sunlight Pearl: 169
Chapter 12: Years of Longing: 183
Chapter 13: A Rock and a Hard Place:................ 195
Chapter 14: A Single Move :........................211
Chapter 15: Diabolical: 227
Chapter 16: Liet Than: 241
Chapter 17: Sunlight Strike: 267
Chapter 18: Dancing Snowflakes: 285

CHAPTER 1

A Disastrous Beauty

The long-awaited wedding of the town magistrate's dear son had become a massacre.

The reception was going to be extravagant: the tables were laden with delicious-looking food, the mouthwatering aroma that filled the air was heavenly, and the wine was exquisite. The guests themselves made a colorful picture in their finery—though it seemed every one of them had come armed to the teeth.

By the time Dong Tu arrived, everyone was dead.

Bodies were piled haphazardly on top of each other. Some had been hacked to pieces. Blood and gore pooled on the floor, sprayed the walls, and spattered the dead's faces, even as it stained their clothing a deep, rusty red. Dong Tu was shocked into a horrified silence.

The situation had escalated.

Could she have caused this slaughter?

It all began ten days before, on a late winter afternoon. The people of Vinh Phuc, young and old, had flocked to the pub. A fire blazed in the hearth at the center of the room, where guests sat warming themselves with strong wine. As they sat talking, exchanging gossip and rumors and spreading news, a stranger stepped through the door with a short burst of cold winter air. The stranger was tall and slim, and their shining black, hip-length hair flowed out from beneath a hat that had a veil that fell in front of their face. It was impossible to discern whether they were a man or a woman from the way they moved.

The stranger seemed to have brought the winter sky inside with them: their luxurious, high-collared robe was the same crisp, cool blue, and as they walked, the white clothes beneath the robe were reminiscent of shifting clouds.

"Could you tell me where I might find a security escort?" they asked.

Everyone in the pub answered at once, all of them directing the stranger to the Luu family's dojo.

"You know, *that* dojo!" one of the townspeople added, and was immediately cowed into silence by the shushes and warning looks thrown their way.

"What dojo?" the stranger asked, peering around the room from beneath the veil. No local person would have asked that question.

In a low voice, one man explained, "The Luu dojo is the most prestigious martial arts school in the district. They teach students, and they offer their services as guards. Their people escort carriages and shipments. They have an honest work ethic and are brave, capable people. Their business has boomed over the last two years, and every shipment they escort arrives safely. Thieves don't dare to come near their carriages, and they've become the largest escort service in the region."

"And?" the stranger pressed, growing impatient.

The man beckoned them closer, then continued in a whisper.

"The eldest daughter of the Luu Family, Luu Dong Tu, is young and beautiful, both inside and out—and she is a very skilled martial artist. The Luu dojo got famous because she had a love affair with a high-ranking member of the Poison Legion, a man called Obsidian, one of the Kings of Poison. He's a cruel man who never hesitates to kill, which is why no one dares to mess with the Luu family. Crossing him means death."

"'Love affair' is an exaggeration," another man argued. "It's been more than two years since Dong Tu came back, and there's still no sign of Obsidian."

"I heard that because of Dong Tu, the King of Poison nearly lost his life many times. Why would he risk death if he hadn't been in love with her?" a woman pointed out.

Another man asked, "If it was such a strong relationship, why did he leave her for two years?"

"What was the relationship between the King of Poison and Dong Tu, then? Is it still going on?" the stranger asked.

Luu Dong Tu was old enough to be married, but no matter how beautiful and talented she was, she was doomed to be single forever because of her association with the Poison Legion. No man would show the slightest interest in her unless he had a death wish. Who would dare to flirt with the lover of the infamous Obsidian?

Most of the people in the pub were already tipsy by the time the stranger pressed for more information, and had gradually moved away from discussing the haphazard story, instead contemplating the marriage possibilities of the local beauties amongst themselves: who was at the age for dating, who was interesting, if there was any chance with them or not.

It seemed their time was up.

The veiled stranger paid for their wine and left.

———

Night was falling as the stranger arrived at the Luu dojo, and there, in addition to the Luu family, they found a tall, handsome young man and seven young women, all of them dressed in spotlessly white clothes.

Mr. Luu introduced them.

"This is Bach Duong, son of the famous General Bach. Today is a blissful day," he said. "So many people have come to visit!"

The stranger in the veiled hat bowed their head slightly in greeting as Bach Duong swept his beautiful eyes over them from head to toe. Dong Tu herself came and served tea, and the stranger took the opportunity to study her closely from behind the veil.

Were the people of Vinh Phuc out of their minds? Compared to the true beauties of the world, Dong Tu was merely mediocre. Sure, she had adorable chubby cheeks, bright eyes, and a pretty mouth, but she was a bit short. Was this small woman really a famous fighter? Was it true that the King of Poison had willingly risked his life for her? There was no way to tell which parts of the story were true and which were embellishments.

The stranger couldn't help but wonder if the reputation of the Luu family's security service had been as inflated as Dong Tu's beauty.

Dong Tu felt the guest's judgmental stare and looked away uncomfortably. But like everyone else, she still took her own measure of the stranger: they were the same height as Bach Duong—who was very tall for a man. Even when sitting, their slim, well-proportioned body seemed to tower over her. Their height and physique seemed to belong to a young man, but the flower brooch, the veiled hat, and the polished fingernails were clearly feminine.

After accepting the tea, the stranger finally removed their hat and placed it on the table. A cold breeze gently lifted their hair as they (needlessly) smoothed it back down, and everyone in the room stopped and studied their face for the first time. The stranger was extremely beautiful, a striking and even blend of masculine and feminine: their phoenix eyes were long and clear, and their nose had an exceptionally high ridge; the dimple between their nose and lip was as clear as a drop of water, and their lips were pouty and visibly soft. Their face was perfectly proportioned and glowing with a touch of soft pink blush and red-stained lips.

Teardrop earrings framed their face, and the stranger looked like they'd been plucked from a dream, stunning in ways that drew the beholder in and left them hypnotized. Looking at them felt like floating on a boat in the middle of an autumn lake, so absorbed that time and place melted away. Anyone, regardless of romantic preferences, would have found an ideal in this androgynous beauty.

The Luu family gasped as the stranger's extraordinary face registered. Bach Duong tilted his head and ran his fingers over his chin, smiling softly with instant infatuation.

Dong Tu surreptitiously clicked her tongue, wondering how to address the stranger.

"My name is Tuyet Hoa Phi Vu." The stranger introduced themselves in a warm, deep voice. The name was both evocative and beautiful: *snowflakes flying in the wind*. It suited them well.

"I heard your dojo provides the best protection in the region. Is it possible to safely escort me to my home, Snowflake Tower in Lac Do, within seven days?"

Tuyet Hoa Phi Vu told the gathered group that they had fled from their home to avoid an arranged marriage, only to discover that in doing so, they had put their entire family in danger. They had decided to return and accept the marriage, but the trip was long, and they were weak, with no martial arts training. They needed an escort to protect them from robbery and rape.

"What a terrible plight, beautiful! How can I help?" Bach Duong cried, and then he kissed her hand.

Dong Tu thought, *The stranger must be female! Bach Duong would never have kissed a man.*

The sudden kiss startled Tuyet Hoa Phi Vu. She pulled her hand back angrily, and as she stared at Bach Duong in offense, her eyes began to tear up.

Dong Tu grabbed Bach Duong's collar and shoved him away, stomping on his feet and glaring at him until he retreated to another seat. Bach Duong had a bad habit of kissing women without their consent. He had been criticized for it many times, but still hadn't learned his lesson.

Tuyet Hoa Phi Vu took a handkerchief with lace-embroidered flowers from her robe and carefully wiped at the spot where Bach Duong had kissed her, still visibly upset that he had dared to touch her. Her offense reminded Dong Tu of those highborn ladies whose virginities were so belligerently guarded, as if Bach Duong had stolen her innocence away with that single kiss.

"Don't worry, Miss Tuyet Hoa," Dong Tu consoled her. "We will escort you home. I will accompany you personally."

Hearing that, Tuyet Hoa Phi Vu looked unpleasantly surprised.

"Miss Tuyet Hoa Phi Vu, please don't worry. Our Dong Tu is truly a skilled fighter. If you feel uneasy, we can arrange two more lead escorts to accompany her," Mr. Luu quickly added.

Mr. Luu saw Tuyet Hoa Phi Vu's look of dissatisfaction and, guessing that it might be because of how little Dong Tu seemed compared to her, he reassured her that while Dong Tu was small, she was so talented no ordinary thugs could surpass her. The trip would not take them through dangerous areas, and Dong Tu would easily keep them safe.

"All right then," Tuyet Hoa Phi Vu accepted with a nod. She was still a little skeptical, but having seen how Dong

Tu handled Bach Duong's impetuous kiss, she was more prepared to let their reassurances put her at ease.

Tuyet Hoa Phi Vu finished her tea, then slowly lowered the cup, pushed her silky hair back behind her like a dark stream, and placed two gold taels on the table. She stood up, her earrings swaying, glanced at Bach Duong—whose eyes followed her with amorous longing—and headed off.

―――

Dong Tu and Tuyet Hoa Phi Vu departed the next day, accompanied by two lead guards and Dong Tu's adopted brother, a young man named Bao Thuong. The route from Vinh Phuc to Lac Do passed through many small districts and villages, residential and commercial areas, with many things to see. The only part of the route that would require caution was a forest known to be a haven for bandits.

The first day of the trip went by without incident.

The biggest danger was that Bao Thuong kept staring at Tuyet Hoa Phi Vu, and picked flowers for her along the way. Dong Tu had to remind him several times to mind his manners. Tuyet Hoa Phi Vu was a client, and if he treated her disrespectfully it could damage the Luus' reputation.

Bao Thuong usually kept his distance from the Luus' clients, but he had never seen such beauty before. Lady Tuyet Hoa stood almost a head taller than he did, but she was as beautiful as a painting, and he had hope. Fortunately she wasn't offended, and sometimes covered her mouth to giggle at his silly behavior.

Dong Tu had been sympathetic to Tuyet Hoa Phi Vu's situation from the moment they met: she too had been robbed of the freedom to choose the man who would share her life. Though she would surely live in wealth, her days would be bland, lifeless, and lonely. She already felt that Tuyet Hoa Phi Vu was a beautiful person with a pleasant personality who did not deserve her fate, and before long, they were as close as sisters.

On the second night, as the travelers were eating dinner, Tuyet Hoa Phi Vu asked her, "Do you have a lover yet?"

It had been a long time since anyone had asked Dong Tu that question. In recent years, her private life had been made so public, she felt everyone in the world knew more about it than she herself. According to the rumors, Dong Tu had a relationship with Obsidian of the Poison Legion, who possessed the fabled Storm Pearl—and his every move was newsworthy. Dong Tu had become famous because of him. She shook her head.

"I've heard the King of Poison has black snow falling all around him because of something called the Storm Pearl," Tuyet Hoa Phi Vu prompted.

Dong Tu nodded, but the challenge for she and Obsidian was not only that black snow fell with his every footstep. There were many other obstacles between Dong Tu and

Obsidian, not the least of which being if they ever met again, they wouldn't even be able to touch one another.

"The whole of Obsidian's body is extremely poisonous," Dong Tu explained. "Anyone who touches him will die sooner or later." No one knew if fate would favor them in this life. Dong Tu hoped to meet him again one day, but it had been more than two years since she'd had any news of him, and her hopes were fading.

"You must move on and find yourself a boyfriend," Tuyet Hoa Phi Vu told her. After all, they hadn't seen each other for more than two years, and they couldn't touch each other even if they did meet.

A bright laugh interrupted them.

"How daring of you! Did you know what you just said could've gotten you killed?"

Dong Tu looked up to see the woman who had been sitting at the table by them for some time. The woman stuffed her mouth with food, chewed, and let her fingers trail over Tuyet Hoa Phi Vu's cheek. Dong Tu didn't recognize the woman's face, but she immediately knew who it was from that movement alone.

It was Switch, the Skinwalker, one of the Monstrous Eighteen. She was known for her ability to steal others' faces and wear them as her own—and she was a friend of Obsidian's.

"You're talking nonsense. If Obsidian had heard what you said, you'd have a hard time staying alive." Switch winked, still stroking Tuyet Hoa Phi Vu's cheek. "My, your face is so beautiful!"

It was often said that beauty is a burden that brings only bad luck, and it was especially true when the person who admired that beauty was none other than the Skinwalker herself. Switch had been born faceless, and had developed a covetous passion for stealing the faces of the most beautiful people she could find.

"What a waste of such a beautiful face. If she's gonna be killed by Obsidian, why not let me have her face first!" Switch said. Suddenly she jumped up and squatted on the table before Tuyet Hoa Phi Vu, her hands clasping that beautiful face.

Bao Thuong and the two Luu guards pulled out their swords while Dong Tu pushed back her chair and stood up.

"Don't move!" she ordered. The two guards and Bao Thuong were no match for Switch. "Switch, please don't. Please." Her voice trembled slightly: Dong Tu knew that she was no match for the mutant, either. She would have to rely on their friendship to make her listen.

"I like this face! What are *you* going to do?" Switch laughed. "Are you going to cry to your lover?"

It had been a long time since Dong Tu had seen her, but Switch hadn't become any easier to deal with.

Bao Thuong and the two escorts prepared to defend Tuyet Hoa Phi Vu, but instead of helping them, Dong Tu pushed all three away with the palm of her hand. Switch was a creature of the Whispered World, and was an exceptionally, inhumanly gifted martial artist. The more people attacked her, the more lives would be lost.

Switch stood, grabbed Tuyet Hoa Phi Vu's shoulders, shrugged, and with a swift wind-walk, the two of them disappeared—leaving only a bright, echoing voice behind.

"Let me try this new face on!"

Dong Tu passed a hand over her face. A client hadn't been kidnapped on her watch for a very long time. Even worse, the kidnapper was *Switch*.

Over the years, Dong Tu had come to understand Switch's habits. To swap faces, she needed a secluded place where she could gather her chi, her inner strength. And in addition to stealing faces, Switch liked stealing entire identities. She would want to have a drink and chat with Tuyet Hoa Phi Vu for a while before swapping their faces.

Dong Tu hurriedly called for the shopkeeper and asked if there were any deserted areas or abandoned houses nearby.

Switch had indeed brought Tuyet Hoa Phi Vu to an abandoned hut nearby. She pushed Tuyet Hoa to the floor and pulled two bottles of wine from within her shirt: she'd realized that Tuyet Hoa Phi Vu wasn't trained in any kind of fighting, so she wasn't in a rush. She wanted to find out who this beauty was, and get to know the identity she planned to steal.

Tuyet Hoa Phi Vu didn't appreciate being pushed down. She dusted off her blue robe and stood, then raised a hand to catch the bottle of wine Switch had tossed at her. Switch smiled with satisfaction.

"Such a brave girl! Ordinary people would have been crying, pleading for mercy!"

"I'm on my way home to marry some good-for-nothing. What do I have to fear? I would be just as glad to die here." Tuyet Hoa Phi Vu tipped her head back and drank straight from the bottle.

Switch narrowed her eyes. The girl's manner was very familiar, and her response was suspicious. Was this prey truly brave, or was she so frightened she'd become calm? Tuyet Hoa's demeanor reminded Switch of Dong Tu: hadn't the time she kidnapped Dong Tu been a similar situation? That day, Obsidian had walked in and messed up her process, making it impossible to steal Dong Tu's face. She would not miss the opportunity this time. Switch and Tuyet Hoa Phi Vu would swap faces *and* bodies, and while she would live the life of Tuyet Hoa Phi Vu, Tuyet Hoa Phi Vu could do anything she wanted with Switch's body.

"I don't like to be indebted to anyone. If you have anything left unfinished, a will, or even the desire to kill someone, I will do it for you!" Switch informed her generously.

Tuyet Hoa Phi Vu shook her head.

"No need to kill anyone." Her face turned ice cold. "Switch, aren't you afraid of getting in trouble with Obsidian if you harm me?"

Switch shrugged.

"Obsidian has been missing for two years, why would I be afraid?

"Don't you find it strange?" Tuyet Hoa Phi Vu asked. "Because of Dong Tu, Obsidian nearly lost his life twice. It can't be easy for him to cut all ties." Her gaze was eerily fixed, as if she were seeing through Switch.

Switch wasn't worried. She was officially one of the Monstrous Eighteen herself: if anyone wanted to fight, she would fight. Besides, it was Tuyet Hoa Phi Vu she'd messed with, not Obsidian's woman.

"So you aren't afraid of anyone in the world?" Tuyet Hoa Phi Vu asked.

"No, no one!" Switch laughed.

A voice interrupted them.

"You had better fear Liet Than!" The voice belonged to a figure who entered the hut carrying a bag.

"Who?" Switch asked incredulously. She heard the sound of wine bottles clinking together, and some kind of metal glinted in the light of the fire crackling in the fireplace. Switch canted her head and watched the new stranger carefully; she swung her hand and Switch caught it—and ended up holding a bottle of wine.

"Yes, more good wine!" Switch brought the bottle to her nose and breathed in deeply, reveling in the rich fragrance, and then she took a savoring sip.

Tuyet Hoa Phi Vu watched with wary eyes. She lifted her hand to catch a bottle of wine from the newcomer, reluctantly sniffed it, then put it down.

The stranger said, "Switch, this is your unlucky year. Be careful with Liet Than. Don't say I didn't warn you!"

The warning clearly angered Switch.

"Stargazer, if you want to say something, just spit it out. What the hell is Liet Than?"

The new stranger was Stargazer, the more mystical of the Monstrous Eighteen, an elderly woman whose words of prophecy were as accurate as those of the gods.

CHAPTER 2

Unmatched Strength

Dong Tu searched all night. When she reached the hut, only Stargazer was left, sitting calmly on the floor eating oranges. Nearby, a streak of fresh blood marred the ground, and broken bottles of wine were scattered everywhere.

"Stargazer? Why are you here?" Dong Tu asked. They hadn't seen each other in a while, and Stargazer's presence was a welcome surprise.

"I've just been sitting here, waiting for you." Stargazer smiled. "It's been nearly two years. I wanted to see if you had gotten any taller and prettier. I was right, you have."

Stargazer had, for some reason, been keenly interested in Dong Tu for quite a while. But in that moment, for Dong Tu, seeing Stargazer was like finding treasure.

"Did you see Switch with a very tall lady?" she immediately asked. "Switch kidnapped her." She glanced around, noticing the scattered blood stains for the first time—and felt her stomach lurch in realization.

"The blood! Is it Lady Tuyet Hoa Phi Vu's?"

Stargazer waved a hand, unconcerned.

"Not at all."

"What happened here?"

The old woman shook her head.

"Switch is having a bad year. She had a little...clash, earlier. Nothing to worry about. She'll recover."

"How about Tuyet Hoa Phi Vu?"

"Safe."

"So where is Tuyet Hoa Phi Vu now?" Dong Tu asked, continuing to fire off questions. Tuyet Hoa Phi Vu was no fighter, and neither was Stargazer, so it was unlikely that the blood belonged to the old woman, either. Still, there it was; perhaps someone had recently come to fight with Switch and saved Tuyet Hoa Phi Vu.

Stargazer took a deep breath.

"What you are looking for is in the cave under Tien Thuc waterfall. This is not a lucky year––beware of water-related accidents. And now, it's time for me to go."

"Wait!" Dong Tu stopped her. Knowing that Tuyet Hoa Phi Vu was safe was reassuring, but she wasn't finished. She had been looking forward to reuniting with Stargazer for a long time, and still had so many questions, but a pair of them burned more insistently than the others.

"Do you know how Obsidian is doing? I've learned the Sunlight Strike. When can I see him again?"

Stargazer swallowed the last bite of her orange, dusted off her trousers, and stood up.

"Child, I came all this way to see you after two years and you're only worried about Tuyet Hoa Phi Vu and that Obsidian. You still haven't even asked how I am doing!" she scolded, but there was no real bite to her tone.

A continued rush of questions threatened to come spilling out of Dong Tu, but Stargazer's talent and time were as precious as gold, and sunrise was upon them. It had been a busy night, and it was time for breakfast.

Dong Tu held her hand and refused to let go. Stargazer had said that if Dong Tu learned the Sunlight Strike, she could see Obsidian again, and Dong Tu had dedicated everything to learning the technique: she had searched out and poured over every bit of information she could get her hands on, training day and night with all her hope hanging on the promise of that prediction. But she hadn't seen anything special about the technique for many years.

What was the point? she thought. *What was she getting at when she directed me to practice it?*

"You don't feel anything special because of your chi," Stargazer explained, as if reading Dong Tu's mind. "As I said earlier, what you're looking for is in the cave under Tien Thuc waterfall!"

Dong Tu just blinked at her. Stargazer stared silently for a moment, then huffed and added:

"You should look for Liet Than."

"Liet Than?" Dong Tu repeated, confused.

"Your fate with Obsidian depends on Liet Than," Stargazer insisted. She added nothing more, and hurried away with her beloved bag of jewels. Her hands were tied: every time she revealed the truth about the future, she felt her life get a little shorter. Her hair would turn a bit more gray, her skin would show a few more wrinkles, and her stomach would need more food. She had also found that the more she spoke, the easier it was to be wrong, so recently she had changed her tactics. Speaking more ambiguously and less overall made her predictions more likely to be correct.

Dong Tu watched her go in disappointment. For many years, there was only one thing she wanted to know—the whereabouts of Obsidian. Yet each time she asked, Stargazer gave her a different answer. She was beginning to acknowledge that Stargazer's predictions were fuzzy, with no definitive beginnings or ends.

And even if she had knowledge of the future, it would still be difficult for Dong Tu to change fate itself.

Two days later, following Stargazer's instructions, Dong Tu went to Tien Thuc Falls in search of Switch and Tuyet Hoa Phi Vu—where, lost in thought, Dong Tu slipped and fell straight down the waterfall, disappearing into the depths.

She had forgotten the prophet's warning.

She woke to the sound of a waterfall pounding in her ears.

Dong Tu came to consciousness slowly, and as her eyes blinked open, she took mental stock of her body and surroundings. Her head ached like it was being hammered, her whole body was sore, and between the dull roar of the water, the dark dampness of her surroundings, and the hard, uneven floor beneath her, she realized she had to be in a cave. Dong Tu felt around with her hands, trying desperately to remember how she'd ended up there, but she could barely remember her own name, let alone the events that had led to this. She stopped her search in shock: there was a straw mat underneath her! Her heart began to race as she realized someone had to have brought her there—and it stopped entirely when she realized she was wearing someone else's clothes.

As her vision cleared, Dong Tu spotted a fire flickering deeper inside the cave. She fumbled her way unsteadily toward the fire and into another chamber: the cave's ceiling expanded far above her, and it opened at the top to reveal a vivid sunset. A clear stream flowed over her bare feet, and soft green moss grew along its banks. But without her memories and not knowing if she was even safe, Dong Tu found herself too frightened to continue onward. As she turned to leave, she stumbled on a rock and fell to her knees.

Dong Tu jumped and looked up as a hand appeared out of the darkness; a young man stood there, bent forward to help her to her feet.

"Be careful not to get all wet again," he said, a smile evident in his voice.

Dong Tu couldn't make much out in the darkness as they walked, but his hand was warm and strong.

"Last name Ly, first name Minh Lam," the young man introduced himself. He led her over to the fire, where the flames lit up the cave and cast shifting shadows on the walls.

Ly Minh Lam was young, probably about Dong Tu's age. He had long bangs that fell to his cheekbones, and he would shake them out of his eyes with a graceful flip of his head. His face carried a certain elegance, with a high, slightly curved nose and a smirking mouth, and a mole sat just beneath one eye. It seemed to add an accent to every smile and glance, in ways that spoke of mischief and play. Ly Minh Lam was also fairly tall, with slim shoulders and long limbs, but he was leanly muscled in a way that made Dong Tu sure he was well-versed in the martial arts.

He was also wearing only underclothes; as Dong Tu looked closer, she realized she was wearing his outer layers. Whoever he was, he certainly didn't seem like a bad person. After considering him for a while, Dong Tu finally dared to speak up.

"Did you bring me here?"

Ly Minh Lam nodded, his lips parting in a smile.

"Don't mention it. I help anyone who's in trouble."

Dong Tu performed a gesture of thanks for saving her life. The pair fell silent, and she took the opportunity to take a closer look around the stone cave.

"Are you...the only one living here?" she asked hesitantly.

Ly Minh Lam raised an eyebrow.

"Why do you ask?"

"Did you change my clothes?"

"Oh, this is about your wet clothes?" Minh Lam laughed. "The way you acted, I thought it was more serious. It's not spring yet and the water is cold. If I hadn't changed your clothes, you would have frozen to death!"

The full ramifications of being changed out of her wet clothes struck Dong Tu then, and she flushed bright red.

"D-did you see all of me?" she stammered.

"It's not like there was much to see," Minh Lam answered, shrugging.

Ly Minh Lam's attitude didn't make her feel any better. Men and women weren't supposed to see each other like that! Not even Obsidian had seen her naked, but now a complete stranger had. How could he be so blasé?

"I've saved many beauties from the waterfall," Minh Lam chuckled, his body shaking with mirth. "You're not the first. I'm a lucky man."

The more Dong Tu blushed, the more he laughed, and the more he laughed, the more her embarrassment melted into anger. Falling off a waterfall, being knocked unconscious, and nearly dying from cold excused Minh Lam from having to hold with propriety when he'd saved her, but she wished he would behave more like a gentleman! Maybe he had saved her life, but she still wanted to punch him so badly. It was not a laughing matter!

"Well, did you do anything *else* to me?" Dong Tu asked cautiously.

"Do what?" Minh Lam shot back, feigning ignorance.

"Like—like..." Dong Tu couldn't form the words. She was already too embarrassed to get her question out.

"Like kissing you while you were unconscious?" Minh Lam said seriously. He wasn't laughing anymore, and stared through her with an uncomfortable kind of knowing. The words turned her to ice.

He was obviously referring to Obsidian, but despite the plethora of rumors, very few people actually knew Obsidian had kissed her like that—which meant he knew exactly who she was, and who Obsidian was. Between his build, his attitude, and his knowledge, Dong Tu realized: he had to be connected to the Monstrous Eighteen!

Minh Lam raised an eyebrow at Dong Tu's suddenly panicked expression.

"Well, well! Perhaps the rumors were true!" He reached out to grab her, and Dong Tu ducked away instinctively. Not knowing for sure if he wanted to test her fighting skills or if he was reaching for something else, Dong Tu lashed out with a kick; Minh Lam blocked it, and the two found themselves in a full-blown fight.

It was easy to see he was being gentle with her, but she still struggled to block him. After two failed moves, Dong Tu had to dredge together all of her chi and every scrap of knowledge she had to counter Minh Lam. It didn't take her long to understand that he was way out of her league, but she couldn't let herself give up. Ly Minh Lam changed tactics abruptly, and rather than continue his attacks, he instead gathered his chi to form a whirlwind in his palm. The wind gradually grew into a tornado, forming a protective barrier around him, and all of Dong Tu's moves just bounced off the wind like it was a shield.

Minh Lam pressed forward, pinning her to the ground. The force of the winds whirling around him kept her there until she became too tired to struggle, and when Dong Tu finally gave in, he released his chi, brushed the dust off his shirt, and scoffed at her.

"You're not very good. Do you want to learn my Whirlwind technique?"

Dong Tu scrambled up from the ground, still angry, and glared at Ly Minh Lam. *This young man has some formidable strength,* she thought. *That move he did just now, Whirlwind or whatever, seemed like it was entirely internal.* Dong Tu could no longer tell whether he was good or evil, her friend or foe.

Seeing that the situation was becoming tense, Minh Lam held up his hands in surrender.

"I've heard rumors about you for a long time, and I just want to see how good you were. Please don't hold it against me. Or are you still angry about me changing your clothes? I was joking about that; Tuyet Hoa Phi Vu did it. Are you happy now? No hard feelings?"

Upon hearing that tidbit, the tension in her body finally, visibly relaxed.

"Wait, you know Tuyet Hoa Phi Vu?"

Minh Lam nodded.

"The other night, I passed by a hut and saw someone in danger, so I helped her out." He wagged a finger at her in mock reproof. "Lady Tuyet Hoa has more manners than you, so she politely thanked me for saving her life instead of punching her savior like you did."

Dong Tu blushed again, but before she could speak, another person interrupted them.

"My darling hero, please stop making fun of Lady Luu." The voice came from a tall figure who entered the cave. The light of the fire illuminated her beautifully radiant face as she drew closer: Tuyet Hoa Phi Vu smiled and tossed a string of freshly caught fish toward Minh Lam.

"Aha, dinner is here!" Minh Lam was delighted. He took the string of fish and threaded them onto a stick, ignoring Dong Tu and Tuyet Hoa Phi Vu as they were reunited.

Dong Tu gasped quietly and embraced her friend; Tuyet Hoa Phi Vu appeared to be perfectly healthy, and Dong Tu felt like a burden she had been carrying for days finally fell off.

———

The smell of campfire and delicious grilled fish was fragrant in the air. Dong Tu was relieved to learn that after she had surfaced just beyond the base of the waterfall, Tuyet Hoa Phi Vu had indeed been the one to change her clothes.

"Oh, come on! What's the difference, whether I or Tuyet Hoa Phi Vu did it?" Minh Lam complained.

"Of course it's different!" Dong Tu fired back. "Have you never lived in a civilized society? Men and women obviously can't freely undress each other."

Tuyet Hoa Phi Vu was a bit more masculine than Dong Tu, but she was still a woman. It was different between women.

Ly Minh Lam ignored her, grinning to himself as he grilled the fish. Tuyet Hoa Phi Vu rotated the grilled fish and glanced at her companions. Dong Tu followed her friend's eyes down to the fish and noticed that Tuyet Hoa Phi Vu had many finger-shaped burns on her hand.

With a start, Dong Tu realized that the wounds were characteristic of Switch's attacks. She scooted closer and took Tuyet Hoa Phi Vu's hand to examine the wound. The taller woman pulled it back, but not before Dong Tu caught her pulse. It was worryingly weak.

"Your heart rate is very weak. Are you injured?" Dong Tu began to look her over more closely. Tuyet Hoa Phi Vu shook her head.

"You should let me give you a little strength," Dong Tu continued anyway. "Your chi is so weak, you could get sick if you're not careful."

Her friend shook her head again.

"It's normal for me. When I was born, I almost died, so I've always been a little sickly. You don't need to worry."

Dong Tu was still concerned. She knew that being saved by Ly Minh Lam after facing Switch was definitely not a small matter for her friend. Perhaps Tuyet Hoa Phi Vu was traumatized, but was doing her best to hide it.

But talking about Switch had reminded Dong Tu of something.

"Oh great hero, how did you save Lady Tuyet Hoa from the hands of the Skinwalker?" she asked curiously. "Were you really able to beat Switch?"

Switch, of course, would never have given up Tuyet Hoa Phi Vu without a serious fight. In order to bring Tuyet Hoa Phi Vu to the cave, someone would have *had* to defeat her.

"Oh, it was nothing," he replied with a careless wave of his hand. "She was no serious opponent. I just put in a few slaps and that was that. I've always hated people who like to bully others. I gave her a good beating."

Dong Tu was still doubtful. Switch was one of the Monstrous Eighteen, and almost no ordinary people could beat her. Minh Lam could see her skepticism in her face.

"Follow me," he said, waving her over with a fish skewer as he stood up.

Following the sound of his footsteps, Dong Tu and Tuyet Hoa Phi Vu fumbled their way into another, darker chamber. It held only a small mat in the corner, and someone was lying there, motionless.

Dong Tu approached the mat. Recognizing the clothes that Switch was wearing the day before, she rushed over to help her up—but Switch didn't move. Her head just lolled limply onto Dong Tu's chest. Dong Tu tried to wake her, but Switch still didn't respond. That was when Dong Tu realized: her face was gone. She had no eyes, nose, or mouth. Nothing. Just blankness.

"S-Switch?" Dong Tu stammered. "Switch, what happened to you?"

Switch's whole body was as soft as noodles, and no matter how hard Dong Tu shook her, she wouldn't respond.

"Ly Minh Lam, what have you done to Switch?!"

"Don't worry, she's okay." Minh Lam leisurely chewed a bite of fish. "That's what she really looks like. Without another replacement face, she can't talk. Her pressure points are all locked up, and her chi has locked itself in, so she won't die––but from now on, she can't harm a soul."

Dong Tu put her head to Switch's chest and listened to her heartbeat. It was still beating normally, and her pulse felt steady as well. Minh Lam was telling the truth.

She was shocked. There was no way Ly Minh Lam was just a commoner. He had to be a master, to beat Switch like that: Switch had always been arrogant, walking around like she was the queen of the universe, but she was also strong and skilled enough to back her arrogance up.

"Who are you?" she asked Minh Lam, pulling herself out of her thoughts. "Are you one of the Monstrous Eighteen?"

"What qualifies someone as one of the Eighteen?" Minh Lam raised his eyebrows. "I don't concern myself with the rumors of the world."

"Are you Liet Than?" Dong Tu tried again, finally remembering her conversation with Stargazer.

Ly Minh Lam stopped chewing and frowned at her. Blowing at the bangs which covered his eyes, he narrowed his eyes further and studied her rather than answer. The pale mole under his eye seemed to laugh at her.

"Wait a second, you know about Liet Than too?" Tuyet Hoa Phi Vu hesitantly interjected.

It turned out that, for her own unknown reasons, Stargazer had told many people about the mysterious Liet Than. Dong Tu, Tuyet Hoa Phi Vu, and Switch had all received a prophecy involving those two words.

Minh Lam waved for everyone to return to the first cave, leaving Switch to lie by herself. Dong Tu followed, but kept looking back over her shoulder at Switch's powerless body. She was worried about the other woman, but she knew that if Minh Lam had wanted to kill her, he would have done it already. *Switch has always been a wanderer, causing trouble and harm everywhere*, Dong Tu reminded herself. *If she just stays here, incapacitated, who knows? It may be better for everyone in the long run.*

Returning to the campfire, Minh Lam finally finished eating his fish. He stretched, patting his stomach, but even though he seemed to be stuffed, his belly didn't look any bigger. After many years of practicing martial arts, his abs were rock hard--a meal of fish didn't affect them at all. Refreshed from the stretch, he jumped onto a rock.

"Which one of you two beauties would like to sleep with me tonight?" he called out playfully. "Or do you two girls just want to sleep together?"

Tuyet Hoa Phi Vu picked up a pile of gravel and threw it straight at him. Minh Lam didn't even bother to dodge--the pebbles never reached him. They broke into fine powder before his face as if they had hit an invisible wall.

"No worries! I'll just sleep alone...again..." Minh Lam moaned in mock self-pity. He laid down, facing the stone wall, and fell asleep almost instantly.

His snores echoed off the cave walls.

Dong Tu lay down, but she couldn't sleep. Thoughts whirled through her head. Who was Ly Minh Lam? Did his strength have anything to do with the Sunlight Strike? What or who was Liet Than? *Was* Ly Minh Lam actually Liet Than? After two uneventful years, why was Liet Than being mentioned so often? Could it be that Stargazer wanted to tell Dong Tu to learn from Minh Lam so that she could improve and use the Sunlight Strike to its fullest extent?

Dong Tu huffed in frustration and sat up, only to see Tuyet Hoa Phi Vu still awake by the fire. She went and sat next to her.

Tuyet Hoa Phi Vu stared into the flames, absentmindedly rubbing the wound on her hand. Her gaze was even more wistful and distant.

The burns Switch left on Tuyet Hoa Phi Vu's wrist must be sore, Dong Tu thought. Without asking questions, she took her friend's hands and used her chi to help heal the wounds, slowly transferring her inner power to Tuyet Hoa Phi Vu.

Tuyet Hoa Phi Vu was startled at first, then gently squeezed Dong Tu's hands. It was cold in the cave, and so were her long, slender hands. When Dong Tu transferred chi, her fingers began to warm up. Tuyet Hoa Phi Vu fondly stroked Dong Tu's hands and watched with intent curiosity as the waves of energy slowly entered her body.

Dong Tu guessed Tuyet Hoa Phi Vu had never been given energy like that before, especially when she began to tremble. At first the strange sensation scared her, but it didn't take long for her to relax into it.

"Take a long breath, like this," Dong Tu instructed reassuringly, "then slowly exhale. Try to relax your body, Lady Tuyet Hoa."

Tuyet Hoa Phi Vu obediently followed Dong Tu's lead, and she looked up into Dong Tu's face with gratefulness heavy in her gaze.

"Do you feel more comfortable now?" Dong Tu went on. With a bit of Dong Tu's inner energy, she should feel a little warmer.

Tuyet Hoa Phi Vu nodded.

"Yes, it feels much better. Thank you, Miss Luu."

Dong Tu nodded, and continued to give Tuyet Hoa Phi Vu energy.

Inner energy, which many normal people had, was different from physical strength. Physical strength was used when one lifted heavy objects or exerted power. It made the body move, and was a result of physical muscles. Inner energy, or chi, was the flow of invisible energy inside the body. Unlike physical energy, not everyone knew how to tap into it. Martial arts masters mainly worked to control and enhance their chi, setting them apart from ordinary people.

Dong Tu was no martial arts master, but had learned enough to gain at least some control over her own chi. She could utilize her chi to treat minor injuries, or enhance her strength during a fight.

There were many levels of martial arts masters above Dong Tu, with their respective talents depending on control of their chi. For example, most masters could use their chi to fly like a bird. They could also use chi to master fighting techniques that would allow them to battle dozens of people at once.

The highest level of all was that of great masters like Switch, or any of the Monstrous Eighteen. Those masters could use their chi to move mountains and perform many other extraordinary acts. It was why Dong Tu was certain Minh Lam had to be a great master himself, something she continued to ponder over as she rubbed Tuyet Hoa Phi Vu's hands.

She could tell just from that simple act that her friend belonged to the class of people without chi. When their hands touched, Dong Tu immediately knew that Tuyet Hoa Phi Vu had never transferred inner energy or practiced martial arts. Tuyet Hoa Phi Vu was very young and healthy, but on the inside, her small chi was weak and fragmented and effectively nonexistent.

With chi as frail as hers, Tuyet Hoa Phi Vu should be walking around like a very old person, Dong Tu realized. She should have been sick, near death's door. Yet regardless of her weak chi and the things she'd endured, Tuyet Hoa Phi Vu retained a remarkably calm appearance. Dong Tu secretly admired her strength.

Her friend's body grew warmer, and her face began to look more and more fresh. Clasping Dong Tu's hands in appreciation, Tuyet Hoa Phi Vu leaned back into her chest and slowly fell asleep. Dong Tu smiled. She wrapped her arms around Tuyet Hoa Phi Vu as if embracing a little sister, and then drifted off to sleep as well.

Unlikely circumstances had led to friendship, and the challenges they faced had given birth to love; and Dong Tu and Tuyet Hoa Phi Vu remained in each other's embrace for the rest of the night.

CHAPTER 3

Lingering Memories

When Dong Tu woke up the next morning, Ly Minh Lam had already left with Switch.

Dong Tu and Tuyet Hoa Phi Vu helped each other out of the cave. They struggled to climb back up the falls, searching for the road that would take them back to the rest of their escort. The path was steep and rocky, precarious even during the day; and at night, they would lean against each other for warmth beside the crackling fire.

To Dong Tu, Tuyet Hoa Phi Vu didn't *look* like a lady in need of protection, neither in appearance nor personality. Her height and bearing put off a constant air of strength and dignity. After days of climbing, her makeup had worn almost entirely away, and out of the corner of her eye Dong Tu began to mistake her features and temperament for those of a man. Tuyet Hoa Phi Vu had clear eyes, and an enchanting stillness and peace that was magnetic. One could see clouds drifting in the sky when looking into her eyes, like transparent ice at the end of winter, reflecting heaven and earth, plants and trees. They were pure and fresh.

Dong Tu looked at her own reflection in the water. It was early spring, and plants were beginning to wake and stir. Winter's chill still lingered, but green shoots and buds were already pushing their way out into the air. She splashed water over her face, the startling cold zinging through her body and waking her up properly. Tuyet Hoa Phi Vu did the same, and Dong Tu watched as the spring water streamed in rivulets down her nose, forming a straight line down the center of her face and becoming a gleaming highlight on her lips. There was no powder left on her face, and without her dangling earrings and long hair, there would be no way to differentiate between Tuyet Hoa Phi Vu and a beautiful man.

Dong Tu thought it was just a show. Inside, Tuyet Hoa Phi Vu's spirit was fragile, just like her name—a snowflake dancing in the wind, pretty as a painting. But with one touch, the snowflake would melt into water.

Dong Tu no longer saw Tuyet Hoa Phi Vu as a client in need of protection, but also as her newest younger sibling. Dong Tu tried to help her as much as she could, picking wild berries and giving Tuyet Hoa Phi Vu anything else she found that was edible. Dong Tu even took the lead, on the lookout for any paths that she deemed too dangerous. If there were any suspicious sounds, she drew her sword without hesitation, and Tuyet Hoa Phi Vu was indescribably grateful.

Several days later, Bao Thuong and the two guards were finally found. It was Tuyet Hoa Phi Vu's wedding day, and the group was still more than two days away from Lac Do.

Worry drew lines of stress along Dong Tu's face and sat heavy in her eyes. She didn't know what would happen if they were a few days late, whether the other woman's in-laws would make things difficult for the Tuyet family or not. And she knew if she was worried, Tuyet Hoa Phi Vu had to be as well, and checked in with her regularly to make sure she was okay.

Tuyet Hoa Phi Vu was very good at hiding emotion. Happiness, sadness, worry, fatigue, jokes or seriousness, all were barely visible. Her default expression was calm, confident and a bit thoughtful. Even Dong Tu, who had been by her side day and night, could barely read her expressions, which mostly consisted of only two emotions. First was contemplation: Tuyet Hoa Phi Vu sometimes seemed to be pondering over something, like there was something she wanted to say but couldn't. It wasn't anything strange, and Dong Tu suspected she was worried about her upcoming marriage, and felt too awkward to express it.

Second was curiosity. Dong Tu often caught Tuyet Hoa Phi Vu's eyes watching her movements with some combination of curiosity and admiration, even when she wasn't doing anything remotely extraordinary.

"What does that look mean?" Dong Tu asked her one day.

"I was born like that," Tuyet Hoa Phi Vu replied, trying to brush it off. Pretty people often had a naturally curious-looking face, they couldn't blame her for it.

"But you don't look at Bao Thuong like that, do you," Dong Tu pressed. That got Bao Thuong's attention, and with no other way to worm herself out of answering, Lady Tuyet Hoa gave in.

"You're so small, but you always act like everyone's big sister. It amuses me." Tuyet Hoa Phi Vu raised her hands to measure their heights. Even when standing, the top of Dong Tu's head didn't even reach the taller woman's chin, but she always treated Tuyet Hoa Phi Vu like a weak little kid. Tuyet Hoa Phi Vu found it funny.

"Tuyet Hoa Phi Vu, I advise you not to underestimate me just because I'm short," Dong Tu snapped. "Your safety depends on me. In fact, you should address me as your big sister from now on."

Tuyet Hoa Phi Vu had begun as their client, but their relationship had changed, which meant they needed to address each other more properly. Dong Tu might have been short, but she was still the stronger of the two.

"All right, big sis," Tuyet Hoa Phi Vu agreed. "Whatever you want."

———

Only one day away from Lac Do, the group decided to stop for the night in the neighboring district. Spring had just begun, and with it the cold was finally fading, the soil warm enough for seeds to bloom. The Spring Festival was in full swing, and the stores had been packed with people buying and selling saplings and seeds, trinkets and treats, all afternoon. Just like the plants, people woke up after the cold winter months, and they milled about the town, talking and laughing and eating to their hearts' content.

"Let's buy some new clothes!" Tuyet Hoa Phi Vu proposed excitedly. Without saying another word, she pulled the group into the biggest clothing store on the street. The store owner greeted them with a big smile on his face as Tuyet Hoa Phi Vu generously pulled out her purse. She told the owner to bring out the most precious brocades: she wanted to buy new clothes for each and every one of them, to replace the clothes dirtied after days of travel. Dong Tu and Bao Thuong politely declined, but Tuyet Hoa Phi Vu refused to be swayed, and they resigned themselves to the fact that their ward absolutely would not be taking no for an answer.

Tuyet Hoa Phi Vu had been dubious of Dong Tu's abilities, but the other woman had impressed and touched her with how hard she'd struggled to ensure her safety. She fully intended to pay Dong Tu back by buying her gifts, and pampering her as much as she could.

"Dong Tu, this set really suits you!" Tuyet Hoa Phi Vu called, after rummaging around for a long while. She had turned the shop upside down just to find a beautiful pink dress, which she held in front of Dong Tu and nagged her to try on.

Dong Tu reluctantly obeyed. It had been a *long* time since she last went shopping for clothes, and even though her family's business was successful, they could never have hoped to afford anything of that caliber. Pastel pink, the dress was extremely feminine, with many lace and flower patterns embroidered along the fabric like the kind wealthy women wore. Dong Tu was a martial artist; she rarely got to wear anything like that. Putting on that kind of fancy, feminine clothing made her squirm internally with an uncharacteristic shyness she hadn't felt in a long time.

Tuyet Hoa Phi Vu's face lit up in delighted astonishment as Dong Tu finally came out in the dress.

"Wow!" she cried. "You're so beautiful! Like a freshly polished diamond! See? There are no ugly women. Only busy ones."

Dong Tu had her doubts. She turned to the large mirror in the center of the shop and studied her reflection, her hands smoothing absently over the fabric. The dress, so lovely with its rare fabric and meticulously detailed embroidery, made Dong Tu look like a gentle and refined lady. It had been more than two years since Dong Tu had last seen Obsidian, and as she looked at the girl in the mirror, she wondered: if he met her again now, would Obsidian still recognize her?

Dong Tu had matured. She was older, a bit taller, more lady-like. Over the past two years, Dong Tu had practiced in her family's dojo day and night, and tried her best to learn the Sunlight Strike. It hadn't done much for her chi, but thanks to the physically demanding nature of her studies, her body had developed into a shape that was both graceful and strong. She wasn't the same young, innocent thing Obsidian had met any longer.

Obsidian...I wonder how he's doing.

Dong Tu was lost to her own thoughts for a while, staring blankly at her reflection. She hadn't realized Tuyet Hoa Phi Vu had been standing behind her. Tuyet Hoa Phi Vu eased Dong Tu's hair out of its bun and tried to slip a jade hairpin into place, but Dong Tu hurriedly waved her hand. She couldn't bring herself to accept such an expensive gift.

Tuyet Hoa Phi Vu signaled the store owner to bring in more and more hairpins; she was clearly someone who was accustomed to spending exorbitant amounts of money. Tuyet Hoa Phi Vu slowly brushed Dong Tu's hair and then put the pin in its place. Placing one hand on Dong Tu's shoulder, Tuyet Hoa Phi Vu used the other hand to gently raise Dong Tu's chin and directed her attention to the mirror.

"Dong Tu, look. It suits you very well," Tuyet Hoa Phi Vu whispered. As she spoke, her breath washed over Dong Tu's ear and sent chills rolling over the smaller woman's skin.

The pin made it even harder for Dong Tu to recognize the woman in the mirror before her. Facing her was an elegant lady with long, beautiful hair, looking like true nobility. On top of that, she could see the beautiful Tuyet Hoa Phi Vu standing behind her, meticulously inserting the hairpin and combing her hair. The reflection struck Dong Tu with a sense of both familiarity and strangeness: once again, her height and seriousness made Tuyet Hoa Phi Vu look like a beautiful man. From a certain angle, Tuyet Hoa Phi Vu's face even reminded Dong Tu of Obsidian. It hit her hard, and together with the light from a dazzling sunset, for a moment she felt like she was in a dream.

Tuyet Hoa Phi Vu felt like a sister to her. But the mirror reflected the glittering image of a man tenderly cradling a woman in his arms, like a couple who were very much in love.

Time seemed to stop. Bao Thuong and the other guards, the store owner, and the customers all froze mid-motion like vibrant statues; the words they spoke halted on their lips. Even the fluttering silk sheets froze in midair.

Bright gold evening sunlight and the chill of early spring filled the room. *Had* springtime even come?

In a flash it was no longer Tuyet Hoa Phi Vu but Obsidian that Dong Tu saw standing behind her, caressing her hair, dressing her up like royalty. She couldn't see his face clearly, but she knew in her heart that it could be no one else but her Obsidian, and it knocked the breath from her lungs. He was right there...she could embrace him simply by turning around...

The pain of his absence had begun to dull eventually, but to see him there brought the ache right back, hot and sharp. Tears flowed down her face as Dong Tu clasped the hand on her shoulder. She turned around to look at him, to hold him in her arms.

Yellow-gold sunlight suddenly went dark. The sun had fallen far enough that it left the shop in shadow, and the store owner turned on the lights. Everything that had been frozen snapped back to life.

The teardrop-shaped earrings, angular face, transparent eyes, straight nose, and pouty lips—Dong Tu suddenly awoke, too. A completely different face looked down into her own, and she realized it had always been Tuyet Hoa Phi Vu. Dong Tu released her hand in sudden embarrassment.

A slightly puzzled expression flickered across Tuyet Hoa Phi Vu's face, but she tucked her confusion away for later.

"I'm buying all of these," Tuyet Hoa Phi Vu announced instead, awkwardly waving her hand to the owner.

"Dong Tu, you look like a princess," Bao Thuong complimented. He couldn't just ignore the first beauty he'd ever fallen for to run after a new one.

"How are you related to Bao Thuong?" Tuyet Hoa Phi Vu asked. The first time they'd met there had been an introduction, but after the events of the last several days she had completely forgotten. Dong Tu explained that Bao Thuong wasn't just any patron in the Luu's dojo, but was their adopted son. According to the order of hierarchy, he was Dong Tu's elder brother.

"You two don't even look alike," Tuyet Hoa commented. But of course they didn't, because Bao Thuong was an adopted child. They weren't bound by blood.

Bao Thuong had lost his family when he was a child, and was brought back and raised by Dong Tu's father. Thuong had only been two or three years old at the time, and Dong Tu had been a newborn; her mother had nursed them both. The corner of Tuyet Hoa Phi Vu's mouth twitched when she heard that: the two of them had to be extremely close.

"Of course," Bao Thuong agreed. "The two of us grew up learning from the same teacher, eating off the same tray, sleeping in the same place, bathing in the same stream."

Dong Tu stopped his blabbing after that. It had been one thing when they were kids, but now they were all adults; talking about eating and bathing together sounded so *weird*.

Tuyet Hoa Phi Vu examined Bao Thuong from head to toe. How funny the sisters of the Luu family were! Dong Tu seemed to have no idea that Bao Thuong had romantic feelings for her, apart from his brotherly love, but Tuyet Hoa Phi Vu merely chuckled to herself. She was in no rush to bust him.

There were evidently two obstacles for anyone travelling the road to Dong Tu's heart. The first was Obsidian, the King of Poison, her rumored lover. The second was her (adopted) big brother, sticking to her day in and day out, hoping to one day have a chance to shift from brother to lover himself.

Tuyet Hoa Phi Vu clicked her tongue and shook her head to herself.

Winter was coming to its end, but the wind was still freezing. Tuyet Hoa Phi Vu was wearing men's clothes like Bao Thuong, but the two looked completely different. Bao Thuong was a broad-shouldered, broad-chested, muscular martial artist, while Tuyet Hoa Phi Vu was slender, tall, pure and transcendent. One was wearing tight clothes, the other wore an elegant, silky shirt that fluttered in the cold wind.

As soon as she put on the male costume, Tuyet Hoa Phi Vu stole the gazes of everyone in the vicinity. Not long after they left the store, either because she was sick of being ogled or because she was freezing, Tuyet Hoa Phi Vu dragged everyone into a restaurant. She spent freely and happily once again, and filled the table with expensive wines and delicious food. Bao Thuong and the other two guards ended up drunk as skunks.

For Tuyet Hoa Phi Vu, however, the more tired she was, the more she could drink. As soon as Bao Thuong finished one cup, Tuyet Hoa Phi Vu drank another one. The three men drank so much that they ended up on the ground, faces bright red, too drunk to tell which way was up. And Tuyet Hoa Phi Vu continued to drink calmly, entirely unaffected.

Woah, she does have an amazing skill after all! Dong Tu thought as she drank. Tuyet Hoa Phi Vu's alcohol tolerance and intake could bankrupt even her own wealthy family.

Normally Dong Tu would never drink to the point of uselessness. But all night spent sitting opposite Tuyet Hoa Phi Vu meant that somehow wine continuously poured itself into her mouth, and it wasn't weak wine, either. Before she knew it, her head laid flat on the table. The last image imprinted in her mind was Tuyet Hoa Phi Vu glancing at her with the same affectionate gaze Obsidian had. Was it Dong Tu's imagination? Was it the alcohol? Had Tuyet Hoa Phi Vu just turned into Obsidian?

Dong Tu only faintly felt Tuyet Hoa Phi Vu carrying her back to the room later that night. On the way, images of the moon playing tag with the clouds in the deep darkness, and trees and flowers, flashed through her mind. Everything whirled and wobbled; a teardrop-shaped earring was swaying next to an angular face similar to that of Obsidian.

Obsidian, why are you wearing Tuyet Hoa Phi Vu's earrings? Dong Tu wondered fuzzily. *Tuyet Hoa Phi Vu, how did you grow stubble?!*

Even after melting into the bed, Dong Tu hadn't known whether the person who had carried her was Tuyet Hoa Phi Vu or Obsidian. She blinked hard, trying to calm herself down, but what she had seen was still whirling around in her head. Reality and fantasy mingled, and in Dong Tu's dreams, the jumbled images kept warping. Tuyet Hoa Phi Vu's eyes, then Obsidian's eyes; Tuyet Hoa Phi Vu's lips, then Obsidian's lips...the teardrop earrings...

Dong Tu looked closely and then a strung-out smile broke out across her own pretty mouth. It was Obsidian who had just put Dong Tu to bed!

"Don't go," Dong Tu begged softly, clutching Obsidian's hand. She pulled him closer. Dong Tu wanted to see his face more clearly, wanted to hug and kiss him like she'd been dreaming of doing for so long. She was vaguely aware of the tears that stung her eyes and the taste of salt on her lips, but none of that mattered. He was *there,* and she pressed a sweet kiss to his lips. Obsidian gazed at her with the same fondness and longing.

"Phong, my love, do you know how many years I have longed for you, how badly I've wanted to find you?" Dong Tu felt him respond to her kiss, but then he gently pushed her away. A cold towel covered her forehead, and instead of Obsidian responding, it was Tuyet Hoa Phi Vu.

"Dong Tu, you're too drunk," she murmured in concern.

After days and days of tiresome traveling, Dong Tu had caught a slight fever, and with the addition of the alcohol, she had lost all sense of control and had mistakenly kissed Tuyet Hoa Phi Vu.

Dong Tu looked so *heartbroken,* and it puzzled Tuyet Hoa Phi Vu. Her eyes, which could fill the sky with melancholy, were so sorrowful that it left Tuyet Hoa Phi Vu shaken. *Maybe her kiss was for me?* she wondered briefly.

Tuyet Hoa Phi Vu left Dong Tu for a long time, and then decided to return to check on her. Dong Tu remained fast asleep, unaware of Tuyet Hoa Phi Vu going in and out. The taller woman touched her forehead; Dong Tu's fever had gone down, but she was still muttering in her sleep. Tuyet Hoa Phi Vu leaned in to listen. Dong Tu softly, miserably repeated just two words.

Don't go.

"I'm not going anywhere...I'm here," Tuyet Hoa Phi Vu whispered to calm her down. Tuyet Hoa Phi Vu awkwardly watched Dong Tu for a long time, then pulled a pillow up to sleep next to her.

Only when the morning sunlight seeped in did the two wake up.

Dong Tu opened her eyes and saw Tuyet Hoa Phi Vu lying next to her, face to face. Tuyet Hoa Phi Vu's long eyelashes, full lips, and steady breathing almost made Dong Tu scream out. She thought a strange man had trespassed her room!

Tuyet Hoa Phi Vu woke up, startled by the way Dong Tu's body had jumped in her own surprise.

"Last night you weren't well, so I stayed here. I don't remember when I fell asleep," Tuyet Hoa Phi Vu explained, and covered her mouth as she broke into a yawn. It didn't seem like she'd slept well. Tuyet Hoa Phi Vu shrugged, then stretched, as if she had nothing more to say. Then she looked at Dong Tu curiously.

"Do you remember what happened last night?" she asked.

Dong Tu shook her head. It wasn't that she didn't remember: Dong Tu briefly recalled thinking that Obsidian had been by her side all night, and the two of them kissing; and she knew Tuyet Hoa Phi Vu had been the only person there, so Dong Tu guessed that she had been so drunk she had hallucinated. But she didn't want to trouble Tuyet Hoa Phi Vu, so she didn't take it further than that.

Meanwhile Tuyet Hoa Phi Vu wished Dong Tu *had* remembered the previous night, and though she decided not to call up the incident, she glanced reproachfully at Dong Tu all day.

Dong Tu had been her first kiss.

CHAPTER 4

The Gentle Man

Lac Do was where they finally had to bid farewell.

Tuyet Hoa Phi Vu didn't want to bring the whole group home where they could be dragged into a potential mess, so she said goodbye at the district's gate; and because she'd dressed herself as a man, when she and Dong Tu parted at the gate, they looked like a loving newly-wed couple sending each other off. So many things had changed in the week and a half they'd been travelling together: where once there had been dubious skepticism and awkwardness on both sides, there had blossomed a beautiful friendship, and before she knew it, tears began to fill Dong Tu's eyes.

"Good luck, Lady Tuyet Hoa!" Dong Tu exclaimed, trying to hide her worry. The trip had taken nearly ten days, which was way past the wedding date, and it had sounded as if Tuyet Hoa Phi Vu had real reason to fear for her family's safety.

Tuyet Hoa Phi Vu nodded, and she awarded Dong Tu a rare smile. Even after ten days, even to Dong Tu, she still betrayed few of her own emotions. That fact made her smile all the more precious.

After saying goodbye, Tuyet Hoa Phi Vu turned to leave.

"Wait!" Dong Tu called out, and ran to hug Tuyet Hoa Phi Vu for the second time. She knew the heaviness in Tuyet Hoa Phi Vu's shoulders, even if it was barely a hint, and she knew the steady step of someone forcing themselves forward despite their deepest desires. She'd been forced into a wedding too, once upon a time. It had killed her.

Literally.

"Tuyet Hoa, if you need anything, or if we have the chance to meet again, don't forget me," Dong Tu earnestly reminded the other woman.

"And me!" Bao Thuong added.

Tuyet Hoa Phi Vu smiled again, this one small and rueful, and stroked Dong Tu's hair; it was the only comfort she could think to provide. While tears poured down Dong Tu's cheeks, Tuyet Hoa Phi Vu's eyes remained dry—and if someone who didn't know what was really going on passed by, they could easily have mistaken Dong Tu for the woman being forced to marry.

Tuyet Hoa Phi Vu leaned down and pressed a gentle kiss to Dong Tu's forehead.

"Dong Tu, my big sister...you are so sweet."

Dong Tu didn't want to let go of Tuyet Hoa Phi, but the taller woman gently pulled away. Dong Tu watched, her heart aching with every pulse, as Tuyet Hoa Phi Vu's ethereal figure faded away. It hurt just like leaving Obsidian had hurt, and Dong Tu couldn't stand it: Tuyet Hoa Phi Vu was so fragile, and forcing someone as rare and delicate as she into an arranged marriage was nothing short of cruelty.

And yet there was nothing she could do.

Dong Tu, Bao Thuong and the two extra guards stood at the district gate in silence, staring, for a long time after Tuyet Hoa Phi Vu took off.

Dong Tu's heart remained heavy for the rest of the day. Bao Thuong began vomiting around noon: he no longer felt the need to save face after saying goodbye to Tuyet Hoa Phi Vu, and finally gave in to the nausea his massive hangover had caused. Dong Tu helped him over to a tree so that the pair of them could sit in the shade, where another traveler sat just off to one side with his head down. Seeing that Dong Tu was carefully helping Bao Thuong drink some water, the traveler looked up and asked for a sip.

Only then did Dong Tu realize he was seriously injured. Blood dripped from his sleeve and drenched the ground beneath him, and when he took the water Dong Tu offered him, he accepted it with only one hand.

He hid a blood-stained blade in his cloak with the other.

"Are you...okay?" Dong Tu asked warily. She tried to decide if he would be a danger to their small group as she fished the supplies to help stop the bleeding out of her bag, which the injured man gratefully accepted.

"Thank you, lady," he thanked her tiredly. "My name is Ly Tuyen. May I ask for your name, and where you're from? If I ever travel near in the future, I will come and repay your kindness."

"My name is Dong Tu, and my family name is Luu. I belong to the Luu dojo in the Vinh Phuc district," Dong Tu told him. The Luu family had started to gain a reputation in the martial arts world, and it felt good to be able to speak her family's name with pride.

Ly Tuyen's eyes narrowed.

"Luu Dong Tu..." he repeated the name like it was one he'd heard before. "May I ask if you're the Luu Dong Tu who was in a relationship with the King of Poison?"

Dong Tu shrugged.

"It's been a long time since I last saw him. I didn't realize it would be such a popular topic," she added to herself. The story had traveled much further than she'd ever anticipated.

"Well, there are many legends about the King of Poison, but I didn't believe you were real until now. What a coincidence..." Ly Tuyen trailed off ominously, his eyes glinting sharply in a way that made her heart stop. She realized in that moment that the stranger *was* a threat—and that she'd not only given him her name, but also where she *lived*. Ly Tuyen started to reach for Dong Tu, but something stopped him. He looked above them with a glare, gathered every piece of energy he had left, and fled.

Dong Tu turned her head just in time to see Ly Minh Lam come floating down beside her.

"Dong Tu, you have to be careful. That man would have killed you," he told her seriously. "Now come with me to Snowflake Tower. Tuyet Hoa Phi Vu needs you."

Dong Tu's heart gave an awful lurch, and her whole body turned cold: Tuyet Hoa Phi Vu had to have been in trouble. Did it have anything to do with them returning a few days late? Was it her fault?

When they reached Snowflake Tower, they were met with the space that had been so beautifully decorated, having instead become the site of a vicious slaughter. Broken dishes, torn banners and cloths—and bodies, bloody, ruined bodies were piled everywhere. Tuyet Hoa Phi Vu's entire family was piled among the dead. The sight shocked Dong Tu into silence, and hot, horrified tears rolled unchecked down her cheeks. Dong Tu picked her way through the mess until she found her friend, her sister, and pulled her close.

"Tuyet Hoa Phi Vu, I'm so sorry! This is all my fault!"

Tuyet Hoa Phi Vu had been able to keep her face as cool and collected as ever up until that very second. With Dong

Tu's arms around her she broke down, clinging to the woman who had become so dear, and began to sob. Ly Minh Lam and Bao Thuong also tried to hug the two crying women, but Tuyet Hoa Phi Vu pushed them away.

"Dong Tu, you have to take care of me!" Tuyet Hoa Phi Vu cried, burying her head in Dong Tu's shoulder. "You're all I have left! You can't leave me!"

"I won't leave you, Lady Tuyet Hoa," Dong Tu reassured her shakily. "Would you mind coming to live with my family? We're not rich, but at least it's safer than staying in Lac Do alone. We can adopt you, and make you one of our own."

"I will stay with you for my whole life," Tuyet Hoa Phi Vu insisted. "Wherever you go, I will follow you."

Dong Tu nodded.

"I understand. My poor little sister..."

Adding someone to a family was easy, but Dong Tu and the Luu family would never be able to make that tragedy up to Tuyet Hoa Phi Vu, even if they took care of her for a hundred generations. Dong Tu finally pulled away, and knelt down and bowed to Tuyet Hoa Phi Vu.

"Lady Tuyet Hoa, I *will* find a way to repay this debt."

Tuyet Hoa Phi Vu also knelt down, and took Dong Tu's hand in both of her hands. Her face was glazed with tears, her lovely eyes shattering to look upon.

"It's not your fault, Dong Tu," she denied. "I blame myself for having such an ill-fated beauty, a beauty that has brought disaster to my family."

Ly Minh Lam pursed his lips, covered his face, and turned away. Lady Tuyet Hoa's family had been destroyed. It wasn't Dong Tu's fault, but the truth was still the truth: Tuyet Hoa Phi Vu had nothing and no one left. If she hadn't accepted Dong Tu's invitation, her only other option would have been to travel with him instead.

Bringing Tuyet Hoa Phi Vu into their family presented more problems than Dong Tu had known to anticipate. The first problem? Keeping Tuyet Hoa Phi Vu safe was no easy task.

That fact made itself even more abundantly clear on the way back to Vinh Phuc, as they crossed by Tien Thuc Falls where Dong Tu and Tuyet Hoa Phi Vu had been saved by Ly Minh Lam for the first time: someone had been waiting for them.

That *someone* was a still-faceless Switch.

Switch was powerful enough that even after being immobilized so totally, it hadn't taken much time for her to free herself. She had hidden in the caves around Tien Thuc, and despite several days of searching, not even Ly Minh Lam had been able to find her. And as she'd remained hidden, she'd boiled with fury: she was one of the Monstrous

Eighteen, and yet a complete stranger had managed to strip her of her precious face! It was an absolute disgrace, and if she couldn't find a way to take revenge and save face, her reputation would be ruined throughout the Whispered World—forever.

The longer she'd had to stew in her own rage, the angrier she'd become. Switch swore on her own infamous name that if she ever ran into Ly Minh Lam and the others again, she'd tear them all into a hundred pieces!

Switch remained in hiding for many long days, allowing her body—and just as importantly, her chi—to recover from her embarrassing loss; and after days of waiting, she finally got her wish. Dong Tu, Ly Minh Lam, Tuyet Hoa Phi Vu, Bao Thuong and the two guards appeared by the waterfall, talking and laughing loudly without any thought of potential danger.

Like prey walking straight into the mouth of a predator, Switch thought with dark glee. Using her chi to guide her, Switch burst from her hiding spot and barreled straight for the group. Without a face, Switch couldn't shout out; but had she had a mouth, she would have screamed:

Liet Than! You will die by my hands!

Tuyet Hoa Phi Vu suddenly found herself caught between two expert martial artists as Ly Minh Lam used his Whirlwind technique to block Switch's attack. Tuyet Hoa Phi Vu was blown up into the air with the force of the wind, and Dong Tu sprang forward to catch her without hesitation and without any thought given to where they stood. Tuyet Hoa Phi Vu came crashing down into Dong Tu—and they both went tumbling over the edge of the falls.

The next thing Dong Tu knew was darkness.

Which brought them to the second problem. When Stargazer had told Dong Tu to beware of water-related accidents, she hadn't only meant the one time.

The first thing Dong Tu began to notice was being gently, rhythmically ground against rocks and pebbles. Next was the vague awareness of being soaked to the skin by icy water. Finally, as Dong Tu began to wake properly, she realized the dull, constant roar in her ears was the sound of the Falls rumbling in the background. She blinked her eyes open and began to cough up water, her skin stinging with cold and the abrasive grit of the bank beneath her cheek. Her body had clearly been battered around by the rushing waters, judging by the way she ached from head to toe, and her throat and lungs burned from the water she'd inhaled and was trying to clear. It took a moment to register just what had happened, before she remembered the fight with Switch and the fact that she had fallen over the edge alongside Tuyet Hoa Phi Vu.

Dong Tu began to pull herself out of the water completely, crawling weakly up onto the bank, and as she crawled she lifted her head higher and began to search the area for Tuyet Hoa Phi Vu. Fortunately she caught sight of the other woman close by, lying motionless at the edge of the water like a piece of wet cloth. Dong Tu quickly crawled closer.

No one else seemed to be around. She couldn't see or hear the guards, Bao Thuong, or Switch and Ly Minh Lam. Perhaps the latter two were still battling it out at the top of the cliff. Dong Tu gathered her chi and began to use the energy to chase the freezing cold from her body, and once she began to feel the unpleasant prickle of feeling returning to her fingers and toes, she turned her attention to Tuyet Hoa Phi Vu once more. Dong Tu called her name, and tried to brush the wet hair plastered to the other woman's face out of the way.

Tuyet Hoa Phi Vu didn't move. Her skin, already pale as the moon, had taken on an unhealthily white pallor. She too was drenched like a piece of paper soaked in the rain. But it was her stillness that terrified Dong Tu: Tuyet Hoa Phi Vu lay there on the bank as motionless as a corpse. Dong Tu leaned down and pressed her ear against Tuyet Hoa Phi Vu's chest: the taller woman's heart still beat, but it was weak and uneven, and she wasn't breathing.

"Don't you die!" Dong Tu hissed, panicked. She drew on her own chi and let the energy sink into Tuyet Hoa Phi Vu, trying to bring the other woman back into balance: what little chi Tuyet Hoa Phi Vu had was blocked, preventing its flow. Maybe it had been the surprise of the fall, or the shock of the icy water to her system; maybe she had swallowed too much water and was nearly drowned. All Dong Tu knew as she frantically folded her hands together on Tuyet Hoa Phi Vu's chest and began compressions, trying to work with her own chi to bring her back from the edge, was that she would never forgive herself if Tuyet Hoa Phi Vu died.

"Miss Tuyet Hoa, please—keep trying—!" Dong Tu repeated her plea over and over as she worked. She leaned down to listen again, jerking the fabric of Tuyet Hoa Phi Vu's shirt out of the way so she could reach bare skin and listen even more closely. If she was fast, she could still save Tuyet Hoa Phi Vu from imminent death. But the other woman's chest was still cold, her heartbeat still disjointed. Her skin had begun to fade to a sickly grey, and her lips were turning blue.

"Tuyet Hoa Phi Vu! Tuyet Hoa Phi Vu!" Dong Tu called her name several times, shaking her by the shoulders. Still, there wasn't any movement. "Wake up! Please, don't die!"

Casting about for anything else that might help in desperation, Dong Tu remembered a trick she'd been told of years before. She didn't know if it was real, or if it would even work, but she had nothing left to lose. Dong Tu squeezed Tuyet Hoa Phi Vu's nose, lowered her head, put her lips to Tuyet Hoa Phi Vu's mouth and blew with all her might.

Nothing changed. Dong Tu didn't give up.

She didn't keep track of time as she alternated between trying to spur Tuyet Hoa Phi Vu's heart back into rhythm and trying to get her to breathe again, but after what felt like an eternity, Dong Tu slowly realized that Tuyet Hoa Phi Vu's lips were warming up—and after a beat longer, they started moving. Her eyes stayed closed, but they roved beneath her lids as if she was looking around, and her thick lashes moved just so with each turn. Tuyet Hoa Phi Vu's face became rosier, and her lips began to tremble; and while Dong Tu couldn't see it, the corners of her lips curled just so.

Dong Tu finally felt Tuyet Hoa Phi Vu's warm breath wash gently over her own lips, and as she paused, she could feel the other woman's heart return to a regular, if unusually fast, rhythm.

It had worked!

Dong Tu heaved a heavy, shaking sigh of relief.

Tuyet Hoa Phi Vu continued to breathe on her own, and since the immediate danger seemed to have passed, Dong Tu began to take stock of herself and their surroundings once more. The closer she looked, the more she noticed—and what she noticed turned her pink.

Dong Tu was practically on top of Tuyet Hoa Phi Vu, one hand still left on her chest, the other still cupping Tuyet Hoa Phi Vu's cheek. Tuyet Hoa Phi Vu, lying beneath her, had slid her hand up to hold Dong Tu's arm.

When Tuyet Hoa Phi Vu opened her eyes, the two were looking straight at each other. Dong Tu had never looked so deeply into someone's eyes, not once. Even when she'd been with Obsidian, Dong Tu had been too overwhelmed by it all to let herself have something so intimate. Tuyet Hoa Phi Vu's eyelashes were still wet, and her clear eyes reflected the clouds of the early spring sky; Dong Tu found herself unable to look away, lips still hovering above Tuyet Hoa Phi Vu's own lovely mouth, and as Dong Tu stared, Tuyet Hoa Phi Vu seemed to lean up just the smallest amount and close that slight distance. Their lips touched once more.

Had Tuyet Hoa Phi Vu just *kissed* her? Or had that been an accident?

Dong Tu slowly pushed herself up, flushed and confused, and decided to distract herself from thinking about it too closely. Instead she sat back enough to get a good look at the rest of Tuyet Hoa Phi Vu since she was awake and apparently well—and froze as her gaze passed over the other woman's throat. The thing that caught her eye was something it had snagged on just moments before, but she'd been too focused on keeping Tuyet Hoa Phi Vu alive to give it a thought.

She wasn't busy anymore.

Usually covered by high, elegant collars, the column of Tuyet Hoa Phi Vu's throat wasn't slender and smooth. Right before her eyes was the prominent curve of Tuyet Hoa Phi Vu's larynx, sharper and more present than they ever were in women. Dong Tu gasped quietly, and before she could control herself, she ran her fingers down Tuyet Hoa Phi Vu's throat, right over the bump—and then down even further. She'd already bared the other's chest in her panicked determination, which meant she was free to see and feel the shape of Tuyet Hoa Phi Vu's chest. What she found astonished her, and presented the final issue with adopting Tuyet Hoa Phi Vu into the family as her sister: Tuyet Hoa Phi Vu wasn't a woman at all!

Like everyone else, Dong Tu had been uncertain of what to make of Tuyet Hoa Phi Vu at first. Their androgynous beauty had been enchanting and yet utterly baffling when it came to any form of polite address. But now the knowledge hit her like a bell being rung in her ear, like a flock of crows suddenly bursting out of the trees around her, like an owl swooping silently out of nowhere to catch an unseen mouse by her feet.

How could she have been so blind?!

Tuyet Hoa Phi Vu's impressive height was only reasonable for a man.

Tuyet Hoa Phi Vu's strong jaw was only reasonable for a man.

The breadth of his shoulders, the depth of his voice, his mannerisms, his clothing—*everything* was indicative of Tuyet Hoa Phi Vu's being a man. Sure, Tuyet Hoa Phi Vu chose to wear those glittering teardrop earrings, to wear makeup like he was a lady, had chosen to veil himself when he'd first come to Vinh Phuc...but surely those things had a reasonable explanation?

What was ridiculous was the fact that it had taken Dong Tu so long to realize it when the two of them had been inseparable for nearly two weeks.

Tuyet Hoa Phi Vu remained absolutely still as Dong Tu had her revelation, still holding her arm, one hand resting at her waist. And he stayed still, his gaze fixed on Dong Tu, as the young woman scrambled to her feet.

Dong Tu stared at Tuyet Hoa Phi Vu for a long time, her eyes as round as the pebbles on the shore in her consternation.

Above them the clouds floated on.

Cold water continued to flow along the stream, gurgling its merry music.

The waterfall above them thundered relentlessly down, creating a frothy white foam that floated on the churning surface of the water at its base, and clung to the rocks in and around the pool that formed where the water met the earth.

A flock of crows passed overhead, calling out to each other.

And after a long, long time...

Dong Tu shouted so loud her voice seemed to split the heavens.

"OH MY GOD!" she screamed. *"OH MY GOD!"*

After days of being so close, Tuyet Hoa Phi Vu turned out to be a *man?!*

Every event of the past ten days came shooting back through Dong Tu's mind like lightning-fast arrows. The night they'd spent in the caves with Ly Minh Lam, Tuyet Hoa Phi Vu had changed her clothes! Tuyet Hoa Phi Vu had doted on her the entire trip, being openly affectionate and sweet—when he'd taken them all shopping, he had hugged her, brushed her hair! Tuyet Hoa Phi Vu had carried her to her room after she'd drunk herself stupid, slept next to her at night, held her hands, touched her face—

Dong Tu could still taste his lips from minutes before!

Tuyet Hoa Phi Vu sat up, pulled his shirt closed and raised his hands to cover his chest.

"Big sister, did you just defile my manly body?" Tuyet Hoa Phi Vu's teardrop-shaped earrings glittered in the light as he moved, and again as he tossed his head to shake the water away from his beautiful face.

"Y-you—you—you're a man!" Dong Tu exclaimed, scaring off whatever birds were left in the vicinity.

Miles and miles away, Bach Duong sneezed.

"That's strange, why am I getting goosebumps? I must have caught a cold...."

———

As it turned out, Tuyet Hoa Phi Vu being a man wasn't even the most complicated part of adopting him into the Luu family. Dong Tu and the others had failed in their mission to return Tuyet Hoa Phi Vu home within the allotted seven days, and as a result, his entire family had been wiped out. Dong Tu's family accepted that responsibility without question. The problem was, Tuyet Hoa Phi Vu firmly refused to be anyone's junior when it came to establishing him within the family's hierarchy.

Dong Tu had intended to bring Tuyet Hoa Phi Vu back to be her younger sister. After her revelation, however, there was no way he could be the second or third lady of the Luu family; he wasn't a lady at all. Tuyet Hoa Phi Vu then proposed his own solution: marriage. Both he and Dong Tu's engagements had ended (and begun) horribly. If Dong Tu married him, he would become her fiancé, and thus a member of the family.

It was a solution that would kill two birds with one stone.

"Are you crazy?" Dong Tu shouted him down indignantly. She was still mortified by the entire ordeal, and furious with him for letting it go on so long.

"Your engagement. Were you being forced to marry the magistrate's son?" Xuan Thu, Dong Tu's sister, asked.

Tuyet Hoa Phi Vu shook his head. It had been Bach Duong and Dong Tu who'd mistaken him for a woman from the start, and then everyone else had gone along. It had been convenient in more ways than one, not the least of which being that being a "girl" gave him the chance to stay close to Dong Tu. It hadn't been something he'd been in a hurry to give up. But his marriage?

"It's not that I was being forced to marry the Lac Do magistrate's son, the Lac Do magistrate's son is me," Tuyet Hoa Phi Vu explained.

"You are the son of Lac Do's magistrate?!"

"I am," Tuyet Hoa Phi Vu affirmed with a nod. The family broke out into gasps and whispers of shock and interest.

No wonder he spent so excessively: he practically screamed of wealth from his clothing to his manners. But why was the first son of the Lac Do district forced into a marriage?

The story was a cursed one. Tuyet Hoa Phi Vu had always been disastrously beautiful, drawing the gazes of all who saw him, and covetous desires were never far behind. One such greedy individual had been a young woman from the Nhung family. They were a superficial group, but they were dangerous. The moment Tuyet Hoa Phi Vu had reached marriageable age, she'd demanded they be wed.

"I didn't care for Lady Nhung. She was plain, and... weird. But she liked me whether I liked her or not, and while my family had power, hers is extremely wealthy and is known for using violence to get what they want. Our hands were tied: if we didn't want any trouble, I had to marry her."

No one in the room was any less astonished by Tuyet Hoa Phi Vu's explanation. A woman being forced into a marriage against her will was a sad occurrence, but it wasn't unusual. But for a man to be forced like that...it was truly an eye-opening tale.

And at the end of it all, poor Tuyet Hoa Phi Vu, the beautiful and stylish son of Lac Do's magistrate, had ended up with nothing.

As the room calmed down, Dong Tu's father came up with his own solution.

"Well, let's decide your role based on your age. Mr. Tuyet Hoa, how old are you?"

Tuyet Hoa Phi Vu paused for a moment. He looked at Dong Tu and tried to guess her age: he'd heard that she'd been very young when she met the King of Poison, no more than fourteen or fifteen. If it had been two years since, surely she had to be sixteen or seventeen. Her face was far too young and fresh for her to be any older than that.

"I'm eighteen," Tuyet Hoa Phi Vu replied, obviously lying. Dong Tu's father smiled and shook his head.

"Eighteen? So, Mr. Tuyet Hoa, Dong Tu will be your elder sister, and Xuan Thu will be your younger sister. That's the final decision."

Tuyet Hoa Phi Vu pursed his lips, cursing in his head.

"Mr. Tuyet Hoa, you are free to keep your own name. But if you're afraid of being pursued, you can change your name to Luu Dong Trung: Middle of Winter. That way, you can start a new chapter in your life." From Dancing Snowflakes to Middle of Winter, Tuyet Hoa Phi Vu would still be able to keep the essence of who he was, without the danger of remaining attached to his old family name. "What do you think?"

"Luu Dong Trung isn't bad," Tuyet Hoa Phi Vu mumbled to himself. He looked back up and bowed to Dong Tu's father, the head of his new family. "Father...from now on, please let Dong Trung take the refuge in the Luu family."

"Let that be the final decision," Mr. Luu agreed. "From now on, our family will have a new member: Luu Dong Trung. You will be a good brother to my daughters."

CHAPTER 5

Newcomers

Luu Dong Trung, formerly known as Tuyet Hoa Phi Vu, was a human version of an onion. Each layer that was peeled back seemed to reveal a completely new person, and the more one peeled, the more tear-inducing he became—both in sadness and in hilarity. He'd started as a cold, classy, mysterious individual, and then became the resilient damsel in distress Dong Tu had believed him to be; he'd been a miserable beauty trying to save his family, did a complete about-face and morphed into a flirtatious man—and the latest layer showed him to be an extremely determined little brother.

He embraced his new, frugal life once he'd been adopted into the Luu family. Luu Dong Trung didn't wear any makeup, unlike his previous incarnation; he dressed like a man, acted like a man, and no longer wore his glittering teardrop earrings. With his cold beauty given up, he became a respected, soft-spoken (and dangerously silver-tongued) student. He was still as calm as ever, and as it turned out, his calm was the product of indefatigable cleverness and intelligence.

Luu Dong Trung was always a step ahead of...everyone.

Mr. Luu recognized that Dong Trung's strengths lay in his smarts, and assigned Dong Trung to manage the administrative duties of the dojo. He was responsible for client consultations, keeping their books, and tracking their numbers, and he managed it flawlessly. Under his direction, the Luus' most profitable ventures shifted: the majority of their income had previously come from their services as armed escorts between districts, but after he took control, women flocked to the dojo to learn. Enough came that while Luu Dong Trung had no real chi, and hadn't bothered to learn martial arts because of it, he began to study a variation of the Sunlight Strike that Dong Tu had studied closely so that he could help the family teach.

Dong Tu had yet to unlock any real power in the technique, and had not seen its application in a real fight; but what she did notice, and what the rest of the women who came to their dojo noticed, was that it was remarkably good for their health. With some tweaking here and there, the Luu family created their own special technique using the Sunlight Strike and marketed it as a way to improve fitness and beauty. They weren't wrong: those who came to study found themselves slimmer and more flexible. Their skin looked healthier, their cheeks rosier, and their eyes shone with new vibrance.

Dong Tu found herself wondering if perhaps Stargazer had told her to learn the Sunlight Strike two years before just to make her more attractive to Obsidian.

Luu Dong Trung became a teaching assistant during classes, but his presence seemed to be as much of a hindrance as it was a help. He was no less handsome than he had been before, despite his plainer style, and his own body had been sculpted all the more finely from his own training—which meant that the more often he came around to adjust the students' postures and positions, the more often the students intentionally adjusted themselves in ways that required a little more correcting. He was a sensation, and all of the women in their district seemed to adore him.

But none of that mattered.

Luu Dong Trung's heart was set on Dong Tu.

As time went on he had his name legally changed, and when he returned, he pulled Dong Tu aside.

"Luu Dong Tu, whenever you change your mind...you are still welcome to call me your husband," he reminded her. Yes, he had become her brother in part because the entire Tuyet Hoa family had been annihilated, but the moment she was ready, he would *happily* take the upgrade. Being adopted into the family had been a good way to get his foot in the door.

Dong Tu stared at him without blinking. As always, his face was as still and smooth as ice on a lake in the middle of winter. He flirted playfully with her all the time, and she couldn't decide if he was joking, or telling her the truth. What a weird man.

Of course, trying to determine whether or not Dong Trung was genuine was all the more difficult when he liked to play mind games. One day he caught Dong Tu's gaze and held it intently, his sparkling eyes piercing straight through her.

"Do you know why Obsidian hasn't contacted you in so long, Dong Tu?" he asked softly. Dong Tu found herself morbidly curious.

"Why?"

"Because he wanted to end your relationship. Obsidian is one of the Monstrous Eighteen, the King of Poison, and you—you are a normal girl. You're not from the Whispered World, you barely know anything about serious martial arts. Those people are masters. You're from completely different worlds, and he knows you will only get in his way. He also knows that being near you only ever brought disaster to you and your family," Luu Dong Trung explained.

The words stung like salt in a wound. Dong Tu hadn't expected an answer like that, and she couldn't help the way her eyes suddenly brimmed with thick, burning tears. Dong Trung paused for a moment and studied her in mild confusion, surprised by the tears. His usually stoic face pulled into a concerned and empathetic frown.

"He did it for you. He deliberately cut off contact because he hoped you would forget him, and live a long, safe, happy life away from the Whispered World," he pointed out softly. "It was Obsidian's wish that when he volunteered his life to save you from the poison, you would be able to go home to your loved ones."

Luu Dong Trung watched as Dong Tu absorbed his bittersweet comfort. After a second, he pulled her into a gentle embrace and bent his head to whisper in her ear.

"He wanted to save you so that you could find another handsome man, who is able to pamper and love you the way you should be loved. A man who can bring you happiness, and peace...who can give you a simple life away from all that death and darkness."

Dong Tu frowned, and finally realized what he had to be doing. Her suspicions were immediately confirmed as Luu Dong Trung whispered again: he began to paint a picture of the cold-hearted Obsidian and his cruel but noble sacrifice, abandoning her so that she could be free. Dong Trung spoke of fishing, planting trees; he talked of starting a family, having children, picking flowers in the spring and bathing in the river in the summers, watching the leaves turn in autumn—and curling up in warm blankets with another handsome man in the winter. That other handsome man was him, of course: Tuyet Hoa Phi Vu. And as he wove his words together, he pulled away from her ear, bending closer and closer until there was almost no space left between them.

All he needed was a sign from Dong Tu, and he could end his speech with the opening kiss of yet another historic chapter in Dong Tu's love life.

But Dong Tu was not so easily deceived. She kicked Luu Dong Trung, and straightened up as tall as she could so she could smack him in the neck.

"You're full of crap!"

"Aren't I the type of man Obsidian wanted for you?" Dong Trung asked as he dodged Dong Tu's assault. "I'm handsome and tall, I'm not some dangerous fighter, and I'm not involved with the Whispered World! I love you no less than Obsidian, and which one of us is by your side, every day, straightening your clothes, taking care of you, doing anything you ask?"

In his defense, Luu Dong Trung wasn't wrong. He *was* handsome and tall; on a scale from one to ten, he was an eleven without question. He was clever, intelligent, and aside from his own weird idiosyncrasies, he was normal. Harmless. Safe. But to Dong Tu, the most important questions still remained unanswered.

Was a marriage to Luu Dong Trung really what Obsidian would want for her? Was that the real reason she hadn't heard from him in so long? Or had something else befallen him?

If that was the case, Dong Tu wondered if Obsidian would strangle Dong Trung in furious jealousy if he returned to find her married to someone else. She didn't know how he'd react if he returned and found out she had another lover at all. Dong Tu forgot Luu Dong Trung's presence entirely as she lost herself in her thoughts: *would* Obsidian be jealous? Would he be sad? Would he be happy for her?

The last question hanging heavy in her mind was also the most painful.

Had Obsidian already forgotten her?

Dong Tu's heart ached as she remembered that in his own world, Obsidian was constantly accompanied by women she could never measure up to. Dao Que Chi and Ivy were both deadly yet ethereal beauties: Dao Que Chi was tender and elegant, while Ivy was powerful and lascivious, and both of them were master martial artists in the Poison Legion, which Obsidian helped to lead. She could easily picture Obsidian with either one of them.

Meanwhile, Luu Dong Trung was right. Dong Tu had already been shown that there wasn't any place for her in Obsidian's world, not unless so many things changed...and she wasn't sure her life in Vinh Phuc could handle everything Obsidian's presence would bring. The two of them having any kind of future together seemed like an impossibility.

Life in Vinh Phuc had been quiet and peaceful for two years. Luu Dong Trung's adoption had brought change, but it hadn't up-ended their whole lives. Yet it seemed the journey to take Tuyet Hoa Phi Vu back to Lac Do had triggered a new stream of strangers, all coming to visit the Luu family—all coming because Ly Tuyen, the man Dong Tu had helped on the side of the road, had begun to spread the information she'd foolishly given him throughout the Whispered World.

At first the visitors were innocuous, only coming because they'd heard the story of Dong Tu and the King of Poison and *had* to see the woman who'd stolen Obsidian's heart for themselves. The Monstrous Eighteen were as elusive as they were famous, but Dong Tu gave them a concrete touchpoint, and every visitor tried to grill her on all things Obsidian: about the black snow that fell wherever he went, about his mysterious behavior—they even asked about his clothing, his mask and gloves.

"I heard he's very handsome!" Ryujin, one of the guests, said. "Is it true? What does he look like?" What she really wanted to know was if he was handsome and *single,* or if he had promised himself to Dong Tu.

Ryujin was no ordinary woman. Her eyes were large and catlike, and her gaze pierced like a knife; some of her hair had been twisted and tied into little horns atop her head, which hung down to her shoulders in a shining blue sheet. Ryujin's mouth was ever-pouting, but though her expression was often haughty, she seemed to be friendly despite her heavy rebellious streak and a belief that there was no reason to smile or laugh just to make someone else feel better.

No one really knew when Ryujin arrived. She'd just appeared one day, hanging upside down with her feet hooked in the rafters, and interrupted an ongoing conversation. She wore large, metal hoop earrings, a similarly large silver necklace, and tight leather clothes with more metal accents. She was never seen without a small knife, and went back and forth between picking her nails with it and tossing it from hand to hand.

Ryujin also happened to be one of the Monstrous Eighteen. Like all the other members, she was skilled beyond most anyone else in the world when it came to martial arts; and like the rest of the masters, she preferred to keep the company of those who matched her in skill and knowledge. But there weren't many people who were as talented as she was, let alone in the same age group, which meant that if she wanted to find a lover who was young, talented, *and* handsome, she was going to be forced to find them within the existing Eighteen. It was next to impossible, which was why she'd leapt at the chance to come see Dong Tu for herself.

Like...*everyone* from the Whispered World when meeting Dong Tu for the first time, after having heard the stories and picturing some grand beauty, Ryujin was...underwhelmed by Dong Tu when they finally met face-to-face.

"Obsidian preferred an ordinary girl like you?" she wondered aloud, not caring about how rude it might have been to say it in Dong Tu's presence—just like everyone else. "Does he just have bad taste, or what?"

"Dong Tu reminded him of the normal life he had always longed for," Luu Dong Trung interjected. He then proceeded to analyze Obsidian's entire decision-making process for Ryujin: how Obsidian was kidnapped as a young child and taken to the Poison Legion in the Valley of Life and Death, and how his innate talent and fervor had led to both a promotion and the honor of bearing the Storm Pearl; how he'd been respected by everyone in the Valley, and how his future with the Poison Legion was bright—and how deep in his heart, Obsidian didn't want any of it. He hadn't wanted to master poisons and be embroiled in the constant warfare of the Whispered World. He wanted to return to the light, and be a regular person once more.

Luu Dong Trung reaffirmed the fact that Dong Tu—being able to touch her, be close to her, someone pure and light—had reawakened his dreams of going home again, to be Bach Phong, brother of Bach Duong and the youngest son of the great General Bach.

"He wasn't attracted to Dong Tu just because she was his first love, but also because Dong Tu represented his deepest desires," Luu Dong Trung finished.

"Oh, that's it!" Ryujin agreed with a nod. Dong Tu also nodded. Even if Dong Trung had never laid eyes on Obsidian before, he still understood every nuance of the complexities of Obsidian and Dong Tu's attraction. If the Monstrous Eighteen had been recruiting based on psychoanalytical abilities instead of martial arts skill, Luu Dong Trung would already have been a member.

"Well, well...and who are you, handsome?" Ryujin asked, turning her full attention on Luu Dong Trung. She held his gaze without faltering, and a mischievous smirk curled her lips. He might not have been one of the Monstrous Eighteen, which was disappointing, but he *was* gorgeous. He was handsome enough to make Ryujin rethink her standards: should she set her sights on Luu Dong Trung instead, martial arts skills be damned?

After that conversation, she came to visit...*often*.

Ryujin was only one among the many who came to the Luu dojo to investigate the claims made about Dong Tu and the Poison King. Most of them were peaceful. They would drink tea with the family, eat a few cakes, and ask Dong Tu as many questions as they could think up. They always asked the same questions: did she know where Obsidian was? Just how deep did their relationship go? What did Dong Tu know about the fabled Storm Pearl?

Inevitably, they all came to realize that Dong Tu and the Luu family were nothing more than a normal, middle-class family running a comfortably successful dojo. Most would return once or twice more, hoping for updates; but when no extra information ever presented itself, they stopped coming.

And despite how the people of the Whispered World reacted to seeing Dong Tu for the first time, there were those who liked her the moment they met, and decided to stay for a while. One of those guests was a man named Le Minh, who fell for her charm at first sight. Wherever she went, his gaze followed. He had a small dog named Yibo that walked beside him everywhere he went, and just like his owner, Yibo immediately took a liking to Dong Tu. He had a habit of hopping up into her lap and panting happily, his tongue lolling out the whole time he was there.

"It's a beautiful spring day outside. Would you like to walk with me, and talk?" Le Minh offered one day. Yibo's tail began to wag excitedly, but Bao Thuong and Luu Dong Trung simultaneously objected. If Le Minh wanted to ask Dong Tu anything, he could ask her right there at the dojo. Was taking her outside really necessary?

Bao Thuong and Luu Dong Trung were like feng-shui unicorns, but instead of guarding the house, they shut down every possibility Dong Tu had for a relationship with someone else.

Dong Tu completely ignored them.

Spring was in full swing: the grass had returned, thick and green, and leaves finally sprouted, bright and fresh, from the tree branches. She wanted to go out, enjoy the sunshine and flowers with Le Minh, and talk.

Dong Tu let her fingers trail over flowers and tall grasses as she walked, and the scents of apple flowers and lavender hung sweetly on the air around them. It had been a long time since she'd taken a walk with a man like that, and he watched her with a sweet softness as she moved. Picking a beautiful pink cherry blossom, he tucked it into her hair.

Le Minh was a dignified man. He wasn't unusually tall, but he was still tall enough that he could look Dong Tu in the eye without having to bow down like Luu Dong Trung. He was in good shape, not too thin and not too large, and he was an elegant gentleman as well: he carried a folded fan, and his hair was fashionably wavy.

"The flower goes well with your shirt," he complimented. Dong Tu smiled shyly, but before she could respond, someone else interrupted.

"Thank you! I chose that shirt." Luu Dong Trung had followed them, even though he had clearly not been invited on their romantic excursion. Bao Thuong followed just behind him, and Dong Tu and Le Minh looked at each other awkwardly. They were both shy, unwilling to speak openly if there was going to be an unwanted audience, and they finished their walk mostly in silence.

"You are a traditional woman! How can you go walking with a strange guy like that?" Dong Trung scolded her later.

Bao Thuong nodded his own agreement. It was unacceptable! Girls couldn't take risks like that, it was dangerous!

"If she never talks to men she doesn't know, she'll never have any chance of getting married—"

"—And she'll stay single for the rest of her life."

Luu Tien and Luu Ky, Dong Tu's other two brothers, defended her firmly. The family had six children, seven with the addition of Dong Trung. If no one ever got married and left when they came of age, their comfortable house would quickly become far too small for them all. Luu Tien and Luu Ky were Dong Tu's blood brothers, not adopted, and had no ulterior motives when it came to their sister's suitors. If a visitor seemed like a good man, they happily encouraged Dong Tu to make friends. Dong Tu's younger sister, Xuan Thu, agreed with her brothers: Dong Tu had mourned the absence of Obsidian for two whole years. It had been such a long time, and she needed to move on.

That Dong Tu's other siblings were encouraging her to seek a boyfriend who wasn't him frustrated Luu Dong Trung to no end. What did he have to do to make the family see he was the perfect choice for her husband?

Luu Dong Trung's fixation wasn't just frustrating for Dong Tu. Ryujin and Le Minh were also annoyed by his attachment to her—Le Minh because he was adorably smitten with Dong Tu, and Ryujin because *she* was still interested in Dong Trung. Anyone watching from outside would be able to see troubles brewing in their love lives.

But that wasn't the only trouble brewing.

There had always been people who sought out Obsidian and the Storm Pearl for their own gains. Obsidian was a surprisingly impossible person to track down, considering the fact that the poison that saturated his body combined with the magic of the Storm Pearl in a manner that left black snowflakes falling around him wherever he went. It was a unique phenomenon that should have been immediately recognizable, and yet next to no one had ever seen him.

Now, though…now the people of the Whispered World knew of someone who had. Someone he cared about. And more importantly, they knew exactly where that someone was.

It was Ly Tuyen himself who showed up at the Luu dojo, after finally recovering from his injuries. Whether Dong Tu was certain of where she stood with Obsidian or not, Ly Tuyen was convinced the King of Poison truly loved his ordinary dojo girl. There was no other explanation for the way Obsidian had so readily risked his life for hers—no other explanation for the way he had endured the worst test known throughout the Whispered World, just to ensure Dong Tu got the antidote she needed.

Ly Tuyen firmly believed that if he kidnapped Dong Tu, if he threatened the woman Obsidian loved so much, the

King of Poison would be forced to come out of the shadows and make a deal. He entered the dojo bristling with weapons, his face twisted into an intense glare.

"Dong Tu!" Ly Tuyen shouted. "You're coming with me. And you will come quietly!"

CHAPTER 6

The People at Your Side

Dong Tu hadn't been the only person in the dojo when Ly Tuyen strode in and shouted. Le Minh and Ryujin had stuck around; Le Minh was hoping for more time with Dong Tu, and Ryujin was hoping to tempt Luu Dong Trung away from Dong Tu. Before Dong Tu could properly react, Le Minh cleared his throat and flicked his fan open.

Ly Tuyen drew his sword and attacked, but he had underestimated Le Minh and his fan. He lunged left and was blocked; he darted to the right—and tripped. He fell into the table, pushed himself up, lost his balance again and cracked his head on a pillar, and finally smacked face-first into the floor.

He'd been rebuffed by a man with a *fan*.

Ryujin was still sitting by the table, carelessly sprawled out in her chair. She paid no attention to the fight happening around her, casually using her little knife to clean her nails like it was just a peaceful afternoon. She didn't even look up as Ly Tuyen picked himself up off the ground and came at Le Minh once more.

Until Ly Tuyen came crashing into her.

Ryujin didn't even stand up. She took one irritated look at him, and with a single kick she sent Ly Tuyen careening through the air and straight out of the dojo completely.

Ly Tuyen had lost spectacularly to Le Minh and Ryujin in a matter of *minutes*.

He turned and ran, and with his special talent for evading dangers, he was never seen at the Luu dojo ever again.

He might have been the first of the would-be kidnappers, but he wasn't the last. They never stopped coming, yet Dong Tu didn't know who they were, where they'd come from... she didn't even know what they looked like, because they were all beaten away before she even had a chance to get to them. All she saw were the remnants left over from the fights, scattered across the front courtyard: small blood spatters, broken swords, darts that had been forgotten as their owner beat their escape, and even teeth. It worried Dong Tu, and Luu Dong Trung could see it, so he started waking up early to sweep away the leftovers. From then on, when she woke up in the morning, all she ever saw was Dong Trung sweeping; and if he noticed her watching him, he would stop, flash his innocent smile, and wave his hand adorably like he was merely sweeping away leaves.

"I can't believe it's summer already. Should we go somewhere to avoid the heat?" Le Minh suggested one day. He was beginning to get bored with lazing around: there were only so many times they could drink tea and play chess at the dojo before going mad. Time had flown: spring had ended, and summer had come bringing singing cicadas and scorching heat. Dong Tu was lying on a large, heavy wooden bed in the hall while Dong Trung sat beside her and fed her watermelon.

"Have you ever visited Thanh Liet Lake, Dong Tu?" Le Minh continued. The name caught her interest instantly. Thanh Liet Lake? Was that in any way related to the Liet Than Stargazer had told her about? Dong Tu absently opened her mouth as Dong Trung waved a piece of watermelon in front of her, lost in the possibilities that filled her mind. If Thanh Liet or Liet Than had anything to do with Obsidian, it was worth a trip.

"Thanh Liet Lake? Ah, that's the lake that's jade green and ice cold all year long," Dong Trung interjected knowingly as Dong Tu chewed her watermelon. Le Minh nodded. Thanh Liet Lake was famous for its beauty, and during the summers it was a popular getaway. Swimming and fishing were among the top attractions, and Le Minh was hoping he could steal away on a boat with Dong Tu, just the two of them and his dog, Yibo. It would be the perfect romantic outing, and he knew that as long as he stayed with the Luus, Bao Thuong and Luu Dong Trung would see to it that he never got a private moment alone with Dong Tu.

"Okay, let's go," Luu Dong Trung agreed. He was well aware that he hadn't been invited, but he wasn't going to let Le Minh and Dong Tu take a trip like that alone.

"I'll go too," Ryujin chimed in. She was followed not only by Bao Thuong's eager acceptance, but Xuan Thu's as well. Le Minh sighed, and Yibo barked and whined at his owner's disappointment. Le Minh had no choice: if he wanted to take Dong Tu at all, he would also have to take the menagerie that came with her.

The only people happier about the trip were Dong Tu's older brothers, Tien and Ky. With the big group gone, the house would be quiet and empty for the rest of the summer.

Thanh Liet Lake did not disappoint.

The water was a rich, clear jade green, and its perfectly still surface reflected the sky like a mirror. Tall trees shaded the shoreline and waved in a gentle rush with the breeze. The summer heat was just as oppressive there, but seeing the cool water brought an instant sense of relief. The sound of insects singing was music to their ears—but the arrival of the six-person group, plus Yibo, shattered the serene spell so effectively it was almost comical.

The three men fought over the right to attend to Dong Tu on the journey. Luu Dong Trung was the most dedicated of them all, waiting on her hand and foot, clinging to her hand wherever they went—but Dong Tu had gotten used to that back when Luu Dong Trung had gone by Tuyet Hoa Phi Vu, and had let Dong Tu believe he was a woman. Bao Thuong showed his devotion through luggage duty, a hard job with little praise, and Le Minh...Le Minh carried Yibo. But there was genius in it: Luu Dong Trung and Bao Thuong might have been trying to keep Le Minh from talking to Dong Tu, but Yibo was just as determined to help his master succeed. He continued to charm Dong Tu, whining when Dong Tu strayed too far from he and his master, and whenever Luu Dong Trung tried to cut in while they were talking, Yibo barked loudly enough to drive him away.

After checking in to the guest house and getting their things put away, the group wasted no time in heading for Thanh Liet Lake itself. Luu Dong Trung stripped out of his shirt without hesitation, showing off his lithe, toned body. He dove elegantly into the lake with barely a splash, and his long, dark hair billowed out around him, rippling and swirling prettily as he swam. The way his tall, slender body moved and the way his hair danced beneath the water were almost enough to convince someone that mermaids really did exist.

Ryujin grinned happily as she watched him. She'd decided to keep holding out for a man who could match her skills in martial arts, but that didn't mean she couldn't enjoy what was right in front of her. It would be a waste to ignore that kind of show.

Luu Dong Trung came up out of the water streaming, his gleaming-wet body glistening in the summer sunlight. He saw Ryujin watching him and pretended to cover his chest as if preserving his dignity, and then let his attention be drawn to Dong Tu. He swam over and held his arms open wide.

"Dong Tu! Jump in, honey! I'll catch you!" he called. The double-standard was obvious to everyone, including Dong Tu; and while Luu Dong Trung called out yet again, Dong Tu refused to be taken in. She climbed up into a tree instead and jumped into the water away from where Dong Trung was waiting for her. She remained beneath the crystal clear water happily, opening her eyes so that she could look at the world beneath the surface. It was calm and quiet in a soothing, peaceful way, and the tension that she'd been carrying for months began to melt away as she hung suspended in the cool water.

And then Luu Dong Trung's body appeared in Dong Tu's vision. He ducked down beneath the water, his hair bobbing and billowing around him, and blew bubbles directly into her face. Dong Tu jerked her head up out of the water and began to smack at him.

"What! I was only bringing air down to help you breathe," Luu Dong Trung explained with faked innocence, but there was no hiding the mischief shining in his eyes or in the tiny curl of his lips.

Back on the bank, Le Minh watched Dong Tu and Luu Dong Trung chase each other with disappointment. It was such a waste of a good romantic opportunity, to have the two of them so engrossed in each other instead of he and Dong Tu having the time he'd been craving. And beyond that, Dong Tu's relationships with her adoptive brothers were...complicated.

Dong Tu and Bao Thuong's relationship wasn't too terribly unusual. They'd grown up together, to the point where they'd even bathed together when they were small; and now as adults Bao Thuong was a gentleman, keeping a proper distance between himself and Dong Tu. Luu Dong Trung, however, was a big concern.

He'd only been with the Luu family for a few months, and yet he behaved as if he and Dong Tu were born and raised together. More specifically, he behaved like a two-year-old, innocently holding Dong Tu's hand, leaning over and kissing her cheek at will. Wherever Dong Tu went, he followed, sticking more closely to her than Yibo did a tray of food. And though Yibo tried his best, Dong Trung was still magically there to interfere every time Le Minh found a chance to flirt with Dong Tu.

If Le Minh picked flowers for Dong Tu, Luu Dong Trung would offer to bring Dong Tu the flowers and then claim he'd picked them himself. If Le Minh wanted to fan Dong Tu when the weather was unbearably hot, Luu Dong Trung would beat him to it, and stand there fanning enthusiastically. When flying kites or fishing, Dong Trung always stole Dong Tu's attention away from Le Minh, screaming and tugging at the lines, ruining the moment and scaring away the fish. Luu Dong Trung even showed Le Minh up in a drinking contest one night, drinking endlessly without seeming to feel a single drop. Dong Trung wasn't a wrench in the gears so much as he was a herd of elephants smashing straight through the center of town.

Xuan Thu and Ryujin weren't any help, either. Ryujin was only there *to* watch Luu Dong Trung show off, and Xuan Thu...just didn't care.

Le Minh sighed to himself, trying to come up with ways to salvage the situation—ways to get some alone time with Dong Tu, when she was so closely guarded by Bao Thuong on one side and had Dong Trung sticking to her like sap on the other. It might have been different if Luu Dong Trung had been getting in the way accidentally, but it was far too painfully intentional to pretend anything else. Eventually Le

Minh decided it was time to negotiate with the enemy, and pulled Dong Trung aside.

"Luu Dong Trung, we've known each other for a while now. I think it's time for a serious, man-to-man conversation," Le Minh began quietly.

"Okay," Dong Trung accepted with a small frown. "What is this about?"

"It's about your sister. I really like her, and she isn't promised to anyone. Can you help me get some time with her?"

Luu Dong Trung pretended to think, then nodded.

"Luu Xuan Thu is a beautiful and intelligent person. Of course I'll help!"

"It's not Xuan Thu," Le Minh denied in irritation. Luu Dong Trung's eyebrows rose.

"Then perhaps you like Bao Yen," he guessed. Bao Yen was the youngest daughter, only six or seven years old. "Ewww, Le Minh, you're sick!"

Le Minh couldn't take it anymore. He'd tried to be polite, he'd tried to come to Dong Trung and discuss the matter respectfully, but the other man refused to take him seriously.

"You know I mean Dong Tu!" Le Minh snapped sharply. His upset made Yibo bark at Luu Dong Trung all over again. Dong Trung's playfulness vanished in an instant, and though he smiled, his eyes were as cold as Thanh Liet Lake.

"You don't have a chance with Dong Tu," he denied with an eerie surety.

"What do you mean?" Le Minh demanded. "Do you mean because she loved Obsidian? It's been two years, and he hasn't tried to contact her once. If they were engaged before, the engagement is surely cancelled now."

Luu Dong Trung didn't explain. He merely smirked at Le Minh and waited for him to come to the answer on his own.

Le Minh looked away and frowned in thought. Obsidian...no one knew where he was, or what had happened to him. Was it possible for him to be poisoned and die, after taking all of those poisons in exchange for the antidotes that saved Dong Tu's life? Or maybe, after the news that he had the Storm Pearl had spread, someone had killed him for it. Perhaps he'd even been forced to marry the Cassia of the Poison Legion, Dao Que Chi, and was busy changing diapers day in day out in the heart of the Valley of Life and Death.

Luu Dong Trung waited, bored, as Le Minh pondered over the answer.

"If it's not because of Obsidian, then who?" Le Minh asked again, but all Dong Trung did was slowly tug at his earlobe, as if remembering the weight of the earrings he used to wear. Finally it all clicked.

"You?"

And there it was. Le Minh and Dong Trung were finally having the conversation that confirmed what everyone already knew: Le Minh and Luu Dong Trung were both trying to win Dong Tu's heart. Would either of them give in and bow out?

Of course not.

Each man knew it was time to speed up his own plan, and win Dong Tu's heart before the other could get the chance.

Dong Tu dove into the lake and fought the urge to gasp as the cold, clear water shocked her system yet again. She'd discovered early on that the water was clear enough to see the clusters of moss and colorful fish that lived and grew on rocks and along the lake bottom, and had taken to diving as deep as she could handle, exploring the strange, stunning underwater landscape. Flashes of blue and orange streaked through the water as fish went swimming by; some of them were tiny, silvery things, and others were impressively long. Freshwater shrimp and crabs with round eyes hid between rocks, and freshwater seaweed reached its long fingers out to wrap gently around Dong Tu as she dove even deeper.

The weeds parted and suddenly Dong Tu found herself looking at what looked to be a giant black spider curled atop a pale rock. Why was there a spider in the lake? Was there a breed of black spider that knew how to swim? The spider began moving, and Dong Tu quickly realized it wasn't a real spider at all. Her heart skipped a beat as she realized it was a tattoo—and not just any tattoo. Obsidian wore the same tattoo on his back: it was the mark of the Poison Legion.

She reached out to touch the man's shoulder, desperate to see if it truly was Obsidian swimming just ahead of her, when something pulled her back. Bubbles surrounded her, and Dong Tu let out a little shout beneath the water as a hand closed tight around her shoulder. Luu Dong Trung moved into her line of sight, evidently having dived in to follow her, and he tugged her into a tight hug as she tried to worm and wriggle her way out of his grasp. He ignored her attempts to break free and planted a kiss on her lips, even as she let out another shocked cry and began to choke on the water. That was apparently enough, and he released her long enough to let her kick to the surface and gasp for air.

But Dong Tu wasn't angry with Luu Dong Trung: she was too focused on the man with the spider tattoo. She sucked in another deep breath and dove back beneath the surface, but her vision was still obscured by bubbles. As far as she knew, the man with the tattoo had disappeared.

Dong Tu spent the rest of the day shaken, completely oblivious to the world around her. Dong Trung kept close to her, hoping she'd say something about their kiss under the water, but Dong Tu had effectively forgotten it had even happened. There was only one real thought on her mind: had that been Obsidian under the water?

Le Minh and Luu Dong Trung were completely oblivious to Dong Tu's concerns, and didn't let up in their competition for a second. They might have been gentle on the outside, and most importantly with Dong Tu, but the two of them were both extremely tense when it came to the game they'd begun.

The group settled around a fire by the lake as the sun began to set. Le Minh had been plotting for days to prepare the perfect surprise for Dong Tu: just as the military needed to employ superior strategy to defeat their enemies, so too would he in the war to win Dong Tu's heart. As he saw it, there were four players in the ring: Luu Dong Trung, Bao Thuong, Obsidian, and Le Minh himself. Le Minh knew he would have to out-perform the other three in order to be taken seriously as a suitor, at least in a field that would impress Dong Tu the most. Whoever won would be the man who could do what the others could not.

Le Minh knew he was better than Bao Thuong and Dong Trung when it came to martial arts, but he couldn't touch Obsidian's own skill. In terms of good looks and tenacity, he couldn't hold a candle to Dong Trung's ethereal handsomeness.

But there was one trick left up his sleeve.

As Dong Tu settled herself by the fire, Le Minh pulled a guitar out without a word. Yibo waited excitedly, his tail wagging, as Le Minh settled the guitar across his body; and then he began to play. Music swelled up from beneath his fingers, rich and mellow and enchanting, soaring on the evening air like a bird spreading its wings. Wind blew softly along the surface of the lake and rustled the leaves in the trees like an accompaniment, and just like that, the whole group seemed to fall under his spell. The sunset exploded into color as the forest around them dimmed, reflected in strange tints in the lake's jade-green waters; the girls' cheeks all flushed with soft pinks as the firelight played in flickers in their eyes.

Le Minh's heart leapt as he met Dong Tu's gaze. He was winning, he had to be!

And then a voice rose up over the guitar. Deep yet warm, Luu Dong Trung began to sing along, and he somehow became even more lovely as he did, the music and singing enhancing every bit of his natural beauty. Le Minh looked up in surprise and found Dong Trung watching Dong Tu fixedly, with as much passion burning in his eyes as there was fire reflected in their clear depths. Le Minh faltered, and the music stopped. Never in his life had he ever had a man affect him like that, but in that moment, looking at Dong Trung made his heart beat out of rhythm and then break into a sprint.

And never in his life had he ever heard a voice so beautiful that it had shocked him into stillness.

That was it. He'd lost, he knew it. There was no competing with a man like Luu Dong Trung, especially if he himself was just a little bit smitten with the other man after that.

Luu Dong Trung was still staring at Dong Tu. His gaze seared into hers, intent and intense, like he wanted to melt the sky and the earth away and leave nothing and no one save he and Dong Tu, sitting there alone in the sunset. And yet....

And yet Dong Tu wasn't looking at him.

She was staring at something behind him.

A man stood just behind Luu Dong Trung in the deepening twilight, wearing a black coat and a silver mask. He'd been watching them the entire time. Luu Dong Trung turned to see what she was staring at, and as he did, the stranger vanished into the darkness.

"Obsidian!" Dong Tu cried out, jumping to her feet—but she didn't chase him. She slowly sat right back down as the sounds of the people around her faded away, and she found herself once again lost in thoughts and memories of Obsidian. She was just as robotic later that night as the rest of the group enjoyed delicious food and good wine. Luu Dong Trung and Le Minh fought each other for the chance to serve her food, but her blank expression never faltered.

"That must have been Obsidian," Dong Tu murmured to herself. The rest of the room went still again, and finally Dong Tu came back to herself enough to recount what had happened in the water that afternoon before Dong Trung had leapt in and interrupted. Xuan Thu and Bao Thuong both frowned in sympathy, while Le Minh sat there, still holding his chopsticks, and sighed.

Dong Trung had never been his competitor. Neither had Bao Thuong. There was only one man he had to contend with, only one man in Dong Tu's heart.

Obsidian.

CHAPTER 7

The Eyes Looked, but the Heart Saw

Dong Tu couldn't forget the spider tattoo or the man dressed in black.

Although she'd been underwater when she saw it, and the reflection of the light beneath the surface had been dazzling, she was certain of what she had seen. She knew every inch of that tattoo. Every crest, every line, every change texture.

The first time Dong Tu had seen that tattoo had been more than two years before. She'd cleaned the blood and infection from Obsidian's back after he'd collapsed, and in her fascination, she'd taken the time to trace over the design with her fingertips. Covering almost all of Obsidian's back, the modification had been even more severe than ink pricked into skin: shaped metal pieces had been sewn beneath the skin, and the dark coloring was the result of the caustic poison that had been used to mar and stain Obsidian's back.

It not only left the skin blackened, but had left it roughened as well.

There was no way Dong Tu would mistake it for anything else.

"Are you sure that was Obsidian?" Ryujin asked doubtfully, after catching Dong Tu mulling it over again. "Everyone in the Poison Legion has a tattoo like that."

Dong Tu hummed, but she was uncertain. If it hadn't been Obsidian, then who could it have been? Did the members of the Poison Legion get so much free time that they could just hide in a lake and watch her whenever they liked?

"Maybe Obsidian sent them here to spy on you," Le Minh interjected. "Maybe they lurk in the dark, waiting for you to get a new boyfriend, so they can kill him." It was an unsettling thought for him, the idea that the man he'd thought gone from Dong Tu's life forever might now be around and watching. What if Obsidian appeared and killed *him?*

"That can't be it. Obsidian was never that kind of guy," Xuan Thu denied with a shake of her head. "If he still cared about Dong Tu, he'd tell her himself."

Dong Tu wondered again if Luu Dong Trung was right. Maybe Obsidian really did want her to forget him. Maybe he wanted to set her free, but still loved and cared about her, so he kept watch from the shadows...

Dong Tu felt her throat tighten up. She knew in her heart that Obsidian had never truly left her. He'd been by her side for a long, long time.

From the day she ran across the stranger in the lake onward, she felt like she was being watched. At first it was just a vague, instinctual sense that someone was following her. Soon it became the constant sense that someone was staring at her, like a predator stalking its prey. Sometimes, while walking through the street, the hair on the back of her neck would stand on end like it had when she'd seen the man in the silver mask over Luu Dong Trung's shoulder. Every time it frightened her, and every time she would turn and look behind her.

One such instance left Dong Tu standing in the middle of the road, alone, searching the crowd around her for the figure she knew so well.

That had been Obsidian, hadn't it?

Hadn't it?

One day, as Dong Tu turned back around from looking behind her, she came face-to-face with a series of masks dangling from the booth of a street vendor. It was time for the summer festival at Thanh Liet Lake, which was celebrated with food and water-related games, and everyone who came wore masks. They lined the whole street: human masks, animal masks, masks of all different colors. Even silver masks. Xuan Thu dragged everyone into the booth to see.

There were dozens to choose from, and everyone laughed and teased as they tried them on. Dong Tu walked slowly along the display, carefully inspecting every detail. Pink, silver, black—

Dong Tu stopped and tipped her head to the side, coming back to the silver mask. It reminded her so much of Obsidian's...she reached out for it—

And gasped as it blinked at her.

She forced herself to breathe and looked again. There they were, two eyes staring straight back at her from behind the mask. Before she could react, Luu Dong Trung jumped in front of her wearing a pig mask, shook his head, and shouted, "Oink! Oink!"

Dong Tu pushed him aside in annoyance and looked for the silver mask again, but the silver mask—and the man wearing it—had disappeared. Once again Luu Dong Trung had ruined her chance to see if it really was Obsidian who'd been following her!

Thinking Dong Tu didn't like his mask, Luu Dong Trung deflated, but Dong Tu quickly explained what she'd seen and refused to believe it could be anyone other than Obsidian. Nobody would be able to convince her differently, even if everyone but Xuan Thu tried.

"If Obsidian's been following you, why didn't he just show up and come to the lake with us?"

"He's stealthy. This has to be too obvious, doesn't it? Besides, if he's been sneaking around for this long, what's the point of coming out now?"

The others began to argue over Obsidian's possible motives. But once things began to settle down, the group realized: Luu Dong Trung and Dong Tu were nowhere to be found.

Unbeknownst to the rest, Dong Tu had left the shop and had immediately caught sight of a figure dressed all in black as he disappeared into the crowd. She followed, even as Luu Dong Trung tried to run after her and pull her back; but Dong Tu was small, and melted into the crowd before he could catch her.

The man in black led Dong Tu through town, sometimes stopping to let her catch up. He was tall and broad, and wore the same armored coat she knew so well, and Dong Tu hushed all other thoughts except following him out to the edge of town. They were on the very rim of the district, and the only things around were the crumbling ruins of old houses. The walls still stood mostly whole, serving as perches for the crows, but the tile roofs had long since collapsed into the houses they used to shield. Empty baskets were piled against the walls on the abandoned streets.

The man in black stopped, but he didn't turn around. Dong Tu stopped behind him, panting, but being out of breath didn't dampen her euphoria.

"Obsidian, is it really you?" she prompted breathlessly. Her heart began to pound as he finally turned around and she saw the silver mask along with the familiar coat. Wind rushed through the space between them, kicking up loose dust, as Dong Tu wiped the sweat off her forehead with a trembling hand. Was it really him? She pinched her thigh to make sure she wasn't dreaming, swallowed hard, and slowly approached the man.

The weather turned strange as she came closer: it was midday in the summer, hot and sunny, but the wind whipped the dust up into a swirl that steadily clouded her vision the harder the wind blew. In just three steps it looked like a sandstorm had blown up between them, tearing at the man's coat and mask, and Dong Tu realized the windstorm had nothing to do with the weather.

A powerful application of chi had trapped Dong Tu in a whirling ring of wind and dust, separating her from the man in black and blocking her own figure from view.

"Dong Tu, where are you?" A faint echo cut through the wind, and though it grew quieter as the windstorm began to grow into a true tornado around her, it was just loud enough for Dong Tu to recognize Luu Dong Trung's voice. "Dong Tu...!"

"Obsidian!" Dong Tu shouted in despair. "Obsidian, please don't leave me! I'm right here!"

Suddenly Dong Tu heard the sound of sharp metal slicing through the air, and Ryujin's little knife sank point-first into the ground with a dull thunk. The storm vanished as quickly as it had appeared, and the dust and dirt fell to the ground with a sandy hiss. Left exposed in the mid-summer sun, the man in black hid his face behind his hand and bolted.

Le Minh and Ryujin converged on Dong Tu and demanded to know what had happened, but Dong Tu barely managed to force out Obsidian's name before her eyes filled with tears and her throat tightened, choking off any other information she could have given them. Le Minh and Ryujin looked around, but they couldn't find any clue as to who'd been there, or who might have called up that storm. Luu Dong Trung had also gone missing, until they followed the sound of his voice as he began to call for Dong Tu again.

He'd been blown up into an old tree nearby. Unable to climb down on his own, Dong Trung had held on for dear life and yelled Dong Tu's name, hoping she'd come and rescue him. Ryujin rolled her eyes, jumped easily into the tree, and jumped back down again with Luu Dong Trung cradled in her arms like an overgrown child. They all took some time to calm down, and then Ryujin looked at Dong Tu seriously.

"Dong Tu, do you know who created that dust storm?"

Dong Tu shook her head. She wholeheartedly believed the man she'd followed was Obsidian, and was heartbroken that just before the pair of them had been able to reunite, the chi-force wall had divided them. Ryujin slid her dagger back into its sheath and hung it on her belt. Her brows pulled together in concerned consideration: Ryujin was the strongest martial artist in their group—one of the strongest alive, in fact, as a member of the Monstrous Eighteen. She was capable of incredible things when using her own chi, and yet even her own dagger had had trouble breaking through the mysterious wall.

"Well, the storm was definitely built from someone's chi. And I might not have been able to see him, but the man on the other side was bound with that same chi and couldn't move. Whoever had the power to do all of that must be a real master." Obsidian was famous for his skill with poisons and with the powers awarded him by the Storm Pearl, but the move that had just been used to keep Dong Tu from the man in black wasn't in Obsidian's repertoire. So if he *had* been the man in black, and if he hadn't called up that windstorm, who had? Who would want to interfere in Dong Tu and Obsidian's reunion—and more importantly, why?

That night at dinner, a name popped back up in Dong Tu's mind.

"...Liet Than," she murmured to herself. Luu Dong Trung stopped chewing and looked up. He'd heard the name before, from the unexpected reappearance of Stargazer. The old woman had said the fate of Dong Tu and Obsidian's relationship hinged on that name. She'd said to beware of them, it—whatever Liet Than was. Luu Dong Trung quietly told the rest of the table about Stargazer's words.

"Although I wasn't sure then, whether Stargazer was talking to me or Switch." It had been a warning thrown out into the room at large. He still wasn't sure: he had no powers, no fighting skills, no enemies and no one he wanted to make an enemy—and Switch hadn't been seen since their latest fight. He'd thought the warning was most likely for her.

"In all the years I've travelled and studied martial arts, I've never heard those words," Le Minh said, shaking his head. Yibo licked his nose and cocked his head like he was just as stumped.

Dong Tu had originally believed Ly Minh Lam was Liet Than. Out of everyone in her acquaintance, only he seemed to have the strength of chi required to call up a storm like that. But the incident left no trace of him. Could the mystery still link back to Liet Than? And could it be that Liet Than wasn't a person's name, but something else entirely?

"Liet could simply mean 'cold,'" Luu Dong Trung mused. "It could be alluding to Obsidian, since his power is associated with the snow."

"Or an intimidating aura," Ryujin added.

"It could mean 'frigid,'" Le Minh offered. In reality Liet Than could be anything: the name of a place, a master, a technique, or someone else.

"Hold on a sec..." Ryujin lifted a hand to silence the others. The name was suddenly ringing a distant bell. She snagged a piece of chicken with her chopsticks and sipped her tea with narrowed eyes, trying to squeeze the name from her memory. Ryujin was a simple woman, with simple desires: if it wasn't good food, a martial arts technique, or pretty girls and handsome men, she didn't spare the subject much thought. Where had she heard the name? Were they one of the Eighteen?

"I wonder if the name is on the Whispered World's *Hot List*," Ryujin murmured out loud, and Luu Dong Trung chuckled.

"Is there really a thing called the *Hot List*?" If there was, he had to be at the top of the list, and create some fame for himself. Ryujin met his gaze with utter seriousness.

"Yes."

It was unofficial, but there really was a secret compilation of the most beautiful people in the Whispered World, all in a neat little handbook. That was part of the reason Ryujin was interested in Obsidian: he wore a mask most of the time, but he was still high on the list. She told them all about how Obsidian's name had blown up throughout the martial arts world ever since it had been revealed that he carried the Storm Pearl: he was brought up in every conversation from attractiveness to fighting skill.

Dong Tu blushed when she recalled the first time she'd foolishly removed his mask. She had indeed been stunned into silence by his attractiveness.

Her blush needled uncomfortably at Luu Dong Trung.

"Who's better looking, me or Obsidian?" he prompted. Dong Tu glared at him without answering. Her eyes looked, but her heart saw; and in both her eyes and her heart, who could be more handsome than Obsidian?

Luu Dong Trung leaned in closer, his eyes—clear as Thanh Liet Lake—sparkling with anxiety.

"Dong Tu...look at me, and tell me the truth?"

Xuan Thu separated them with her chopsticks.

"Obsidian is manly, but you're the prettier one," she said, and knew that it would be enough to satisfy Dong Trung. And it was the truth: not even women were as pretty as Luu Dong Trung, let alone Obsidian.

"Between Liet Than and Obsidian, who's more powerful?" Dong Trung asked Ryujin. Ryujin shrugged. She still wasn't sure where it was she'd heard the name, and if he really was one of the Eighteen or some other master, it was clear he might not be so popular.

"Liet can also mean 'paralyzed.' Perhaps it's the handicapped grand master!" Le Minh interjected, glad to be able to get a word in. "A few months ago, a rumor said that there was a martial arts master near Tien Thuc Falls whose entire body was paralyzed, and yet he killed with ease. Perhaps he could be Liet Than!"

"A cold-blooded, murdering, handicapped grand master?" Luu Dong Trung repeated in contempt. "Why would he be interested in Dong Tu?"

"He could be like all the other thugs that have come after Dong Tu lately," Xuan Thu pointed out. "Coming to kidnap her so they can try to trade her for the Storm Pearl."

"But are you even sure the man in black was Obsidian?" Le Minh cut in again, trying to change the subject.

Dong Tu hesitated.

No, she wasn't sure. The two of them had been standing too far apart, the dust storm had been excellent at obscuring his figure...and it had been a long time since Dong Tu had actually seen Obsidian. She wondered if he'd grown taller, or changed in some other way, since she'd seen him last. The tattoo, though, was still unmistakable. The group let the silence hang for a while as Dong Tu lost herself in consideration, until Le Minh decided to speak.

"Dong Tu...why do you think the man in black was Obsidian?"

Dong Tu had been feeling more and more unsafe and unsettled. There had been too many people from the Whispered World coming to her family with malicious intent. Dong Tu knew Ryujin and Le Minh had helped fend them off many times, but there were times the two of them weren't around. The more she thought about it, the more she realized: the would-be kidnappers wouldn't just stop and wait to attack on days when Ryujin and Le Minh were there.

She cursed herself for her stupidity. It was so obvious! There was only one person who could have been protecting her the whole time.

To test her hypothesis, Dong Tu asked, "When Ly Tuyen spread the news about me and my family, did you and Ryujin help defeat them?"

Ryujin shook her head, and Le Minh counted on his fingers.

"Yes, but not many. About two or three guys."

That was all Dong Tu needed. Absolute certainty went through her like a shot: she knew for a fact there had been more than just two or three guys, and if Ryujin and Le Minh hadn't defeated even most of them…it had to have been Obsidian. Perhaps he'd been hiding for a reason, she didn't know. But what she did know was that he'd been silently protecting her the entire time.

Luu Dong Trung saw the hope flare to life in Dong Tu's eyes and started to speak—and stopped himself. He thought for a quick second, then started again, much more gently.

"Dong Tu, you keep holding onto the hope that he'll come back, and you're just fooling yourself. If Obsidian wants you to forget him, do as he asks. Otherwise his effort will be wasted."

Passing spring, longing summer, hoping autumn and decaying winter; she'd spent nearly three years hopelessly waiting for so much as Obsidian's silhouette. That should have been enough, right?

Dong Tu disagreed. It was not as easy as it sounded. The day she and Obsidian had parted ways, as much as it had broken her heart, he'd never explicitly said the two of them would never meet again. He'd gotten himself his goodbye kiss, but she hadn't been prepared. She'd cursed herself over the past few years for not holding him longer, more tightly; for not memorizing the feeling of his breath and lips against hers, or the herbal smell of his skin. There had been no closure in the sudden way they'd parted, and it had left a wound that still ached and bled.

It was only made worse as the memories she did have began to fade into a dreamlike quality, clouded and smoky. His figure had been reduced to the same silhouette she chased in life as well as sleep, and she often dreamed of running after him through dense black snow. Dong Tu always became more lost, and fell further behind, the more she ran. Those dreams saw her waking up shouting his name, and she was always dazed when she went from standing in darkness and snow to lying in her bed in an instant.

Tears began to roll slowly down Dong Tu's cheeks. All she wanted was to stand before Obsidian once more, stare into his eyes, study his face, listen to his voice...she had so many things she wanted to say to him. If he'd moved on and forgotten her, found himself happy with someone like Lady Dao or Ivy...her own inferiority to those women ate at her, but she would still be happy. Relieved. She would still be able to finally find peace and move on. But remaining in the shadows, watching over her day and night to protect her from the evil men who would do her so much harm, maybe even loving her still from such a distance...that much was agony. Being so close and yet so far was nothing but torment.

The mood sagged as the group finished their dinner.

Luu Dong Trung watched Dong Tu worriedly. He couldn't share the ache Obsidian had left in her heart, but how it felt to fall in love with someone and want desperately to be close to them, to the very point of despair? *That* he understood intimately. Dong Tu sat right in front of him, but her heart and soul were gone: no matter how deeply Dong Trung looked into her eyes, how often he leapt in front of her, *kissed* her, the only thing she ever saw was Obsidian.

Dong Tu was running after a ghost, and he was just a shadow.

Sadness covered Luu Dong Trung's face like a thin veil, leaving him as somber a beauty as a gloomy autumn lake.

Dong Tu stayed in her room that evening after dinner, not opening the door for anyone. Around midnight Ryujin opened her windows; her room overlooked the beautiful courtyard, and the sky was clear. Bright, high moonlight glowed silver on Luu Dong Trung's long hair as his tall figure patrolled the space in front of Dong Tu's room, frowning in contemplation. He wasn't fidgety or stiff, but it was clear his mind was not peaceful: he was torn, torn between wanting to protect the peace for Dong Tu and wanting to knock on the door and step inside himself.

Like all summer nights at Thanh Liet Lake, the heat had cooled for the moment. The insects could be heard calling and rustling, and Ryujin raised her eyebrows knowingly as she watched Dong Trung pace. Mortal hearts were tangling like silk, and the relationships between Dong Tu, Luu Dong Trung, and Obsidian were becoming more and more troubling.

CHAPTER 8

A Desperate Desire

After hearing that Obsidian might be lurking around somewhere, Luu Dong Trung stuck to Dong Tu like glue. He became her guard dog, alerting her to any strange sounds, even waiting outside the door whenever she went to the restroom. Predictably, this didn't sit well with her.

"Dong Trung! Obsidian has no intention of hurting me, and even if he *did,* there's nothing you could do! Could you please give me some space to breathe?!" she yelled, once she finally reached her wits' end.

Apparently the answer was no.

Yes, Luu Dong Trung followed Dong Tu because he was worried for her safety, even though everyone knew he didn't have a chance of stopping anyone: all he knew was the Sunlight Strike variation that Dong Tu had taught him, and that was as useful as a plié in combat. In the two years that the Luu dojo had been teaching the technique, it had grown so popular it had spread beyond the borders of Vinh Phuc and on into the Whispered World itself, with absolutely no one being able to make out its true nature. Even Ryujin had declared it effectively useless after taking the time to study it.

The Sunlight Strike was broken into four parts: the first was striking, but the other three were healing. No one could figure out who would want to hurt someone only to heal them, or vice-versa.

"It was created by a husband and wife, right?" Ryujin had pondered. "They probably named it the Sunlight Strike because it sounded pretty. They should have called it 'I was mad at you, but I still love you.' It's like the martial arts equivalent of make-up sex."

But safety wasn't the only reason Luu Dong Trung was following Dong Tu around. In fact, he was far less afraid of her being in danger than he was the chance of she and Obsidian being together again.

From the moment they'd met, Luu Dong Trung had been more and more intrigued by—and interested in—Dong Tu. Her strength and bravery delighted him, and her protectiveness was comforting. He loved the idea of being pampered and protected by a woman so small, and he loved to pamper her in return. Those early days had flown by like a shuttle as the pair grew closer. The longer they were by each other's sides, the more he wanted to protect what they had, to keep building a little world just for them...he wanted to *be* her world like she had become his.

Dong Trung had tested the waters with teasing, flirting comments after he'd come back to live with Dong Tu and her family.

"Let's be together forever," he'd told her, watching her with starry, love-struck eyes.

"We're siblings, of course we're gonna stay together forever," Dong Tu had joked in return. She had missed Luu Dong Trung's true meaning entirely, but her answer had left him pleased. He'd smirked, and batted his pretty eyelashes at her.

"So you won't marry another man, and I won't marry another woman," he'd pressed. Dong Tu had assumed he was being silly when she'd agreed to that too, but more than that, she was just as sure that she wouldn't marry anyone but Obsidian back then as she was in the present. It hadn't been a difficult promise to make. But Luu Dong Trung had assumed Dong Tu had just agreed to be his wife, and he'd spent many a peaceful day under that delusion.

Until now. He'd been awakened from his dream world, and realized the only space left in Dong Tu's heart was for Obsidian.

So Luu Dong Trung had made it his personal mission to replace Obsidian with himself. That was why he was beside Dong Tu day and night. That was why he was constantly trying to undermine her faith in Obsidian and kill any hope of the King of Poison's potential return, and it was why he sought to convince her that she and Obsidian were a poor fit.

That was why he made sure he was the only one she spoke with, the only one she saw.

Luu Dong Trung was there to bring her water so she could wash her face every morning; at night he was there to comb her hair and tuck her in. At lunch he made her tea; in the afternoons he peeled her fruit for her and fanned the flies away. Every move she made got the full Luu Dong Trung service package.

And it had seemed to work—until Dong Tu saw the man with the spider tattoo.

He'd thought he'd been building himself a fortress within her heart, but it had turned out to be a sandcastle, and it came crumbling down the moment the tidal wave that was Obsidian came crashing through her heart again. Dong Trung kept trying, kept knocking, worshipping her like a goddess and bringing her gifts, but she never seemed to notice.

The harder Luu Dong Trung tried, the more she pined for the specter that was Obsidian.

He understood, in a way. He'd studied their story carefully, inspecting every little detail. He knew every moment, every kiss, and he believed the foundation of Obsidian and Dong Tu's relationship was built on their three kisses--especially their last, and most heartbreaking.

He'd even tried to recreate similar scenarios twice thus far, but both times Luu Dong Trung and Dong Tu had kissed, she'd just spent days being mad at him, and their relationship seemed to crack. Dong Tu's feelings toward him—the same platonic love they had developed back when she'd thought Dong Trung was a woman—hadn't changed, but that didn't stop him from working day and night to find a way to recreate that third kiss. He truly believed it would be the one to make her forget Obsidian altogether.

And so Luu Dong Trung carried on, wondering if he could stand to do it for a lifetime.

But even her loyal shadow couldn't keep eyes on her every second of every day, and one afternoon, she managed to sneak away.

Dong Tu was totally oblivious to the battle being waged in Luu Dong Trung's mind, but she *did* have a suspicion that if Obsidian wanted to meet her, he wouldn't be doing it when her brother was around. It would be hard for him, around that many people. So when Luu Dong Trung's guard was down, she snuck off to Thanh Liet Lake by herself.

She was running by the time she made it to the lake, and began calling Obsidian's name as she ran: the lake was deserted, the guests remaining inside for the hottest part of the day, and Dong Tu knew the only person who would hear her was Obsidian himself. The sun shone bright gold, and a hot haze waved over the lake's tranquil surface as she kept calling out.

Her efforts were rewarded after a few minutes.

A rustle of movement tweaked her ear, and she looked up to see the shadow of a person wrapped in a black coat, hidden in the canopy of the trees. He leapt to the ground and bolted, and Dong Tu chased after him.

Just like the time before, she ran after the stranger with abandon; and just like before, when they came to a stop, the area was deserted. They were near the shoreline, separated from the shore only by a large bush, and the only things around were the trees. Even the animals seemed to have vanished, and silence reigned around them. There was no storm, this time. No dust, no whirling wall of chi force keeping them apart. Dong Tu felt as if she'd just struck gold.

Obsidian looked different from Dong Tu's memory. He was still tall, still wearing the black coat and silver mask, but there was something off...

He wasn't wearing his gloves, and when he stopped walking, no black snow fell.

Dong Tu knew in that moment she'd made a huge mistake.

She looked around, looking for anyone or anything that might help, but all she could see and hear were the rustling trees and the vast green lake lapping softly against the shore.

She took a step back as her enthusiasm cooled, and the man removed his mask.

The new man was young. He was average-looking, nowhere near as handsome as Obsidian, and no emotion registered on his face or in his eyes. A spidery shape seemed to rise out of his skin beneath his left eye, likely shaped with the same kinds of metal that had been sewn into Obsidian's back. There was no black staining, but the legs did run up from the lower lid and into his iris. He looked hard, and intimidating, and Dong Tu began to tremble.

"Are you from the Poison Legion?" she asked nervously.

He nodded.

Dong Tu hadn't really needed his confirmation. His tattoo and modifications, his appearance and his outfit...all of them screamed Poison Legion to her. She knew she had to be careful: the body of a high-ranking Poison Master was saturated with poisons, leaving them lethal to the touch, and he wore no gloves. She could only assume that meant he hadn't come there just to talk.

Dong Tu took another, involuntary step back. The stranger walked forward two steps.

"Did...did Obsidian send you here?" Dong Tu asked. He made her uneasy, but she still held on to the blind faith that Obsidian would never send someone to hurt her. The man grinned, crooked and mirthless.

How foolish the girl was.

"Obsidian, well..." he trailed off, but his smile vanished as his face twisted into a stare that was cold and intent. Dong Tu knew then that he had to have had some kind of rivalry with Obsidian, and had likely come for revenge. Her heart began to pound, differently than what her running had caused; she had no sword, and even though she hadn't seen him fight yet, she was sure she was no match for him.

The man unclenched his fists and began to stalk forward.

"Lady Luu, please follow me."

Dong Tu's gaze dropped from his face to his hands. Bare hands, the tips of his fingers all dyed black as if to emphasize how deadly they were—to warn mere mortals off of trying to touch, let alone pick a fight, if they wanted to live. She shook her head and continued to slowly move backward.

The man moved closer.

Dong Tu spun around, trying to reach a nearby tree branch so she could break a stick off and wield it as a weapon—and the man vanished. She froze and looked around her with wide eyes, knowing he couldn't have gone far, and dropped into a crouch when he reappeared and reached for her chin. She curled into herself, covering her face with her hands.

The stranger bent down and playfully ran his fingers through Dong Tu's hair, walking each finger from her hair to her shoulder. She shook beneath his touch, like a deer caught in a trap, just watching the hunter close in. He laughed softly to himself, and it made her hair stand on end. He wasn't in a hurry, and her shaking seemed to amuse him, so he curled his fist around her hair and bent closer.

"What do you want? Why—why do you want to kill me?" Dong Tu demanded, carefully lifting her face to look at him.

"You want a reason? Go ask Obsidian yourself!" The man reached for Dong Tu's face, and she used the stick she'd broken off to parry his hand away.

The man merely smiled.

He slowly pushed the stick out of his way and kept moving closer, and Dong Tu silently begged for some kind of miracle to help her survive.

She got her miracle, but it wasn't exactly what she expected: Luu Dong Trung came pelting through the undergrowth. It hadn't taken him long to track her down, not when he'd followed her so closely for so long. Both Dong Tu and the stranger turned to watch as Luu Dong Trung's slender figure came running from afar.

Dong Tu's heart sank. This wasn't a miracle, this was a massacre! In the face of impending death, threatened by a member of the Poison Legion—with neither Ryujin nor Le Minh in sight—Luu Dong Trung was as good as another dead body.

"Dong Tu! Dong Tu, I'm here, I'm coming! Stop right there, don't you move!" Luu Dong Trung yelled. It took an almost comical amount of time for him to reach them, but for some reason the man in black waited patiently for Dong Trung to come closer.

High-ranking masters in the Whispered World were good at determining another martial artist's skill level just by looking at the way they moved, and could get an approximate read on just how powerful their opponent's chi was based on the force their opponent radiated. Dong Tu could tell the man before her was well trained, possibly even of a higher skill level than Le Minh—and given what she knew of the Poison Legion, he was possibly equal to, or even above, Ryujin. This all meant that the man in black was getting his own read on Luu Dong Trung, and he straightened, watching curiously rather than with any kind of concern. He was waiting to see what the newcomer would do.

To Dong Trung's credit, he wasn't clumsy. He was agile; a little *too* agile really, compared to ordinary people. He was healthy and flexible, but he had lived as the kind of noble who rarely had to lift a finger, let alone get their hands dirty. That much was obvious.

It wasn't helped by the way he winced and groaned as he was scratched by a tree branch.

Dong Tu knew the man in black could see that while *he* was as dangerous as a panther, Luu Dong Trung was no more dangerous than a mouse, and it only made her more desperate.

"No!" she shouted back. "You've followed me day and night! Why would you follow me into death, too?!"

Yet Luu Dong Trung kept coming. He would hold the man in black's attention as long as he could keep it, but he had no idea what to do when he finally slowed and came face-to-face with the stranger, with Dong Tu crouching like a cornered animal at the man's feet. Dong Tu signaled for him to run, and his serious frown softened as he looked at her, but he didn't move.

"I told you. Wherever you are, I'll be." Luu Dong Trung's subtle earnestness faded as his gaze returned to the man in black. His eyes hardened and cooled like chips of ice, and a cold, stern glare settled back on his face. Powerless though he was, and as hard as his heart beat in his chest, he still brought all the haughty confidence of a master to bear. He cut an impressive and intimidating figure. That was why absolutely no one wanted to play cards with him: his poker face was *impeccable*.

If it worked, Dong Tu told herself she'd kiss the very ground he walked on for the rest of her life, but for the moment all she could do was grit her teeth, remain a smaller target, and wait. Luu Dong Trung and the stranger stared at each other for so long Dong Tu's legs started to tire in her scrunched up position, and finally the man in black raised his eyebrows.

"Are you actually going to *do* anything?" The spider under his eyelid twitched every time he expressed any kind of emotion, and his curiosity over such a show of bravery from someone who didn't just feel weak, but hollow like an empty vessel, was fading quickly. The reckless challenge wasn't amusing anymore.

Luu Dong Trung didn't respond. His face remained cold yet calmly emotionless as he stared. What was he supposed to say? What was he supposed to *feel?* Because just then he seemed to feel everything and nothing. Perhaps the three of them could stay like that for the rest of the day. Perhaps they could even stand there long enough for the others to realize what had happened and catch up.

In the end, the first person to make a move was Dong Tu, not either of the two men: she couldn't bear the oppressive silence and the sense of impending doom, and she hated the way it was being dragged out by this weird standoff.

Dong Tu lashed out to shove the man in black aside and bolted for Luu Dong Trung.

"Run," she gasped as she grabbed his hand and began to pull him away.

The moment Dong Tu's hand hit his skin, Dong Trung seemed to come to life. Her touch was like a blast of liquid courage, and he took off running with his eyes fixed on her, weightless despite the fact that death in human form was coming up fast. The man in black hadn't even stumbled when Dong Tu pushed him, and they didn't get as much of a lead on him as the pair wanted. The man in black aimed a palm strike at the two of them, and though the strike missed their shoulders, they still went tumbling to the ground with the force behind it.

Dong Tu had just enough time to cover her face. She squeezed her eyes closed and waited for the veritable touch of death....

Yet none came.

Dong Tu cracked her eyes open to see that Luu Dong Trung had used his own body as a shield, protecting her from the man in black.

CHAPTER 9

For the One He Loves

Dong Trung knelt between Dong Tu and the man in black. He curled over her protectively, one arm braced over her, the other blocking his own face. He lowered his arm enough to glare at the man in black, still radiating that intimidating chill. It was easy to forget just how big Luu Dong Trung really was when he was so tall he looked skinny, but kneeling over Dong Tu like that? His shoulders were strong and broad, and between his body, his fluttering sleeves, and his long hair, he blocked her entirely.

Luu Dong Trung whipped his gaze over the other man with a hesitant kind of consideration, looking almost torn; he settled after just a beat, and his glare deepened. Whatever he'd been trying to decide, one thing was certain: he would never let anyone harm Dong Tu, no matter what it cost him.

The man in black tipped his head and lifted an eyebrow in cool amusement.

"Sacrificing yourself to protect your sweetheart. What a romantic scene," he taunted. It was impossible to mistake Luu Dong Trung's feelings as anything other than romantic when he was clearly willing to die for her. "I hope you're truly ready to die, loverboy."

Luu Dong Trung didn't move a millimeter as the man in black reached out and took hold of his jaw. He didn't even blink as the poison from the stranger's fingers sank into his skin and threads of black poison webbed out across his fear-blanched face, snaking across to the other side. Dong Trung kept staring furiously, determinedly at the other man; but his jaw tightened as he stared, his lips pressed into a thin line. His brow furrowed as he began to tremble.

The lethal cocktail of poisons that had become the Poison Legion's calling card was burning through him and leaving him numb as it spread. And while the others had thought his lack of chi would leave him limp like a noodle, if not outright dead, he *still* didn't drop. Drawing on some unknown reserve of power, he reached out and grabbed hold of the man in black's wrist.

"Dong Tu, run!" Dong Trung forced out harshly, fighting back against the poison while trying to maintain enough strength to hold their attacker. The longer he was in contact with the other man, the more poison suffused his body, but that didn't stop him from grabbing the man's other hand, too. He would do everything it took to give her a fighting chance.

"Dong Tu, *go!*" Luu Dong Trung shouted again. This time the effort was plain in his voice: he was at the very end of his strength, and would break at any moment.

Dong Tu hesitated. She might live if she ran...

But she couldn't leave him.

The moment she decided to stay, the air around them dropped several degrees. Wind rose up, blowing leaves from the trees and lifting petals from their flowers, and surrounded the three of them in a familiar spiral. The usually mirror-still waters of Thanh Liet Lake rippled as the wind beat against its surface, and true waves began to lap at the shores in a choppy rush; the sky, usually reflected perfectly in the water, broke apart as whitecaps began to form. Dong Tu looked around them in shock as, in the middle of a sweltering summer afternoon, snowflakes began to fall. She caught a snowflake on her hand, studied it, and met Luu Dong Trung's equally astonished gaze.

The snowflake on her pale skin was inky black.

Motion caught Dong Tu's eye, and she looked back out at the water. A figure appeared on the far bank and began to fly just above the surface of the water, sending mist spraying up behind them. Dong Tu was able to make out details as they drew closer: they were dressed all in black, with black gloves on their hands, and sunlight glinted off a familiar silver mask and staff. The coat was just as familiar, billowing out behind the newcomer as they crossed the lake, only settling back around them when their feet hit the shore and they began to stalk forward with purpose.

Dong Tu would know that gait anywhere. She didn't even need the black snow that scattered through the air.

There was no one else that could possibly be.

The man in black tore his arms out of Luu Dong Trung's grasp and turned to face the newcomer.

"Obsidian," he greeted coldly.

"Tuong Y Ve. Long time, no see," Obsidian greeted him in return. His voice was unforgettable, and elation and relief both shot through Dong Tu. Her heart was pounding, and her vision seemed to narrow to Obsidian alone.

The two men bowed to each other simultaneously, and Tuong Y Ve drew his own sword from the scabbard strapped across his back. Obsidian didn't pull any other weapon out. Snowflakes began to flurry from his hands, coalescing around the staff and forming a sharp, icy blade along its length. Tuong Y Ve leapt into the air and came tearing down toward Obsidian, and Obsidian blocked the swing; it began a storm of movement that Dong Tu couldn't pull her gaze from.

Both men fought with strikingly similar styles, having been trained by the same people. Tuong Y Ve's moves were fueled by anger, and came one on top of the other without pause. Obsidian was visibly unsurprised and unflustered: he countered every move easily, no matter how quickly they came, already knowing where the other man would strike before he got there.

Dong Tu and Luu Dong Trung held their breath as they watched the battle intently. Dong Trung's teeth clenched up tight as he watched, and his typically smooth, pretty face was twisted up in misery.

In the Whispered World, people rarely got to see the Poison Legion's true martial arts skills: with their lethal touch and the frequent use of poison, their opponents were almost always dead before weapons were even drawn. Obsidian and Tuong Y Ve were both immune, and they weren't going to waste their poisons on each other; so the secret techniques of the Poison Legion were now on full display. It was the kind of rare occurrence that Ryujin and Le Minh would have given anything to see, had they known.

The fighting techniques of the Poison Legion were legendary. Obsidian was their King of Poison and remarkably skilled, and it looked like Tuong Y Ve wasn't terribly far behind. They were truly masters, and there wasn't anyone who could have demonstrated the Poison Legion's might better.

It had been three years since Dong Tu had last seen Obsidian fight, and she had been impressed with him then; but he'd also been injured, and he'd had to accommodate his many injuries every time. This was the first time she'd been able to watch him fight without impediment, and without having to hold back, and she couldn't help but watch with awed admiration.

Tuong Y Ve and Obsidian's fight took them out onto the water's surface itself. The water froze solid beneath Obsidian's feet, again and again, as they wove in and out of the trees and clashed back and forth along the shore. Tuong Y Ve began to alternate between his blade and his palm strike, and the trees around them began to fall under the tremendous amount of chi force that backed the two fighters' moves. Without a single break in his attack, Obsidian called up a whirling ring of icy air around Luu Dong Trung and Dong Tu, to keep them safe.

Dong Tu craned her neck and squinted to watch them fight through the whipping wind; but, unbeknownst to the woman beside him, Luu Dong Trung was beginning to fade. His skin was bloodlessly white and clammy, cold sweat beading on his forehead and along his full upper lip. Perhaps it was the flow of the toxins in his blood, searing along his nerves, making his body twitch—or perhaps it had something to do with the fact that his worst fear was being realized, as he watched *Obsidian* fight Tuong Y Ve to *save Dong Tu.*

He wasn't sure what felt worse: his body dying, or the nauseating stress Obsidian's presence caused.

Luu Dong Trung clenched his teeth harder, jammed his lips that much more tightly together, and curled his fingers into shaking fists.

The fight seemed to last an eternity, but really it was over in the blink of an eye. Tuong Y Ve had never really had a chance against Obsidian, not when he was both the King of Poison and the bearer of the Storm Pearl. Not even splitting his attention and efforts between fighting Tuong Y Ve and protecting the other two on the grass had put enough strain on Obsidian to give Tuong Y Ve the upper hand. With the help of the Pearl, Obsidian's own version of the palm strike hit like a giant shard of ice piercing through the body: it swept through the space and broke Tuong Y Ve's sword into two.

Tuong Y Ve snarled and took off yet again. Obsidian nearly followed him, but then he let his gaze trail back to Dong Tu.

It gave her just enough time to call his name. Not Obsidian; his *real* name.

"Phong!"

He stayed right where he was.

Obsidian stood eerily still, his back to Dong Tu, unsure of how to react. There was only one person on the planet who brought black snow with him wherever he went. Mask or no mask, there was no hiding who he was. Behind him, Dong Tu's face was twisted with misery: tears streamed down her cheeks as she realized he had no intentions of staying. As for him...well. Obsidian was glad she couldn't hear him gulp, and glad he wore a mask so that she couldn't see his own eyes turn red with tears.

His tears froze into black snowflakes the moment they hit the open air.

"Phong...Phong, don't go," Dong Tu sobbed, trying to gather the control to stand and failing several times.

Obsidian gently adjusted his mask so that the salty snow-tears could fall further down his face. Licking one salty snowflake off his lip, he finally allowed himself to turn and face her.

To an extent, Luu Dong Trung had been right. Three years previous, Obsidian had broken it off with Dong Tu, and had intended to keep out of her life forever. Life in the Poison Legion was miserable, and being their most legendary fighter resulted in a stark, solitary life steeped in darkness and murder. His enemies made it impossible to get close to anyone who couldn't handle themselves on their own, but being so saturated with deadly poisons also meant he couldn't touch anyone that wasn't already one of the Legion. Ever. Dong Tu included.

Obsidian had never wanted to mix Dong Tu up in the web of the Whispered World. He wanted her to live the normal, peaceful life he'd been denied; so he set aside his own feelings and desires in the hopes that Dong Tu would be able to forget him and move on. He'd thought that with all those years of separation, Dong Tu's feelings would have cooled, and her pining would have faded away. But there she was, sitting in the dirt, her face shining with tears and agony radiating from every pore.

He wanted to leave, to disappear again and try to close the door on their relationship forever...yet Dong Tu's presence drew him in like a magnet. His legs, so leaden when he'd tried to convince himself to leave just a beat before, stepped toward her automatically. Fighting with Tuong Y Ve was nothing, *nothing* compared to the pain of hearing Dong Tu call his name so brokenly, and he had no defense against her sadness.

They stared at each other for what felt like thirteen years, one standing, the other sitting. Obsidian didn't remove his mask. His mind was still railing against his body: he wouldn't bring her anything but ruin. He took a half-step backward and turned away.

"Phong, *stop,*" Dong Tu pleaded. "Don't go!" She seemed to find her strength, then, and pushed herself to her feet. She dashed across the space between them and threw her arms around him from behind, clinging like she could force him to stay if she managed to not let go.

Obsidian reached slowly up and gently rested his hands over hers. He might not have been able to feel the warmth of her skin through his gloves, but he could feel her whole body shaking against his as she sobbed and held him even tighter. Dong Tu couldn't feel his warmth either, couldn't see the face she'd missed for years...but holding him tight, with his body solid in her grasp and his familiar herbal scent surrounding her, the dam finally broke.

Three years of heartache came pouring out.

Obsidian carefully turned in the circle of Dong Tu's arms and pulled her into his chest.

"Dong Tu," Obsidian breathed softly, smoothing one gloved hand over her hair. Dong Tu could hear the pain in his voice too, quiet as it was, and she knew in that moment that he hadn't been able to forget her, either. The two of them melted into each other, fitting together just as they always had, and for just that second everything was perfect. The beautiful summer sky was blue and cloudless, the lake once again reflecting the sky in its glassy surface. Crickets chirped, cicadas called, bees hummed just out of sight. A breeze washed through the trees, creating music in the rustle of the leaves, pulling at Obsidian's coat and Dong Tu's hair.

Black snowflakes still fell silently around them, but they hadn't been a sad sight to Dong Tu in a long, long time.

A snowflake stuck in Luu Dong Trung's lashes as he watched the two embrace, still burning with poison and sickened with the fear that he'd lost Dong Tu forever in that single moment.

Tears shone in his clear eyes.

"Dong Tu," Dong Trung moaned, startling the distracted lovebirds. "Dong Tu, help me!" Unlike Obsidian, he was totally unafraid to cry in front of beautiful girls. Especially in front of Dong Tu, whom he'd just taken a *poisoning* for.

Dong Tu and Obsidian broke apart and rushed over to Luu Dong Trung. Dong Tu knelt beside him; she stroked his face, checked his temperature, felt his pulse. It had always been weak, and Dong Tu was relieved to find it hadn't dropped any lower. It was an encouraging sign.

Still, Dong Trung continued to act as if he were dying in agony.

"Dong Tu, I have to leave this world, I have to leave you now...from now on you'll have to take care of yourself...don't work too much, don't forget me...don't get married, love me forever..." Luu Dong Trung snuck a sly look at Obsidian as he put on his theatrics, willfully ignoring the fact that the masked man was also listening. Obsidian frowned behind his mask. Dong Trung reminded him of Ivy, a woman who was just as possessive and jealous, and who also nagged just like a child.

The difference was that Luu Dong Trung was obviously a grown man, and a big one at that. To see him whining like a child was extremely weird.

Luu Dong Trung saw Obsidian hesitate, mask or no mask, and continued.

"Dong Tu...my Dong Tu...why am I so cold? Why's everything going dark? Is it...is it because I'm dying?"

Obsidian looked around them skeptically. The weather wasn't even close to cold, the sky was clear and bright—without the Storm Pearl, the summer heat would have melted him beneath all his layers of clothing and the silver mask.

"Dong Tu, my precious..." Dong Trung began to lay it on thicker as he called her name, knowing there was nothing Obsidian could say. "I can't—I can't breathe...my chest is so heavy...and it aches..." He pushed his lips out like he was sucking air through a large straw, positioning himself for the mouth-to-mouth he so desperately wanted. He looked like a dying fish.

Dong Tu's heart stuttered and plummeted with panic, and she frantically wiped the sweat from his forehead. She checked his pulse again, even laid her head on his chest to listen to his heartbeat.

Obsidian nudged Dong Tu aside and knelt close to Luu Dong Trung. He'd told himself he wanted Dong Tu to meet other people and forget him for years, but seeing Dong Tu so upset, her face pressed to the chest of a tall, handsome man... all of the sudden he wasn't feeling so great. He reached out to check Dong Trung's pulse, but Luu Dong Trung recoiled, staring warily at Obsidian.

Obsidian still had yet to take off his mask. The mask had been intended to make him look mysterious and evil, and it did its job—especially when combined with his black clothing and the vials lining his coat. Luu Dong Trung seemed genuinely afraid to let Obsidian touch him, when the picture of the man before him blended with the dark things Dong Trung already knew. The closer Obsidian's hand came, the more Dong Trung pulled away.

It wasn't hard to guess why Dong Trung wouldn't let Obsidian touch him, and Obsidian reluctantly pulled his mask off. He kept his face calm and non-threatening as he met Luu Dong Trung's gaze, trying to show the other man that he genuinely meant no harm. Dong Tu relaxed into a sweet smile and her cheeks flushed red as the mask came off: *that* was the face she knew and loved. His dark eyes, those long lashes...his face hadn't changed a bit.

Luu Dong Trung also flushed, but not because he was charmed by Obsidian's handsome face. He flushed with bitterness and frustration. He'd known there was no way Obsidian could have been ugly or evil if Dong Tu had loved him so much, but he'd always considered himself the superior beauty to Obsidian's unknown handsomeness. But now that Luu Dong Trung could see him, he realized the gap between them was far smaller than he could ever have anticipated. Each man was striking in drastically different ways, and the knowledge tapped into the deep insecurity Obsidian's continued existence in Dong Tu's mind had created.

More than that, with Obsidian's face so close to his own, Luu Dong Trung felt like the other man was staring straight into his soul, like all of his conniving plans to replace Obsidian were all laid bare for Obsidian to see.

Finally Luu Dong Trung let Obsidian touch him. Obsidian frowned as he took Dong Trung's pulse: he was pretty sure Dong Trung would survive for a bit longer. From the look of Dong Trung, the poison hadn't even sunken into his body to reach his organs: it was all trapped in the veins just beneath the skin. The chances of the poison reacting like that were one in a million; he was a lucky, lucky man. Obsidian handed Dong Trung the antidote.

Luu Dong Trung hesitated, and didn't even attempt to take it until Dong Tu assured him that it was the same antidote she'd been given when she'd been poisoned years before. Even so, he was still wary as he tipped the vial back and swallowed it, and listened dubiously as its use was explained. It slowed the poison's effects, giving him a few more days, and that gave them time to find Bach Duong, who had the other half of the antidote and could block the poison permanently. Just as long as Dong Trung *never* used his chi--which he never had to begin with.

He would be okay.

Obsidian was in the middle of explaining further when Luu Dong Trung reached up and touched Obsidian's face. Dong Trung had finally worked through his wave of wild jealousy, and his curiosity was getting the better of him. Curiosity gave way to excitement when he realized: that was the infamous Obsidian kneeling over him, the King of Poison, and he could touch him without fear.

How painfully ironic, that Luu Dong Trung could touch Obsidian when the woman who loved him so desperately could not. Dong Tu would have killed to trade places with him in a heartbeat.

With a childish, victorious joy, almost oblivious to the situation he was in, Luu Dong Trung began to poke all over Obsidian's face. His lips curled with a tiny, silly smirk as he poked Obsidian's eyes, his cheeks, his lips—lips that had kissed Dong Tu. Obsidian jerked back with a frown and pushed Luu Dong Trung's hands away. He wondered where in the world Dong Tu had picked up such a weirdo; even the Monstrous Eighteen were way more normal than Luu Dong Trung seemed to be.

"Don't forget, Mr. Luu, that you still have to take Bach Duong's antidote. Otherwise the poison will start spreading again in a few days, and there'll be nothing we can do to help you," Obsidian reminded him, still frowning. It would be unwise for Luu Dong Trung to piddle around when this was truly a matter of life and death. Luu Dong Trung nodded his head vigorously.

"Got it, got it!"

CHAPTER 10

Precious Little Brother

And just like that, Obsidian and Dong Tu's love story became a three-person tangle. The situation was ridiculous: Luu Dong Trung (who hated Obsidian on principle as a romantic rival) could touch the man, while Dong Tu could not. After years spent pining desperately after her lost love, dreaming of simple things like holding him close, or holding his hand, she was right back to being able to touch him only through a fabric barrier.

Dong Tu grabbed Obsidian's hand and held it tight as they turned to make their way back to the guest house along Thanh Liet Lake's calm shore, and tried to speed up so that Luu Dong Trung wouldn't insert himself into the conversation like he usually did. But Luu Dong Trung knew what she was doing, and he did what he was best at: interrupt the couple. At first he followed Dong Tu, trying to get her to talk to him instead, and then turned his attention to badgering and studying Obsidian. He never once stopped trying to get them to give in and let them travel as a group of three, rather than the couple with Dong Trung trailing along behind.

Dong Tu had a thousand things to ask Obsidian, but with Luu Dong Trung there, she filed most of them away for later and changed the topic.

"Who was that man? Tuong Y Ve?"

"Do you remember the four Kings of Poison?" Obsidian asked in return. Dong Tu shook her head: she only vaguely remembered Gia, another of the Poison Legion, giving her a brief explanation.

"Samsara is the leader of the Poison Legion. There are always four Kings of Poison beneath her, protecting the four quarters of her territory. I am the King of Poison in the northern quarter," Obsidian explained. "The Kings of Poison are supposed to be the strongest and most powerful people in the Legion. We are raised by the rule that the strong will always overcome the weak, so if someone wants to be promoted to a higher rank, they have to defeat their superior and take their place. Apparently Tuong Y Ve wants to take my place."

Tuong Y Ve didn't just want to be a King of Poison: he wanted the Storm Pearl, and all the power and renown that came with it. He'd raised the flag to challenge Obsidian, which meant that either one of them died, or—if Obsidian lost and wasn't killed—he would be forced to surrender his position and be ridiculed by everyone he knew. Historically, anyone demoted that way died either by their challenger's hand, or by suicide, unable to take the constant shame and humiliation that came after. For some reason Tuong Y Ve had challenged Obsidian when he wasn't even in the Legion's stronghold, in the heart of the Valley of Life and Death; and though he'd hunted Obsidian for some time, he had been unsuccessful.

"That was why he came after you," Obsidian finished, looking over at Dong Tu. "He was hoping to lure me out by attacking you."

Dong Tu absorbed all he'd told her in silence, and then cast a shy glance at Obsidian.

"...Didn't you want to leave the Legion? Wouldn't it be better to just hand the Storm Pearl over to Tuong Y Ve?" she ventured quietly. If Obsidian was able to renounce the Poison Legion, they might have a chance to be together.

Obsidian understood why she was asking, but he avoided her gaze and looked away.

"I can't," he replied curtly, and refused to speak on the Legion anymore.

Dong Tu fell silent, but her disappointment was palpable. She'd thought that maybe Obsidian had been unable to leave his position in the Legion, and the knowledge that he could be replaced had given her some hope that she was wrong. What she really couldn't understand was what *kept* Obsidian there. He was Bach Phong, the second-born son of the great General Bach. If he chose to leave the Legion and return to a normal life, he'd be returning to a life of royalty. Wasn't that enough? What was so damned important about being King of Poison?

Once again the gulf between Obsidian's reality and her own threatened to swallow her whole. On one side stood the King of Poison, with his Storm Pearl, immense power, and beautiful women...and on the other was Dong Tu, once again just an ordinary dojo girl from a small town. Dong Tu sighed in dismay. Her world was too small; Obsidian would have to give up far too much. Was that the real reason he'd left her behind for three impossible years?

Forgotten for the moment, Luu Dong Trung merely watched and listened as they made their way back to the guest house. He could read Dong Tu's thoughts in her sweet face, and if anyone had bothered to ask him, he would have had no trouble pointing out the fact that while Obsidian wouldn't leave the Whispered World for Dong Tu, Dong Trung would stay in the Luu family for the rest of his life, just to be close to her. Obsidian might risk his life for her, but he would never stay. Dong Tu needed to forget him and move on.

The knowledge weighed bitterly in his heart, but he couldn't say anything with Obsidian right there. He would have to wait until he could get Dong Tu alone, and it burned him to have to watch as Obsidian and Dong Tu held hands the whole way back.

———

Dong Tu and Obsidian were still holding hands when they got back to the guest house. As soon as they entered the yard, a blue flash startled Dong Tu, and a streak of blue came pelting at Obsidian. Obsidian dropped her hand and leapt into the air, flying higher and higher, but the streak continued to attack him with lightning speed and frightening precision. Obsidian leaned over and curled the blue streaks into spirals that turned into ice; he let them fall to the earth, and they shattered as they hit the ground. Obsidian looked across the yard to see a teenager with shocking blue hair, twisted and tied into knots like horns atop her head, watching him.

It was Ryujin, and if one looked close, they'd be able to see that she was manipulating water with her chi and using it as a weapon. Obsidian dodged and wove, but he wasn't quite fast enough to escape the slicing-sharp jet of water that cut through his coat at the shoulder. He couldn't afford to be careless with her, not when she was one of the Monstrous Eighteen and not some ordinary girl. She almost never jumped in to fight, usually letting Le Minh take care of the problems at the dojo; but seeing Dong Tu approach hand-in-hand with a man dressed solidly in black? One look was all it took to know that the man could be none other than Obsidian.

Ryujin wanted to test the great King of Poison herself.

Most thought her weapon of choice was the little paring knife she kept on her at all times, but in reality it was like a favorite toy, used to pick her nails and cut fruit at most. Her real abilities lay in manipulating water, using it to attack her enemies like a sword. She was using the hot water she'd stolen from the teapots of the other guests, the tables now empty as many ran for cover. No one wanted to be caught in the middle.

Well aware that he was dealing with one of the Eighteen, Obsidian drew his silver staff again and concentrated his chi to turn it into an icy sword for the second time that afternoon. Still hovering in the air, he brought his sword down in a slash, and sharp pins of ice split from its surface and went shooting at Ryujin.

Feeling as if she needed to up the ante, Ryujin shot a jet of water at the large water barrel in the corner of the yard. The metal band holding the barrel together split, the wood exploded into splinters on impact, and the water shot up into the air, turning that same bright blue as her chi infused it. It coalesced into the form of a long dragon, which curled and swept in pretty passes through the air as Ryujin took a moment to show off. It then went dashing toward Obsidian. It seemed to swallow him, enveloping Obsidian in water; and then the blue faded as the whole dragon turned to ice. There was a pause, and Dong Tu and Luu Dong Trung watched in very different kinds of anticipation as time seemed to stand still—

And came back with an explosion of white as the ice burst into snowflakes that came raining down on the yard below, glittering in the summer sun. Ryujin tipped her head back with a proud, satisfied smile, and reached out to catch a snowflake and watch it melt in her hand. She looked back up as Obsidian came floating slowly to the ground, his coat flapping around him.

"You must be Obsidian," Ryujin greeted him, and he smiled.

"And judging by those moves, you must be Thuy Long Than," Obsidian guessed in return, and Ryujin preened.

"You've heard of me, huh? It's a pleasure."

"Of course I've heard of you. Thuy Long Than is famous."

Ryujin relaxed, and the intensity in her piercing, catlike eyes calmed. In the Monstrous Eighteen, she was officially known as Thuy Long Than, the Water Goddess: a teenaged girl who was able to control water and rain.

Dong Tu sighed with quiet relief when it turned out the impromptu battle was just a bit of friendly sparring. Ryujin *had* come to satisfy her curiosity around Obsidian, after all, and one of those curiosities was just how powerful a fighter he really was.

After testing each other's skills, Obsidian and Ryujin took up like old friends, complimenting each other's fighting styles. The rumors Ryujin had heard had not been wrong: he was talented, able to block and counter her moves with relative ease—and he was *handsome*. It pleased Ryujin to know that Obsidian deserved his spot on the Whispered World's secret *Hot List*.

"You've got a cut," Ryujin pointed out, reaching up to close the hole in the shoulder of Obsidian's jacket; she could see where she'd sliced into the skin, too. Obsidian pulled away and lifted a hand to stop her from trying again.

"Be careful," he reminded her.

Across the yard, Le Minh stood hugging Yibo to his chest. He'd watched the whole fight, and for a moment toward the beginning he'd fully intended to challenge Obsidian too, at least for one round. That changed hilariously quickly the moment he saw Ryujin and Obsidian really get into it: he wasn't too stupid to know that he wasn't even close to their level. Instead he set Yibo down, then quietly slipped inside the guest house to ask a waiter to bring tea and dessert for everyone.

Yibo himself growled as Obsidian and the others sat down, but even the dog seemed to notice how adoringly Dong Tu watched the stranger. It didn't take long for Obsidian to find himself with a lap full of Yibo, eagerly waiting to be pet with his tail wagging excitedly. Obsidian did so hesitantly, and for the rest of the evening, Yibo remained by his side with his face tucked into Obsidian's shirt. It was weird for Obsidian, but that didn't stop him from sneakily slipping his hand under the table to rub Yibo's furry head.

For the very first time, Obsidian entered Dong Tu's world. He joined she and her friends while they spent the afternoon playing chess and chatting in the sunshine; he ate dinner with them; he joined them in eating fruits and cakes and drinking tea until the moon crested high in the velvety night sky.

And all the while, he smiled.

Being with Dong Tu made Obsidian happier than anything else he'd ever experienced. No pressure, no challenges, no orders; summer was for going out and relaxing, and he could spend as much time as he liked studying her rosy cheeks, her smiling mouth, and those bright eyes. It satisfied him deeply, in a way he couldn't put into words.

Dong Tu's world was colorful and full of life. Xuan Thu was clever and skillful. Bao Thuong was blunt. Ryujin was one of the Eighteen as well, and never let a single moment go stale. Le Minh and little Yibo were kind and personable, and even Dong Tu's nightmarish little brother, Luu Dong Trung, seemed to have his place.

Obsidian let his eyes wander around the space and the people gathered, lost in his thoughts, when suddenly he met the surprisingly murderous gaze of Luu Dong Trung. Dong Trung looked at him like he would love nothing more than to set Obsidian on fire, and had thrown such glances at him from the very moment Obsidian had appeared—and Obsidian had no idea what he'd done to earn such ire. Luu Dong Trung seemed as bizarrely spiteful as anyone from the Poison Legion or the Monstrous Eighteen.

Obsidian cleared his throat and looked away.

"So did everyone come to Thanh Liet Lake just for fun, or did you have something else to do up here?" he asked, moving himself along.

Le Minh found himself at a loss for words. The trip had been his own idea, a way to get Dong Tu alone for a little while and try to win her over without Bao Thuong and Luu Dong Trung's interference. Then the entire group had volunteered themselves for the trip and killed any hope of it—and then *Obsidian* had shown up and destroyed any hope left alive at all. Yibo seemed to understand his owner's distress, and whined softly, bumping Le Minh with his nose.

Luckily it was Dong Tu who answered first.

"A few months ago I ran into Stargazer again. She told me about this...Liet Than. I don't know what it means. But when I heard the name Thanh Liet, I decided to come and see if the two things were related." She watched as Obsidian frowned in thought, and eagerness flooded through her when she realized Obsidian might have the answers she was looking for. "Have you heard the name?"

"It's the name of one of the Eighteen," Obsidian responded, his frown deepening. He had no idea why Stargazer would have mentioned Liet Than to anyone. Dong Tu shook her head, still as perplexed as she was before with the knowledge that Liet Than might have some connection to Obsidian, and even Switch.

"Few people have met him," Obsidian went on. "He's extremely secretive. He's famous for how powerful his chi is, but they call him Liet Than—Frigid—as a joke, because when he fights he uses his chi and nothing else. I've never met him."

"Stargazer also told me to learn the Sunlight Strike. Maybe she wanted me to find Liet Than and learn from him?" Dong Tu pondered. Obsidian didn't answer. Honestly, Stargazer's prophecies were only right about half the time, and he didn't put much stock in her words. Sometimes he wasn't sure how she'd made it into the Eighteen to begin with.

"I wonder if Liet Than is the same paralyzed master rumored to be at Tien Thuc falls," Le Minh added, scratching his chin.

"I wonder if he's handsome," Ryujin interjected. Again.

Obsidian had no more answers, no matter what questions they posed to him after that. Not everyone among the Monstrous Eighteen actually knew each other; he and Ryujin were a good example. They knew each other by name or reputation, but unless there was some fortuitous convergence like the two of them seeking out Dong Tu, there weren't exactly family reunions where they could meet.

Luu Dong Trung remained silent during the conversation, still wearing that dark, brooding frown. He'd sat in a corner all afternoon with his blood silently boiling, hating every second of seeing the way Dong Tu and Obsidian looked at each other. Unlike Le Minh, he refused to give up trying to win Dong Tu over.

He looked up as a waiter passed by, and signaled for him to stop.

"Bring out the wine!" Dong Trung called.

Obsidian might have been the best at martial arts, but he was still the more beautiful of the two. If he could beat Obsidian in some other field, he might just inch his way ahead. Obsidian didn't sing, so that kind of challenge was out. There was one thing Dong Trung knew for certain he could win at: Luu Dong Trung could drink, and drink, and he would never get drunk.

"Phong, to celebrate your lucky arrival, we should drink! Last man standing wins!" Dong Trung called with fake cheer as the waiter brought out a large tray loaded with dozens of bottles of wine. Obsidian blinked at Luu Dong Trung in disbelief. He was Obsidian, the King of Poison, master of—and immune to—thousands of kinds of poison. If the most lethal toxins in the world didn't make him bat more than an eyelash, why on earth would something as mild as wine? Did the other man have a death wish?

"Don't be ridiculous, Dong Trung. You've been poisoned, you almost died. You shouldn't drink tonight," Dong Tu advised him worriedly. Even Le Minh, who wanted nothing more than to watch Luu Dong Trung crash and burn in his effort to steal Dong Tu away from Obsidian, lifted his voice in agreement.

"You should mind your limits, Dong Trung."

Meanwhile, Luu Dong Trung was completely ignoring them. He slammed his cup back down on the table and stared Obsidian down with narrowed eyes: would he rise to the challenge, or was he too scared to drink?

Obsidian let out a short, derisive laugh. He did hesitate for a second, because he didn't want to cause Luu Dong Trung any harm and he had no idea what the other man's intentions were.

And then a bell tolled midnight like the beginning of a match.

Ryujin snatched a bottle of wine from the waiter, looked back and forth between the two preparing to drink, and smirked calmly.

Luu Dong Trung rolled his shoulders and cracked his neck on each side with audible pops, stretching and popping like he was preparing for a physical fight.

Obsidian merely drew in a deep breath and sighed.

Ryujin poured them both a new bowl of wine, raised the bottle before her, and called:

"Begin!"

Luu Dong Trung grabbed his bowl, gripping it hard like he was trying to break it, and downed it. Obsidian watched the other man's dramatics bemusedly, and instead calmly raised his bowl to his lips, drained it, and set it slowly back down.

Ryujin poured a second bowl for each, and Luu Dong Trung sucked the second one down with equal fervor. Obsidian raised an eyebrow and drank his own second bowl with equally as much calm. The third bowl was poured...and then the fourth...the fifth...sixth...seventh.

Every time Ryujin poured a new bowl, Obsidian and Luu Dong Trung drank like they were downing a glass of water. Obsidian continued his leisurely pace, as if he were drinking tea. He almost seemed bored. Even Luu Dong Trung began to grow bored after the first ten bowls, and his theatrics melted into a robotic rhythm.

Eventually even Ryujin found herself bored, and plopped down with a mung bean cake, letting Obsidian and Dong Trung pour wine for each other. Dong Tu finally poured herself a bowl of wine, took a sip, and winced as the strong wine burned all the way down. She looked back and forth between Obsidian and Luu Dong Trung, saw the aggressiveness in both of their faces, and let out a heavy sigh.

The moon lit up a cloudless night sky. It was still hot out, Le Minh was almost drunk, and Bao Thuong was already passed out on the grass with his mouth hanging open, drooling. Xuan Thu had left to go to bed, which meant that Ryujin and Dong Tu really were the only ones paying any attention, both yawning with sleepiness and boredom. Ryujin wondered how long the competition would last; Dong Tu wondered who was going to pay for all the wine when they were finished.

Hours passed. Luu Dong Trung and Obsidian lost none of their zeal, still drinking tirelessly. They'd lost count of the bottles and bowls they'd drained, and had no idea how many times they'd gotten up to relieve themselves. Up and down, up and down, the cycle was endless.

Obsidian wiped his mouth with a hand and narrowed his eyes at Luu Dong Trung doubtfully. He was skeptical of the other man's seeming unflappability: it made sense for Obsidian to have such a high tolerance, but Dong Trung? No ordinary human could have drunk that much without it coming right back up again. Could it be that Luu Dong Trung was another one of the Eighteen? Aside from Stargazer, were there any other members who lacked sufficient chi?

Even as he turned the problem over in his mind, Luu Dong Trung was also beginning to realize that he'd chosen the worst way to challenge Obsidian. Too much had happened that day, and he hadn't been thinking clearly: of course Obsidian would have such a high tolerance for alcohol, he'd been poisoning himself since he was six. But the most dangerous lapse he'd made was the fact that the longer Dong Trung drank and remained unaffected, the more excuse Obsidian would have to be suspicious of him. He needed to think of a way out, and quickly.

Dong Trung let himself go loose and weak, falling sideways to lean against Dong Tu with a low groan.

"Dong Tu, I don't feel so well," he complained. Dong Tu hurriedly dabbed his head with a towel.

"Is it from the wine? We should stop." Dong Tu felt Luu Dong Trung's forehead with a worried frown to see if he had a fever, and then began to rub his chest to see if it helped soothe away the urge to vomit.

But Obsidian wasn't an idiot. He saw through Luu Dong Trung's ploy, and watched in irritation as Luu Dong Trung obviously used the wine as an excuse to be coddled by Dong Tu. And that wasn't the only thing Obsidian saw through: there was no way Luu Dong Trung was some ordinary man.

No average person could drink that much without needing a doctor. It was impossible!

Obsidian silently removed his glove as Dong Tu worried over Luu Dong Trung. His hand shot out, almost too quickly to see, and he seized Dong Trung's bare wrist and jerked Dong Trung over to him. He grabbed Luu Dong Trung's collar and pulled him in even closer, so close that Dong Trung could feel Obsidian's breath on his cheek; but no matter how panicked Dong Trung became, Obsidian's grip—now wrapped around both wrists—was too strong to break.

Ignoring Dong Tu's gasped demands to know what the hell he was doing, Obsidian smelled Dong Trung's breath, and checked his pulse and blood pressure by touch. As expected, Dong Trung's heart rate and blood pressure were completely normal. They'd drunk the same amount of wine for hours: Obsidian's breath smelled of alcohol, Dong Trung's did not; Obsidian wasn't drunk because he'd developed too high a tolerance...and Dong Trung's body seemed not to absorb it at all. In fact, Obsidian couldn't detect any poison in his body at all, not even from the attack that afternoon.

Not even from the way Obsidian's bare hand touched Luu Dong Trung's bare wrists.

Luu Dong Trung tried to break away, but Obsidian's grip on his wrists tightened until it ached. He cast around for something, anything he could do to get away from Obsidian, and finally he stopped trying to escape at all. Instead he angled his head, leaned in, and planted a kiss right on his lips.

Obsidian jerked back, shocked, and released Luu Dong Trung's hand as he turned his face away and began to vigorously wipe his mouth off on his sleeve. Dong Trung did the same, and looked up to find Obsidian *glaring* at him.

"Do you like men?!" Dong Trung gasped, rubbing his wrists. "I know I'm beautiful, but I'm not a woman! And I only like women—I like Dong Tu! You shouldn't use alcohol as an excuse to get close to people!"

He tried to flip the script on Obsidian and paint the other man as the offender, rather than the victim. Obsidian didn't respond. He poured himself another bowl of wine and sat for a while, calming himself down, and he continued to scrutinize Luu Dong Trung as he did.

Finally he spoke.

"Luu Dong Trung, is there a fragment of the Sunlight Pearl in your body?"

Everyone left in the yard felt their hearts stop.

CHAPTER 11

A Fragment of the Sunlight Pearl

Before she ever mentioned a Liet Than, Stargazer had told Dong Tu that while meeting Obsidian had been a lucky accident, the two of them weren't destined to be together. She'd left Dong Tu with only one instruction and one hope: if Dong Tu found a piece of the Sunlight Pearl, she would be able to be with Obsidian again. She'd asked anyone she could find about the Pearl and its pieces, but no one seemed to have heard of it, let alone understood its purpose.

Dong Tu hadn't heard it mentioned again since she and Stargazer had parted ways.

"That's why you weren't afraid of being poisoned," Obsidian continued cautiously. "You knew the fragment would protect you." Pieces of the Sunlight Pearl weren't as rare as the Storm Pearl, but they were still precious and highly coveted throughout the Whispered World. Luu Dong Trung's gaze whipped from side to side as he tried to think of a way to deny the truth, adjusting his untidy collar tensely... but in the end he knew nothing but the truth would do.

"Yes. I have a piece of the Sunlight Pearl inside me," Dong Trung affirmed quietly. He hesitated for a beat, then drew himself up to his full height and smoothed his hair. He lifted his chin, shoulders back and expression haughty, and began to tell the story.

Tuyet Hoa Phi Loc, a district magistrate, had two sons: Tuyet Hoa Vo Thuong, and Tuyet Hoa Vo Le. The brothers were tall, strong, talented, and learned everything they could. Between the two of them, the pair had a vast pool of knowledge that spanned innumerable subjects, including a deep understanding of the Whispered World and how the various factions and networks all worked with (and against) each other. Years passed, the brothers matured, and their parents assumed they had moved beyond childbearing age.

In a twist of fate, Lady Tuyet Hoa became pregnant with their third child. The baby would be almost a decade younger than his brothers, and because his mother was elderly, they were worried the baby might be sickly when he was born. Lady Tuyet Hoa went into labor in the middle of a winter snowstorm, and their family's mansion fell into chaos as the servants ran back and forth at the behest of the midwife. The labor dragged on for over twenty-four hours, and the Lady's servants shared concerned looks with each other: she was too old to struggle on much longer.

Finally the midwife reappeared.

"It's a boy!" she announced happily, but her smile didn't reach her eyes, and the usual sounds of a wailing newborn were startlingly absent. Mr. Tuyet Hoa and his sons slipped nervously into the room, and after he greeted his wife, the midwife placed his newborn son in his arms. The baby's skin was painfully red against the towel he was wrapped in, and the boy barely moved. It only took a moment for Mr. Tuyet Hoa to realize the infant couldn't breathe, even as the midwife did the math on her fingers: the baby was supposed to have been born in the spring, and was several months premature.

She'd tried everything she could think of to get him to breathe. She'd turned him upside down, spanked him...but nothing worked. He still lay there, silent and motionless. The brazier that lit the room cast dramatic shadows on the family's faces, and every one of them showed heartbreak and grief. In that oppressive silence, the blizzard could be heard raging outside.

The midwife took the baby, placed him on a table, and covered him with a cloth. Mr. Tuyet Hoa picked him up again almost immediately, unable to bear the pain and yet trying to memorize that beloved little face before their time was up. He refused to put his son back down even as he ordered their servants to prepare for a funeral, and kept the baby in his arms as his eldest sons took the time to look at their poor little brother, too. As Tuyet Hoa Vo Le reached out to touch the baby's tiny red cheek, a wrinkled hand wormed its way into the mix and pushed what looked like a pearlescent grain of sand into the baby's mouth.

The room went still as everyone studied the newcomer in shock.

It was an ancient-looking woman in a colorful coat, with multiple strands of pearls draped around her thin neck. She'd snuck into the mansion while the house was hectic with the frenzy of childbirth, and had sat there, drinking tea, waiting for the child to be born. And when it was time, she'd come to bestow a piece of the Sunlight Pearl upon the dying newborn. It had been so small, the only reason it was even visible was because of the way the firelight had reflected off its surface.

"The Sunlight Pearl is naturally hot, but it won't bring him any harm. It is full of life, and will help your son to live. It will also protect him from any poison and any venomous creatures he may run into," the strange old woman explained. Almost as if to prove it, a bright light began to shine behind the baby's purple lips; the light spread throughout his entire body, and for a moment the baby shone as brightly as the sun and lit up the winter night outside the bedroom windows.

When the light faded, the baby's color was returning. He opened his big, clear eyes and began to cry loudly, as if he had finally, truly been born.

"You, little treasure, are going to wreak havoc on the Whispered World. We couldn't let you die like that, could we, no," the old woman chuckled. Mr. Tuyet Hoa and his family all began to realize the baby really would live with a rush of excitement and relief. "Now, I will call you Tuyet Hoa Phi Vu, and you will be my disciple."

The family knelt before the old woman, believing a true, mysterious master had just saved their son's life; but the old woman waved it away like she'd done nothing more than repair a lost button. She didn't need thanks, but she *did* want compensation for the Sunlight Pearl fragment.

———

"Are you talking about Stargazer?!" Dong Tu and Obsidian demanded loudly and in tandem, their voices echoing around the yard.

"Yes!" Luu Dong Trung affirmed with a nod. Everyone looked around at each other in surprise.

"And Stargazer is your teacher?"

Luu Dong Trung nodded again. Dong Tu nearly fell out of her chair: in all the time he'd been living with her family, Luu Dong Trung had never mentioned anything about Stargazer or the Sunlight Pearl! She'd been right to compare him to an onion, but Dong Tu had thought they'd peeled back the final layers months ago. There was so much more to be discovered, or so it seemed: her handsome little brother had turned out to be the student of one of the Monstrous Eighteen, of Stargazer herself!

"Why did Stargazer pick someone so ordinary to be her student?" Dong Tu asked, and Luu Dong Trung frowned earnestly.

"I am not ordinary! She said I would cause chaos in the underworld!"

That was, however, Stargazer's signature line. She said the same thing to everyone, Dong Tu and Obsidian included. It looked as if she'd used the same trick to dupe the Tuyet Hoa family. Obsidian had no faith in Stargazer and her prophecies and ignored everything she said, mostly because the first time she'd met him, she'd told him she had never met anyone who would create such chaos in the Whispered World, and yet had such a short lifespan.

Without knowing Obsidian at all, she had flattered and jinxed him in the same breath.

"Your lifeline is not good," Stargazer had told him. "You'll either face sudden death, or continuously face catastrophes and near-death accidents, perhaps even become disabled."

Obsidian had stripped his gloves off, cracked his knuckles, and stared her down.

"I think you're the one headed for a short lifespan," he'd threatened, but Stargazer had laughed him off.

"You don't have to believe me. I just say what I See."

In fairness to the usually cooky old woman, she had been right about a few things: her warnings to mind the arrow before he was shot in the neck by Bach Duong's own arrow; the fact that Dong Tu's choosing to stay and help him had led to such a tumultuous and short-lived relationship, that sent ripples throughout the Whispered World and had likely changed it forever. But it was impossible to know what predictions were the product of a true gift, and what was just dumb luck.

Besides, Obsidian knew he was well-known throughout the Whispered World, and he held little regard for his own life. Between his position and his possession of the Storm Pearl, the question was never *would* he be killed; it was when, and by whom. His having a short lifespan was no surprise.

Luu Dong Trung was different. He was the son of a magistrate, not a member of the Poison Legion. What was his secret? What made him so important? Then again, Stargazer seemed to be fond of taking any student she could find, and had nearly talked Dong Tu into studying with her, too.

"What did she teach you?" Obsidian asked, wondering what an old woman with no chi and no knowledge of martial arts could have passed on.

"Absolutely nothing," Luu Dong Trung responded, shrugging.

Of course she hadn't. The old lady had been born with the gift of foresight, and that wasn't exactly a teachable skill. Stargazer remained with the family for thirteen years, relaxing and enjoying the noble life rather than working or passing anything useful on to Tuyet Hoa Phi Vu. And when the boy had turned thirteen, she'd decided her responsibility had been fulfilled and moved on, continuing her journey.

Obsidian and Dong Tu both facepalmed as they listened to the story's end, embarrassed by the old woman. It had likely all been a ruse to get the family to take care of her for free the entire time; it would explain why Luu Dong Trung knew exactly nothing of martial arts, despite having been gifted a life-saving fragment of the Sunlight Pearl. And Dong Tu finally understood why Luu Dong Trung's chi was nonexistent, and why his pulse beat like that of a dying man, even though he was strong and healthy. All of his strength came from that tiny fragment.

Dong Tu wondered why Stargazer had ordered her to find all of the fragments of the Sunlight Pearl. Was it because she'd given a piece to one of her students? Or did she intend for Luu Dong Trung to hand over his fragment to Dong Tu, making her able to touch Obsidian without fear again?

Luu Dong Trung managed to follow Dong Tu's train of thought exactly.

"Any fragment of the Sunlight Pearl you take merges with your body, just like the Storm Pearl," he interjected. "I can't give it to you. If I remove it, I'll die."

Obsidian opened his mouth to move them past *that* subject, but it was too late. Dong Tu had already seized upon the exact detail he had hoped beyond hope she'd missed.

"Just like the Storm Pearl?" she repeated. "What's that supposed to mean?"

"The Sunlight Pearl is safe, benevolent. Especially in pieces, it runs no risk to those accepting it and isn't picky about who it will merge with. Anyone can consume it. Depending on the person, it can make them stronger, protect their life...neutralize the effects of poisons, venoms, and even alcohol. With certain people, it could be used to advance their own martial arts skills or even learn new techniques using its power. It's possible that some of the Monstrous Eighteen carry fragments themselves."

Ryujin, watching silently until that moment, shook her head.

"I was born awesome. I don't have any secret Pearl fragments."

The Storm Pearl, on the other hand, was different. It picked exactly one person with whom it was willing to merge, and that person was anyone who could withstand the enormous amounts of dark, freezing energy that it contained. When swallowed, the Storm Pearl's energy spread throughout the body, absorbing the hopeful carrier's own chi, and if they weren't strong enough…it drained them entirely, and left them a frozen husk. That was part of the reason for its renown: the trial was far more likely to end in death than success.

And that was part of the reason Obsidian was so feared.

Obsidian hadn't been named a King of Poison because he'd defeated his predecessor, he'd earned it through the trial of the Pearl. His predecessor had been too old to defeat his challenger and had been killed, but the challenger himself had also died in his attempt to swallow the Pearl. For years members of the Poison Legion had died while testing their mettle against its icy energy, one by one, until at last Obsidian had stepped forward to receive it.

Luu Dong Trung carefully went on to explain what he'd meant when he said the two Pearls were similar in effect—when he'd said Obsidian could never remove it.

"The Sunlight Pearl and the Storm pearl…one positive, one negative, one light and one dark, hot and cold…they were created by a single person. They work the same way. Once one is swallowed and merges with its carrier, it doesn't just exist in the body as a foreign object. They become like another heart. They're so interwoven with your life-force that removing one is like ripping out your heart. You'd never survive it."

Obsidian and Luu Dong Trung included.

The more Dong Trung revealed, the more frustrated Obsidian became. He'd never wanted Dong Tu to know any of this. The Pearl was why he couldn't get out of the Legion. With the Storm Pearl, he *belonged* to them. And without it, he died.

"We can't blame Luu Dong Trung for keeping it secret," Obsidian said, trying to shift the subject away from the Storm Pearl. "It's the only thing keeping him alive."

Luu Dong Trung nodded.

"Without the fragment, I would have suffocated and died." He looked beseechingly around at those in the yard still conscious. "Promise me you won't tell anyone else?"

The pieces of the Sunlight Pearl might not have been as rare as the Storm Pearl, but they were still widely sought after, and the only reason Luu Dong Trung had been able to stay alive as long as he had was because no one in the Whispered World knew he carried one. With no chi and no skill as a fighter, if someone wanted to take it, he'd die.

Everyone nodded their assent.

It was exhaustingly late when those who'd stayed up finally got back to their rooms. Luu Dong Trung wanted to follow Dong Tu to her room, but Ryujin began to stubbornly drag him away. She was well aware that Dong Tu and Obsidian hadn't had any time for just the two of them. Luu Dong

Trung caught hold of a corner and clung to it, legs spread wide, grunting and demanding Ryujin let him go as she dragged him backward.

Ryujin succeeded in the end, and when everyone—Ryujin and Luu Dong Trung included—had dispersed, Obsidian and Dong Tu took each other's hands. They walked slowly towards Dong Tu's room, both of them hesitant...both hearts pounding.

Obsidian softly bid Dong Tu goodnight at her door and reluctantly turned back, trying to keep his expression blank. Being reunited with her had been...better than he could have dreamt. But the day had passed quickly, and it was time to return to his own world. No matter how badly he wanted to spend the night holding her, admiring her, memorizing her; no matter how tempting it was to stay a little while longer and silently disappear in the night, rather than face another painful farewell. At least that way he wouldn't have to endure her tears, even if the knowledge that she would be just as distraught come morning weighed heavily on his heart.

His internal debate was interrupted when he realized Dong Tu hadn't released his hand.

"Phong," she said. Obsidian froze, and stood silently for a beat, trying to fight the urge to turn around...

But he couldn't resist.

Dong Tu wrapped him up in her arms as he turned around, holding him tight as Obsidian tucked her close in return. He smoothed his hand up and down her back, over her long hair, and drank in every second as if it were his last. They stood that way for a long time, lit by the moonlight. Time had flown so *fast,* and the separation had been so painful…would they ever be ready to let go?

The pair felt trapped, powerless. They couldn't touch each other, they couldn't *stay* together—they were happy together, but Obsidian was bound to the Poison Legion and Dong Tu couldn't follow him into it. What kind of future could they possibly have?

Almost as if she knew they were sharing the same hopeless thoughts, Dong Tu held Obsidian more tightly. She pressed her face harder into his chest, right into his thick coat, and while he stroked her hair and caressed her cheeks, all she could feel were his gloves. Her heart had calmed in his embrace, but it began to race again, and her breath was coming in shallower and shallower.

Obsidian swallowed down the bitter taste her pain left in his mouth and sighed, knowing she was probably about to cry again. He'd chosen wrong. He should have avoided her; he should have left as soon as he'd beaten Tuong Y Ve back. He was exactly as crushed and desperate as he'd been the day he'd watched Dao Que Chi lead Dong Tu into the next chamber for her antidotes, in the Valley of Life and Death.

Healing for her, likely death for him...and a wedge between them forever.

Time hadn't dulled his feelings. It had only strengthened them. And he knew when they finally said goodbye again, their shared sorrow would be so much worse.

Dong Tu lifted her face out of Obsidian's chest and looked up into Obsidian's beautiful eyes, once again met with those thick, long lashes. The moonlight lit up the room enough to illuminate her own sweet, round eyes, and to sparkle off the tears gathering at the edge of her lashes. She gathered every ounce of courage she had.

"Phong...stay with me tonight?" she asked.

Obsidian gently squeezed Dong Tu's shoulders. He'd been fighting the desire to return to her for three years, but those three years became *nothing* in the face of her beloved eyes, filled with heartbroken tears and hesitant hope. He knew that despite the cool, impassive expression on his face, his eyes screamed all the things he couldn't show—and he knew she'd see the way the fight bled out of him with that single request. His expression softened, and his gaze warmed as he tried to hide his smile.

He failed: those dimples would always give him away.

Obsidian nodded, his own eyes sparkling; and with Dong Tu on his arm, they walked into her bedroom and closed the door.

Tomorrow would take care of itself.

CHAPTER 12

Years of Longing

Warm light chased the darkness away as Dong Tu lit some candles. She gently blew away the smoke that curled up around them, and smiled to herself as the steady little flames cast a rosy glow on their skin. A bath had been prepared by the maids: the nights were almost as hot as the days in summertime, and fresh flower petals floated invitingly on the surface of the refreshingly cold water. Smoke from burning incense swirled around the room in tiny trails, and its scent was intoxicating.

Dong Tu undressed and slipped into the cold water, blushing deeply. Obsidian sat beside the tub as she soaked, his face resting on his hand, and his eyes took in every move she made with unadulterated adoration. He had barely changed from how he'd looked in the old days, when he and Dong Tu had watched the stars at Hoa Hon Palace. His gaze softened under those gorgeous, long lashes as he relaxed.

Dong Tu had thought they would be awkward and embarrassed around each other, especially as she bathed; but their gazes were fixed on each other for the whole night, and being completely bare around each other felt so *natural*. She did notice small changes as she studied him, like the way the scar on his neck had faded with time. But the way he watched her as she chattered was still so sweet. She told him about how things had changed for her family over the years; she told him about Luu Dong Trung, her adopted brother, who seemed bratty and mischievous--but who was truly kindhearted, and pampered her like royalty.

Obsidian listened, but his attention was still on her, not on what she was saying. He helped her scoop up water to wash her hair and body, lost in his own thoughts: for the past three years, being separated from Dong Tu had hurt more than any wound he'd ever received. In the Valley of Life and Death, out of sight, the ache of her absence had been agonizing; but with her right there before his eyes, soaking in the bath and watching him with such affection...with her soft lips sparking sweet memories, everything he'd tried to forget came raging back even more vibrantly.

He couldn't say when he'd fallen in love with Dong Tu. The first time he laid eyes on her in that thatched hut, he'd been injured and in pain and dying for some rest. Seeing Dong Tu had sparked frustration and exasperation: he'd been sick and tired of Switch and her gang capturing innocent people and using them as playthings to curb their boredom. No, Obsidian's first impression of Dong Tu was that she was nothing more than a comely young lady. Not beautiful, not extraordinary, but pretty enough.

He'd never anticipated their fates becoming so intertwined. Not when they'd accidentally 'kissed' in that hut; not when he'd deliberately kissed her beside her own coffin at her family's dojo; not when he'd kissed her goodbye in the Valley. And he had *never* expected that, three years later, they would be together again.

Just a breath away.

Dong Tu guessed Obsidian's thoughts as he sat beside her in silence, his expression so pensive. After all, he hadn't been the only one pining for years. Her rambling had been intended to hide the way she couldn't find the words to express what she was feeling in that moment. Not when the second he'd removed his own shirt and exposed that familiar tattoo, a lump had risen in her throat.

Obsidian had always hidden himself beneath layers and layers of clothing, and his frightening silver mask. But once he removed them all, the marks left in his skin from his time with the Poison Legion told a different story. The spider tattoo, worked into his skin with poison, metal, and fire by Dao Que Chi. The scar on his neck from being shot with an arrow by Bach Duong, his own brother. His outfits and bearing were all designed to scare the Whispered World and keep them all at bay...but beneath it all he was a battered and sad young man.

"It's been three years," Dong Tu said finally. Silence filled the room after she spoke, but she had to find *some* way to begin to bleed out the sorrow in her heart.

Obsidian nodded. In what had felt like the blink of an eye, Dong Tu had gone from a teen to a young woman. She was still the same girl, dressed in his shirt at Hoa Hon Palace; yet now she looked like a woman, pouring water over her bare skin in the bath. He would never understand why he hadn't noticed how beautiful she was when they'd first met, with her round, vulnerable and yet resolute eyes. Her delicate mouth brought pure radiance to her face when she smiled. As he watched her, the flower petals caught on her wet neck and shoulders.

"I missed you," Obsidian blurted out. Dong Tu hummed noncommittally.

"You missed me, and yet you vanished without a single word for three years. I waited for you for so long, I almost turned into a rock."

She was talking about the rock on Hon Vong Phu mountain. The natural rock formation took the shape of a woman carrying a child in her arms, looking over the ocean, waiting for the husband that had abandoned them.

"Only three years," Obsidian teased. "I heard some people waited thirteen."

"Three years are enough to wear a woman out. I wonder how it would feel to wait thirteen years."

"You *want* to know how a rock feels?" Obsidian laughed, but Dong Tu didn't smile. She nodded. It left Obsidian perplexed: he was good at concealing emotions, not communicating them, and trying to figure out where Dong Tu was going was even harder.

"I wonder what that rock looks like. Have you seen it?" Dong Tu continued. She'd heard various versions of the tale before, but she'd never had the opportunity to see the mountain with her own eyes. "Is it really a natural rock that looks like a human, gazing into the distance, expecting a man that will never return?"

"...It looks like she's worn out with longing," Obsidian said quietly.

"It looks like she's worn out with longing," Dong Tu repeated just as softly. No one knew if rocks really had feelings, but human hearts clearly did.

"The first year, the rock thought it was all some twisted joke of destiny. Not real. She didn't think she was left behind...she thought there had been some mistake. Maybe he'd forgotten his way home. It felt so real, and yet so much like a dream," Dong Tu continued her speech as if Obsidian hadn't interrupted.

"In the second year, the dream turned into overflowing anger," Obsidian continued for her. "Angry at one's self, angry with their circumstances, angry with fate."

"...And in the third year, the anger faded, but sadness remained. She knew she'd done nothing wrong, knew that he hadn't forgotten her...but she didn't know what to do. All she could do was surrender, and collapse in despair," Dong Tu sighed. Obsidian bowed his head, avoiding Dong Tu's gaze, but after a moment Obsidian looked up.

"Did you know the husband left because he found out his wife was really his sister?" Obsidian asked. "He couldn't let his sister suffer, and he couldn't continue to live in that ridiculous situation, either." Obsidian's voice softened as he spoke, and he watched Dong Tu intensely, trying to communicate all the things he couldn't bring himself to say with his eyes.

Dong Tu said, "So he chose to leave? Leaving her behind in suffering and confusion? Was that really the right choice, when it eventually led to both of them suffering in the end?"

Obsidian swallowed and fell silent.

"The wife was left to silently endure, alone, without a chance to choose her own path for herself," Dong Tu went on, frowning at Obsidian. "How could one person decide the outcome for the both of them, without even asking what she wanted?"

Obsidian wanted to explain, but he didn't know *how*. And worse, he was realizing just how wrong he had been…

"He was just trying to bring her happiness."

"But she was in despair, because he left her," Dong Tu pointed out disapprovingly, her voice choked with tears. The candlelight flickered in her eyes and gleamed off her tears. She continued, her voice soft but resolute. "Phong. You and I are not blood siblings."

Obsidian was amazed. The Dong Tu he'd known before had been like a kitten, small and innocent and naïve. But she'd grown, become more determined, and she was no longer unquestioningly obedient. Her eyes fixed on his own.

"I don't need to be a skilled fighter to wander the world. Even if I'm poisoned for my entire life, as long as I don't use my chi…just being by your side is enough."

Obsidian's gaze dropped to Dong Tu's lips and didn't move away.

Dong Tu leaned in to kiss him, but was stopped by his finger against her lips, the flower petal on his finger the only thing separating their skin. They stayed that way for a long time, still staring into each other's eyes; Dong Tu's eyes gleamed in the candlelight, inviting, asking the question only Obsidian could answer.

Obsidian's finger moved, carefully keeping the petal between his finger and her skin. His touch trailed down her chin, skimmed along her neck, and gently followed the highlight of the warm candlelight reflected on her wet skin. Dong Tu was truly prepared to give up everything to be with him. But he'd lost everything, and he couldn't let her suffer that same fate. In the Poison Legion, your life always hung by a thread...and he would rather leave her with the chance to go, than think about what might happen to her because of him. Obsidian sighed regretfully and bowed his head to avoid Dong Tu's look of utter disappointment.

Disconcerted and abashed, Dong Tu caressed the ends of her hair that were floating on the water. She'd confessed her every feeling, but still he'd turned away.

Obsidian was aware that he'd made mistakes, but he had no regrets. His first mistake was stealing a kiss from her beside her casket at the dojo. The second was kissing her goodbye. Perhaps he really wasn't supposed to decide for the both of them by himself, but he knew one thing for certain: he couldn't, wouldn't let Dong Tu be poisoned again, and he could not let her be caught up in the Poison Legion.

Dong Tu stood, and Obsidian wrapped a towel around her wet body and lifted her from the water. She clung to him as tightly as she could around that thin layer of fabric, and refused to let go—adamantly enough that he finally let her sit in his lap. He positioned them so that not even her shoulders would accidentally brush his skin, but Dong Tu could feel his self-control beginning to slip, little by little.

They were stuck. Their faces were so close together, their bodies only separated by a piece of cloth...the distance was as thin as a strand of hair, and yet it felt like a chasm.

Dong Tu could feel Obsidian's hot breath on her cheek, and she could feel his skin burning through the towel.

The *towel!*

Dong Tu laughed softly. She couldn't believe she hadn't thought of it before! She looked at the fabric separating them and pulled it up to cover the lower half of her face. She met Obsidian's gaze, her own eyes glittering, and she could tell the same realization was just striking him, too. Obsidian relaxed, letting Dong Tu lean against him, and with the fabric between them, he kissed her gently.

They melted into each other, her soft, supple body and his hard muscles, lips still locked; they were as close as they could get without their skin touching.

Was it truly a kiss when their lips and cheeks only touched through a layer of cloth? Could it possibly be lovemaking, when skin never touched skin, but their legs still found ways to entangle, their bodies still wrapped around each other?

Obsidian's eyelashes brushed Dong Tu's cheeks as his hands smoothed over the curves of her body. His lips and breath caressed her hair, her neck, her breasts. They shifted, until Dong Tu reclined in the bed, her legs wrapping around Obsidian's strong body again, pulling him closer with that same, thin towel still between them. Obsidian's hands found her hips, gripping her tight so that when he ground against her, and when she rocked up into him, their movements began to blend together in a seamless rhythm.

His gaze was like the moonlight flooding through the window, lighting across her face, shining along every strand of hair—burning itself into the furthest corners of her mind in ways she'd craved for years. The candlelight continued to cast a rosy glow on their faces and bodies, and black snowflakes caught on their hair and lips as they moved together. Three years of longing poured themselves into every touch, though it felt like a dream when their bodies were so close and yet still so far apart.

Obsidian held Dong Tu in his arms like that all night, and Dong Tu continued to cling to him, his muscles as solid as steel. She couldn't touch his skin, no...but she was satisfied as long as he was beside her.

Dong Tu buried her face in Obsidian's chest and listened to his steady heartbeat through the towel. She felt his warmth, breathed in that comforting herbal scent. It was like the old days had returned, back when they'd slept together atop Hoa Hon Palace. That night Obsidian's eyes had seemed to hold the starry heavens in their entirety, but just then they were like flames in the night—untouchable, but fervently intense.

"Phong, I could be with you, just like this, for the rest of my life," Dong Tu whispered. Obsidian nodded, but he was hesitant as he gently stroked her hair.

Would so little be enough for a lifetime?

CHAPTER 13

A Rock and a Hard Place

Obsidian and Dong Tu held each other all night, but Obsidian had a hard time sleeping. His swirling thoughts were a torment, and he couldn't stop thinking about all of the seemingly insurmountable obstacles that lay between them: the toxic touch of Obsidian's skin, the Storm Pearl that bound him to the Poison Legion—and that thin towel providing the only barrier between his front and Dong Tu's warm, bare, sweet-smelling skin.

He again wished to be nothing more than a *man*. Not some martial arts master, not the King of Poison. Just a man living in peace and obscurity by Dong Tu's side.

The night was silent, and the moon was bright as Luu Dong Trung looked out of his window. Across the courtyard, Le Minh also stood at his window, and their eyes met. They'd both seen Dong Tu and Obsidian disappear into her bedroom, and although they both knew the pair couldn't touch each other, they shared the same aching sense of loss.

Le Minh knew he had come after everyone else: after Bao Thuong, after Obsidian, and after Luu Dong Trung. It was sad, in a way, but he knew it was time to graciously withdraw and leave Dong Tu to live the life she so clearly wanted. Yibo whined by his knee, as if to offer his own sympathy.

Luu Dong Trung still refused to go without a fight. He shot a fiercely determined look at Dong Tu's room, his hands gripping the window frame tight, and in the moonlight his fierce expression turned cold and impassive.

His teardrop earrings, which had been absent since he'd been adopted into the Luu family, flashed in the silvery light as he whirled away from the window.

The next morning, Le Minh and Ryujin came to bid everyone farewell at the same time. Le Minh had stayed up for several nights, not just the one before. He was confident in his understanding of Dong Tu's mind, and in his decision to withdraw and find another shore. He hugged Dong Tu as he said his goodbyes, and bowed respectfully to Obsidian as Yibo snuffled his wet nose and wagged his tail.

"Goodbye, Dong Tu. I wish you happiness. If fate allows, we'll see you again soon."

Luu Dong Trung said his goodbyes nonchalantly. There was no friendliness between he and Le Minh. There was no need to pretend they would miss each other, and no need to drag it out. Le Minh offered him a calm, understanding smile and wished Luu Dong Trung good luck: Obsidian's return had made Luu Dong Trung's journey to Dong Tu's heart most arduous. He was young and desperately in love, and Le Minh silently sympathized. It would come gradually, but eventually Luu Dong Trung would understand.

Unlike Le Minh, Ryujin was leaving because she wanted to go to Tien Thuc Falls and find this Liet Than. She was curious to know which one of their hypotheses about his name was correct: was he genuinely paralyzed? Was his technique simply misunderstood? Or was he so powerful he didn't even need to blink to destroy his enemies?

"I want to go too," Dong Tu admitted. She turned to Luu Dong Trung. "Do you want to go home with Xuan Thu and Bao Thuong? Stargazer told you to be careful of Liet Than, right? It might not be safe for you to come with us."

Luu Dong Trung frowned in frustration and stormed out.

Dong Tu followed him, and caught him by the lakeshore; Luu Dong Trung had run slowly enough for Dong Tu to keep him in sight, but fast enough that she wouldn't be able to physically stop him until he was sure Obsidian hadn't chased them. Then he stopped, turned, and looked at Dong

Tu with a sulking pout, his gaze stung and earnest. He didn't look like himself, either: he looked like Tuyet Hoa Phi Vu, with his eyeliner and his soft-pink lips. His dangling earrings framed a face that looked so much younger and more innocent. Beautiful, but not the Luu Dong Trung they'd all gotten used to.

He didn't wait for Dong Tu to ask him a question. All the bitterness in his heart came pouring out unprompted.

"I have been by your side for *months!* But the moment you saw Obsidian, you abandoned me and ran off with him. Was everything I did for you worth *nothing?*"

Dong Tu blinked in confusion. What was she supposed to say? Obsidian had always had her heart, long before Luu Dong Trung had ever entered her life. Where had this jealousy come from?! She knew Dong Trung had been acting bizarrely for a while, but this was different. What was going on?

"Dong—Dong Trung, you've always been worthwhile," she stammered, not sure how to comfort him.

Luu Dong Trung continued to sulk, shuffling his feet, too agitated to keep still. He didn't want to be her little brother, her little shadow, forever. He'd shown her affection in every way he knew how for so long, and yet he'd been nothing but a joke to her. Obsidian's reappearance had finally made the possibility of losing Dong Tu blatantly obvious in ways it hadn't been before.

"Dong Tu, have I only ever been a joke to you?" he asked, his sharp eyes glistening with tears. His eyeliner made the color of his clear eyes even deeper.

"I've never considered you a joke," Dong Tu denied, but there was some hesitation: she'd thought he was joking *with* her.

"Do you love me?" Luu Dong Trung continued.

"Of course I love you! We're family! If you don't love your family, who else are you supposed to love?"

"Then do you love me, or Obsidian?" he pressed.

"It's different kinds of love!" Dong Tu insisted. It was the first time she'd ever admitted to loving Obsidian out loud, and if he'd known, it would have broken Obsidian's heart to know that her first admission was spoken to Luu Dong Trung and not him.

Luu Dong Trung's expression shifted again. His lovely eyes went from insistent and dramatic to absolutely frigid once more, and he frowned seriously, his voice deepening to match. Gone was the soft, sweet man he usually was with Dong Tu, replaced with an air that was suddenly, frighteningly predatory.

"Dong Tu, I don't want you to love me like a child! I don't want you to see me as just your little brother! What do I have to do to make you love me like you love Obsidian? Do I need to be one of the Monstrous Eighteen, like him?"

Dong Tu took a nervous step back. She'd never seen a change like that come over Luu Dong Trung. The last time he'd changed so dramatically he'd revealed himself to be a man, and not a woman like she'd thought. How many more layers to him were there?

"I don't love Obsidian because he's one of the Monstrous Eighteen, with all kinds of martial arts knowledge!" Dong Tu denied, shaking her head. She was aware that Luu Dong Trung sometimes seemed to have low self-esteem, but his suggestion gave her the impression that Dong Trung thought he was Obsidian's match in every other way save his infamy and fighting prowess. In truth, Dong Tu secretly wished that Obsidian and Luu Dong Trung could swap places. If Obsidian had no martial abilities like Dong Trung, their relationship could have been perfect—for a long, long time.

"Is it because I'm not strong and masculine like he is?" Luu Dong Trung kept on, his usual gentle and elegant manner continuing to waver.

Dong Tu shook her head. Of course that wasn't true. All of the comparisons Luu Dong Trung made between himself and Obsidian were far too shallow, and the pair were far too different in every way to even accurately compare them. The two of them were like...heaven and earth. Dong Tu's love for Obsidian was like a flash of lightning in the heavens, overwhelming, struck from the very first moment. For

Luu Dong Trung, it was like rain soaking into the ground, sinking deeper and deeper, layer after layer.

After three years, everything Dong Tu felt for Obsidian was still as intense, still as passionate. He still made her legs shake. He still made her heart pound.

Luu Dong Trung was like an extension of herself. Always beside her, comforting and steady.

Luu Dong Trung wasn't strong and hard like Obsidian. His qualities were different. During the months they'd spent together, little moments had permanently etched themselves onto he and Dong Tu's hearts and memories. Despite being such an elegant, scholarly type, when rain came and the wind tore at their clothes, he used his arms and body to shield Dong Tu, trying to keep her dry while he was soaked to the bone. Once, when Dong Tu had hurt her leg, he'd carried her—even when he was breathless and drenched in sweat. Even when they had a long way left to go. When she was sad, he made her laugh. When she was happy, he insisted she give him affection and love in return. Anyone watching from the outside would have assumed they were madly in love.

Obsidian had sacrificed his life for Dong Tu's, but he'd made it clear he'd rather let her burn in despair and love her from a distance. Luu Dong Trung was always there. Always close by. He was gentle in moderation, and sometimes sacrificed everything he had, everything he could. He always demanded her attention, but, sad or happy, she could always count on him.

No. They were too different to compare, and nothing could ever explain the logic of the heart. One love was tumultuous and shook her right to the core, imprinting itself on her heart, bringing her to the highest highs and the lowest lows. The other was as calm as the lake beside them, eternally serene. Luu Dong Trung wasn't inferior to Obsidian in any way, and she did want the kind of steady love he offered her... just not with him. She didn't have the words to explain why, either, when she didn't understand it herself.

But Luu Dong Trung couldn't see Dong Tu's thoughts. He didn't understand her feelings. All he saw was this rivalry, and that his rival was one of the Monstrous Eighteen; and his misunderstanding led him to the belief that Dong Tu saw his gentleness as his shortcoming, that he couldn't be loved if he wasn't as powerful and impressive as Obsidian. His face flushed with anger, and his eyes took on a murderous gleam.

"This whole time, you've really only considered me your little brother? Is that even possible? We're two grown people, a man and a woman nearly twenty years old. Can we truly think of each other as just siblings?"

If Dong Tu didn't like the sweet, gentle man he was, then Luu Dong Trung would give her the opposite. For so long he'd quietly kept up his place as a lovely little brother in order to get close to her. He'd done everything he could, and the hard work he'd put into making her fall for him had only succeeded in establishing himself as a sibling, killing any idea of romantic love. He'd been restrained, caging his true nature like a wild beast.

Luu Dong Trung caught hold of Dong Tu's shoulder and leaned in close, studying her face from mere inches away. A light breeze caught his hair and drew it across her cheeks. Dong Tu didn't try to warn him off in case he only wanted to hug her or kiss her casually, like he had before. He was poetic and gentle, but he was unpredictable, too.

Dong Trung's eyes fell to Dong Tu's full lips, and his fierce gaze relaxed as he realized what she must have been thinking.

"I've kissed you so many times...and you never felt anything?" he asked softly, doubt still lacing his tone. He was beginning to wonder if perhaps the shadow Obsidian cast was so long, Luu Dong Trung's love genuinely had not registered the way he'd thought it had. Perhaps she really did only see him as her younger brother.

Dong Trung cupped Dong Tu's face in one hand, and let the fingertips of his other hand trail over her skin. He traced the shape of her lips with tender care, letting his touch ease down her chin and neck, much like Obsidian had the night before. The difference was that while Obsidian's familiar touch made her heart and stomach flutter...Luu Dong Trung's made her thorny and stiff with discomfort.

"Dong Tu?" he pressed, his eyes filling with disappointment. He hadn't expected her to just stand there in silence. He let his hand tighten around her neck, and Dong Tu braced for the possibility of his forcibly trying to kiss her. If he did, she wasn't sure she would hold back, and that would end with him seriously injured. And he *wanted* to kiss her.

Instead he curled forward and dropped his head onto her shoulder, moving his hand back up to touch her chin.

"Dong Tu, I don't want to be your brother!" he cried, rubbing his face against her shoulder. "Tell me, what should I do?"

Tuyet Hoa Phi Vu didn't want to be her friend, and Luu Dong Trung didn't want to be her brother. He hadn't held her hands back then because he'd wanted to be sisters. He hadn't bought brooches, combs, and silks for she and her family because he wanted to be adopted.

"I put the brooch in your hair because I wanted you to be beautiful while you're with me. I bought you clothes because I wanted you to enjoy fine things. I didn't feed you, offer you tea, massage your sore muscles, brush your hair... just because I thought it was my duty as a brother. It wasn't a joke when I kissed you in the lake. Did you really not get it?"

She *hadn't* gotten it, and for the very first time Dong Tu finally saw what she'd been missing. And she could see how, in his mind, she'd been so careless and heartless. She thought of Luu Dong Trung the same way she thought of Bao Thuong, and had never noticed how long Dong Trung had been drowning in the suffocating depths of unrequited love. Dong Tu reached out to stroke his hair and pressed their cheeks together, her heart filling with regret.

"I'm so sorry...I was so thoughtless!"

Luu Dong Trung lifted his face from her shoulder. His eyes were overbright with tears, and teardrops clung to his lashes like morning dew. He leaned in, slowly closing the distance between them, his eyes once again on her lips...and this time, Dong Tu couldn't bring herself to punch him.

A gloved hand grabbed his shoulder, and Luu Dong Trung shot a furious glower at the person who'd just interrupted their kiss.

Dressed in black, with a spider tattooed under his left eye—the gloved hand belonged to Tuong Y Ve.

Tuong Y Ve didn't care about keeping Luu Dong Trung and Dong Tu from kissing. All he wanted was the girl. After his fight with Obsidian, he'd realized there was no way he'd beat the King of Poison in a fair fight. But he *could* win with tricks, and his fight with Obsidian had confirmed Tuong Y Ve's most important suspicion: Obsidian's weakness didn't lie in his physical body. His weakness was the woman who'd wandered carelessly away from him without a word. And while Tuong Y Ve had no interest in Luu Dong Trung, it seemed fate had handed him both people on a silver platter.

But Tuong Y Ve wasn't the only one present on the lake's shores. As Tuong Y Ve stole Dong Tu and Luu Dong Trung away, another man stood and watched from afar. With bangs that split in the middle and a mole under his eye, the man wore white clothes and leather pants. Leather straps crossed his body, with a leather cape draped around his shoulders, and his hands were wrapped in thin leather straps as well. The figure was recognizable despite the distance, and if anyone had spotted him, they wouldn't have needed to see his face to imagine the mischievous smirk that was sure to be dancing across his lips.

Ly Minh Lam, the seeming guardian of Tien Thuc Falls, stood watching as Dong Tu and Dong Trung were dragged off; someone they hadn't seen in more than half a year.

As Dong Tu and Luu Dong Trung were being kidnapped, Ryujin was well on her way to Tien Thuc Falls. The journey to find Liet Than hadn't been difficult so far, and the closer she drew, the more rumors she was able to needle out of the locals.

"They say Liet Than is from the Thanh Liet district," one person had told her.

"He's young, not an old, weak man."

"No, no...he was a mutant. A few days ago there was a woodcutter who caught a glimpse of the thing and heard screams. He ran away for dear life, and he was frightened so badly he was sick for days."

Ryujin was glad that at least she'd found a source who'd actually heard and seen evidence of Liet Than with their own ears and eyes. She found the old woodcutter, got what information she could, and ignored the trembling old man's warnings to stop looking for Liet Than. Per his reluctant instructions, she followed the cliffs along the top of the falls in the direction Liet Than was said to haunt.

Tien Thuc Falls was part of the oldest sources of water in its district. It began at the very top of the mountain, cascaded down through Tien Thuc falls, and finally fed into Thanh Liet Lake itself. While the lake was quiet, the falls thundered angrily down the mountain, kicking up thick mist and forming a roiling, riotous pool at the waterfall's base. The area Ryujin crossed into was deserted, and had been since the rumors of Liet Than had begun to circulate through the area, scaring off hopefuls and locals until it was completely empty. While strolling through and enjoying the beautiful landscape around her, Ryujin stumbled upon a series of wild, beautiful rock caves. Water rushed through the rocks, and the sounds of the waterfall echoed all around her.

A groan cut through the rumbling sound of the falls, and Ryujin followed the sound curiously. Before her was a tall, deep, dimly-lit cave, and as she crept through, she found caves within the cave. Even in the dark, surrounded by rocks, with the encompassing sound of the falls making it easier for someone to sneak up on her, Ryujin wasn't afraid: water flowed around her in every direction. What did Thuy Long Than, the Water Goddess, have to fear?

In the dim light she spotted a man lying in a pile of rubble and fabric, as if stuffed into a rock. He looked like a sand bag in an old cloth, and as she drew closer she realized his whole body was completely stuck beneath a huge rock, with only the ends of his hair showing. It was from the owner of the hair that another wordless moan oozed. Ryujin was sure the moment she saw the weird spectacle that no normal human would voluntarily end up trapped like that, only to lay there, moaning. Was the stranger Liet Than? Had he gotten a taste for piling himself in rocks and crying?

Ryujin also wondered if it was the malformed man, the paralyzed master with no arms and legs they'd all heard about.

She levitated the rock enough to liberate the poor man. He was still wrapped up like a package, but managed to roll out from under the rock...and that was all. He didn't have the energy to stand up and run. Instead he curled up on his side and let out yet another groan. Ryujin came around to his side, frowning interestedly, and touched the man's shoulder.

He didn't react.

After checking his acupressure points, she realized that his chi had been blocked, his powers sealed away. Ryujin unblocked his chi and the man groaned yet again, his shaking hands reaching out into the air before him.

"Mmm..." The man made a sound, but it stuck in his throat, and the darkness made it impossible for Ryujin to see his face, let alone read his lips. He stretched and, like a starving leper reaching for the first food he'd had in days, his hands hit Ryujin's face and caressed it in apparent appreciation. The malformed man lifted his head and Ryujin gasped: he had no eyes, no nose, no *mouth*. The hands on her face began to smoke, and with a rustling, almost hissing sound, the sides of her face felt like they were beginning to melt. The man tugged hard, and his intentions were clear.

He wanted Ryujin's face.

That wasn't just any random person Ryujin had freed, it was *Switch*. Ryujin sent a barrage of water at Switch and batted Switch's hands off her face, then pulled water from the waterfall into the shape of a water dragon. She rolled Switch out of the cave and out into the waterfall itself; Switch bobbed in the water for a while, and then disappeared beneath the surface.

Switch had been stuck in that cave for months, incapable of escape. And once she was given her freedom, her first order of business had been to get herself a new face—but she hadn't known she'd made the mistake of trying to steal *the* Water Goddess' face. Ryujin watched angrily as the dark shape of Switch disappeared, and then began to gently clean her face.

Both sides of her face were marked with finger-shaped burns. She spat and cursed quietly to herself.

"Guess who, the damned Switch."

Her fury finally calmed, and Ryujin sat and pondered, still pouting. Normally Switch loved to spend her time outside. She'd never heard of the other woman hiding herself away, let alone burying herself in *rocks*. There was no way Switch had done it to herself. So the question became...who had the power to turn Switch into a useless lump like that?

And if the terror of Tien Thuc Falls was Switch, where was Liet Than? And what kind of person was he?

CHAPTER 14

A Single Move

On the other side of Thanh Liet Lake, some distance away from Tien Thuc Falls, the earth broke up into a craggy, winding gorge. Its rocky cliffs split the landscape all the way to the gorge's end: an unfathomably deep, yawning chasm, the bottom of which was obscured by clouds. Tuong Y Ve had decided to set his trap there, using Dong Tu and Luu Dong Trung as bait so that in the end, he could drive Obsidian over the cliffs for good. He hung the pair over the edge of the cliff using only a thin rope and waited for Obsidian to arrive.

It was only when Dong Tu and Luu Dong Trung had been gone long enough to worry him that Obsidian went out looking for the pair. What he found instead was an arrow jammed into the trunk of a tree at eye level, with a note attached to it—and when Obsidian read the challenge, complete with time and date, his face twisted with fury. His staff was in his hand and had already formed into his icy sword before he even threw the letter down.

His hunt was short, and the moment he laid eyes on Tuong Y Ve, he attacked without a word. Tuong Y Ve blocked the swing, the two weapons clashing loudly—

And yet the sound of the frayed rope snapping beneath the weight of Dong Tu and Luu Dong Trung was *resounding*. Ice shot down Obsidian's spine as the short stretch of rope he could see went lax, and Dong Tu and Luu Dong Trung went plummeting down the side of the cliff. Dong Tu desperately grabbed for any rocky protrusion she could get her fingers around with one hand while reaching for Dong Trung with the other, terror tearing the breath from her lungs. She managed to catch a ledge and cling to it, and let out a pained cry as Dong Trung's weight nearly tore her away from the ledge as she stopped his fall, too.

"You're too heavy!" Dong Tu shouted, holding tight to Dong Trung and the ledge for dear life: Luu Dong Trung may have been slender, but he was tall, and height always came with more weight than people anticipated. It was something Dong Tu now suddenly, intimately understood. "Can you see anything to grab?"

Luu Dong Trung flailed as he dangled, looking around with just as much desperation. It made it far harder for Dong Tu to hold on, but she refused to let go of his hand.

"Don't worry," she called to him. "Don't be afraid, I'm here, I've got you!" She didn't know if she could actually hold on long enough for help to arrive or not, but she tried to reassure him nonetheless. Luu Dong Trung looked up at Dong Tu gratefully, still swinging and kicking.

"Dong Tu, you don't have to do this! It's okay! Let me fall!" Dong Trung denied, his voice tight with strain.

"Don't be ridiculous!" she refused. There was no way she was going to let him fall to his death, and they both knew it—but despite her determination, it didn't take long for her hands to start shaking beneath the effort of keeping them both up. The rock she clung to had cut her hand and fingers, and was still digging into her flesh; blood was beginning to stream in vivid red trails down her arm. Everything was going exactly the way Tuong Y Ve had hoped: Obsidian couldn't bear to let Dong Tu fall to her death, and was forced to split his attention between the two threats.

He jumped and floated down to Dong Tu as Tuong Y Ve used the opportunity to launch several attacks at him. Obsidian used one hand to create a shield of snow to block the attacks, and with the other he began to pull Dong Tu and Luu Dong Trung back up to safety. Dong Tu managed to clamber up onto the flat ground at the top of the cliffs; but with her hands numb from the effort to hang on, she didn't feel it when Luu Dong Trung's hand slipped out of her own. He began to plummet once more—

And came to another sudden stop as Obsidian leaned back over the edge and caught his hand.

Their eyes met, and Luu Dong Trung's surprise and curiosity were plain on his face. There, in the middle of a battle to the death, Obsidian had risked himself and taken the time and effort to save his other rival from dying, too.

Which meant he was preoccupied with helping Dong Tu and Luu Dong Trung get to safety when Tuong Y Ve launched another attack that hit Obsidian directly: it pushed him back several steps, but Obsidian didn't waver. Instead he used his chi to expand his snowy shield to cover all three of them, and knelt over them both to protect them with his body, too.

Obsidian, Dong Tu, and Luu Dong Trung might no longer have been dangling from the cliff's face, but as long as they stood at the top, the three of them were still in danger—and Tuong Y Ve was still positioned just behind them, primed to send them flying to their deaths once more.

Tuong Y Ve gathered his chi and began to attack Obsidian continuously. His own power clashed with an odd, clattering sound against Obsidian's snow barrier, and he aimed his hits in such a way that Dong Tu and Luu Dong Trung's very presence would hinder Obsidian. Black snow howled around all four of them.

Obsidian's strengths were well known. He was a master of poisons, lethal with swords, and commanded powerful magic with the help of the Storm Pearl. But the black snow that always followed him was useless. It was true that the snow was only formed when the energy of the Storm Pearl radiated out of him, and that the snow was black because it mixed with the poison suffusing his body; but it was nowhere near enough to give someone normal like Dong Tu even a mild headache.

The only thing the snow could be used for was denoting his physical and mental states, and that was only if you knew what to look for.

When healthy and happy, Obsidian's own chi had the ability to overtake the Pearl's icy aura and lessen the snow that fell around him. But when he was upset, tired, or injured, he receded into himself, and the Pearl's aura was able to run amok without interference. The stronger the Pearl's aura, the more snow came whirling down around him. And the longer he fought Tuong Y Ve while trying to keep Dong Tu and Luu Dong Trung protected, the more exhausted he became—and the faster the black snow fell. Dong Tu and Tuong Y Ve could both tell how hard Obsidian was having to fight just by the way the air thickened with those dark flakes.

It excited Tuong Y Ve, but he knew there was still a big difference between making Obsidian struggle, and finally defeating him.

Right when the battle reached its harshest fervor, someone new appeared.

He'd been standing unnoticed for a while, helping neither side, hidden by the opaque snow that choked the air. It had gotten so bad that he could no longer see the fight taking place, which finally forced his hand: he cleared his throat for attention and stepped forward. Concentrating his chi, the man shot a blast of wind through the air that blew a path right through the center of the falling snow, and allowed him to walk dramatically into the ring.

As expected, everyone went still, and looked up to see just who had the power to tear clean through the snow like he had.

Relief flooded through Dong Tu, and Luu Dong Trung smiled to himself. Tall, young, wrapped in leather and smirking beneath his bangs, it could only be one person.

"Ly Minh Lam!" Dong Tu shouted excitedly. The last time she'd seen him, he'd saved she and Luu Dong Trung from drowning in Tien Thuc Falls, and had beaten Switch in a fight with ease. He'd offered them a safe place to sleep, fed them, and had been kind and cheerful, even if he was also a shameless flirt. Dong Tu knew him to be a powerful master, able to create winds that could break stones into dust, and if her suspicions were correct? He wasn't just Ly Minh Lam, he was Liet Than!

"If Liet Than—Ly Minh Lam—is helping Obsidian, we're going to be okay!" Dong Tu continued.

Meanwhile, Tuong Y Ve was still frozen. He didn't know this new stranger, why he was there, or how dangerous he was. What he did know was that he wanted to capitalize on Obsidian's draining energy and destroy him, so he ignored the stranger and went right back to attacking Obsidian, Dong Tu, and Luu Dong Trung.

"Ly Minh Lam, please save us!" Dong Tu begged over the noise, and Ly Minh Lam immediately began to gather wind, twisting it into a ball in his hands and filling it with bright energy. Dong Tu had only ever seen the small balls of energy that Ly Minh Lam created for fun. Now that he was fighting in earnest, the ball of energy grew bigger and bigger, and the rumbling winds that charged like a train between his hands seemed to suck everything in like a tornado. Dust, sand, and snow filled the sphere as the ball enveloped his body like a forcefield. With a boom like cannon fire, the ball shot straight toward its target, almost too quickly to see.

But the target wasn't Tuong Y Ve.

The target was Obsidian.

The ball and Obsidian's barrier shattered into each other, tearing the snow barrier in half and sending wind rippling out in all directions like a shockwave. Almost like a shard of pure air, the direct force of the attack pierced straight through Obsidian.

He hadn't thought to defend himself when Dong Tu had called the stranger's name with such hope.

Blood filled Obsidian's mask and began to drip out from beneath it. He caught the dripping blood as quickly as he could so that it didn't hit Dong Tu's skin, and turned his gaze on Ly Minh Lam, his eyes burning with murderous rage. Ly Minh Lam was stronger than Tuong Y Ve, and with those two banding together against him, the situation had just gone from bad to worse.

Obsidian threw up a second barrier just in time to block another series of barrages from Tuong Y Ve. Tuong Y Ve wasn't sure who'd just come to his aid, but the enemy of his enemy was very much his friend, and he relaxed as things began to look up.

Ly Minh Lam smirked and began to form another ball of energy, even as Dong Tu sat paralyzed with shock. Ly Minh Lam's attack had cut through that barrier and yet still managed to hurt Obsidian alone, not she and Luu Dong Trung. But why? Wasn't he a friend?!

Did he have some kind of unknown hatred toward Obsidian?

With the knowledge that he'd fallen straight into Tuong Y Ve's trap, and the sudden appearance of some unknown master of indeterminate power, Obsidian knew he couldn't afford to be distracted any longer.

The next time the ball of wind and power came bearing down on Obsidian, he didn't try to dodge. He waited with all the poised restraint of a serpent waiting to strike, and when the ball came close enough he turned his sword and pierced it. It disappeared, but so did Obsidian's giant, snowy wall. Neither Tuong Y Ve nor Ly Minh Lam wasted a second: Tuong Y Ve rained attacks down on Obsidian and other two, while Ly Minh Lam came at them from the front—but their attacks converged and neutralized each other, bursting harmlessly out in all directions, leaving enough time for Obsidian to put his protections back in place.

Obsidian silently lamented the fact that he was still on his knees, still using his body to cover Dong Tu and Luu Dong Trung, his arms spread out wide to hold the barrier in place. He couldn't attack like that, not well, and not when trying to protect an area large enough to shield them from Tuong Y Ve's attacks from the sky, not just the assault from the ground. They were still pinned down on the edge of the cliff, and if he fell, Obsidian was confident that he would most likely survive. But if all three of them fell...there was no way he'd be able to survive while trying to save the others, too.

And Obsidian was doing all of this while injured, likely far more seriously than he wanted to acknowledge. Blood still filled his mask from his nose, pouring down his chin and neck, and he was still trying to angle himself so that he didn't poison Dong Tu all over again. He was stretched too thin, and he needed to find an opening to get them out of that mess. With only Tuong Y Ve, it would have been easy; Obsidian had beaten him once already. But he had no idea what sorts of other tricks Ly Minh Lam had hidden up his sleeve, and to make matters worse, he could see Ly Minh Lam stalking back and forth, silently observing and visibly plotting something that was sure to be unpleasant.

If Ly Minh Lam really was Liet Than, they were in even *worse* shape.

A person could only ascend to the ranks of the Monstrous Eighteen one of two ways. Either they had to be someone of bizarre and exceptional talent, like Switch and her face-stealing or Stargazer and her divination, or they had to be such an incredible fighter, with such overwhelmingly powerful chi, that they earned the awe and respect being a member commanded...and Liet Than's reputation was tied to his remarkable power.

Knowing what he did about Liet Than and the mysterious man's reputation—how he destroyed his enemies without so much as lifting a finger—Obsidian's eyes were fixed unblinkingly not on Tuong Y Ve and his assault from above, but on Ly Minh Lam's every step.

Below him, Dong Tu kept herself curled over Luu Dong Trung, protecting him as much as Obsidian tried to protect them both. She didn't know how long Obsidian would be able to hold his ground against the other two, and she knew it was imperative that she find a way to escape and unburden him so that he could put all of his attention and energy toward fighting, not protecting them. Dong Tu had no idea how to achieve it, but she did wonder if, while Liet Than was so focused on Obsidian, she and Luu Dong Trung could sneak away and try to make their exit.

"Dong Trung, listen to me," Dong Tu murmured softly, her eyes still glued on Ly Minh Lam and Tuong Y Ve. "For some reason, Ly Minh Lam isn't trying to attack you and me. On the count of three, take my hand, and we'll run. Okay?"

Luu Dong Trung looked up at Dong Tu in silence, his face twisted into a wary frown.

"It's okay. I'll protect you," Dong Tu reassured him, thinking he was too scared to go.

A bright, sharp beam of power pierced straight through Obsidian's black, snowy wall. It shot through the space between Dong Tu and Luu Dong Trung's cheeks, cutting Luu Dong Trung; he clapped his hands to his cheeks as the slice began to bleed, his eyes lit up with surprise, and he let out a scream of pain.

The barrier had been torn.

Obsidian's hands trembled, black snow darkening the air far more completely than it had been before, and Dong Tu realized his strength was finally beginning to fade. Luu Dong Trung frowned seriously and tried to sit up. Thinking he was going to bolt in terror, Dong Tu tried to pull him back down, but instead he slid an arm around her waist and held her tight to his body. He sat up completely and placed his free hand in the center of Obsidian's chest.

Obsidian looked down in surprise and stared at Luu Dong Trung's hand in confusion; but when he looked back up at the other man, he saw the same icy, murderous glint Dong Trung had regarded him with days before. He realized in that moment that Luu Dong Trung was not the harmless weakling he'd assumed—but it was too late.

A blade-like beam of silver light shot out of Luu Dong Trung's hand, cut straight through Obsidian's chest, and powered blindingly through the black barrier behind him. Ly Minh Lam's attacks, which hit like a battering ram, had nothing on the amount of power that charged through Obsidian's body. It was like nothing Obsidian had ever experienced, so outrageous that he wouldn't have believed it if it wasn't tearing through him in that second.

Obsidian let out a muffled grunt. He felt like he was being torn apart from the inside out, down to the tiniest molecule, and cold dread washed over him: he knew in that moment he was going to die. The strike blasted him into the air like he was as insignificant as one of his own snowflakes, and his protective barrier crumbled away into a blinding black blizzard.

Still holding Dong Tu tight, Luu Dong Trung levitated them both up into the air after Obsidian. He formed a protective wall of chi around them as rubble and debris went flying, and Dong Tu watched, frozen in astonishment, as the scene unfolded below them in slow motion. None of it felt real. She was right there, staring...but none of it could *be* real. Dong Tu tried to rub her eyes, but when she opened them nothing had changed; she reached out to touch the wall of energy Luu Dong Trung had used to shield her, and yelped quietly when it sent an electric jolt through her body. She wasn't dreaming.

But that wasn't even the most astounding part.

The most astounding part was the fact that the energy that pierced through Obsidian from Luu Dong Trung's hand was something she knew extremely well. For three years, she'd researched it. For three years she'd taught it to dozens of female students at her family's dojo, every day, every morning. And for more than half of the last year, day after day, her sweet little brother had taught right alongside her.

With those familiar slow, graceful, dance-like movements, Luu Dong Trung had taken the seemingly useless Sunlight Strike and, like a carp becoming a dragon, transformed it into an attack so potent it had taken Obsidian down in a single strike, slamming into him with a force thousands of times more powerful than anything Dong Tu could imagine.

"Ph-Phong—?" Dong Tu stammered, her voice tiny in the face of it all. She still didn't fully grasp what was happening—and neither did Obsidian. Concentrating so hard on Tuong Y Ve and Ly Minh Lam, Obsidian hadn't given any thought to Luu Dong Trung. It was next to impossible for anyone to take down the King of Poison with just one strike, and yet Dong Tu's weak little brother had somehow managed it in half a second.

Obsidian's mask cracked and shattered. Fragments fell from the air in a glittering silver rain, revealing Obsidian's stunned face; blood poured from his mouth, nose, and even his eyes. Everything around Dong Tu slowed almost to a stop. Each blink lasted long seconds, and she watched as the blood rolling down Obsidian's face seemed to lift into the air as he continued to fall in slow-motion.

The shock and the sensation of falling were strange to Obsidian, but they were nothing compared to the feeling of the Sunlight Strike itself. It was like someone had reached into his chest, grabbed ahold of his heart, and was trying to pull it straight out. As Obsidian gasped for air, his entire body shaking, light began to stream out of his bloodied mouth. Every artery, vessel, and vein in Obsidian's body followed suit, and as they lit up, the excruciating pain—pain that felt like his body was being torn to pieces—expanded like his blood vessels were all being torn out alongside his heart. The pain was so intense he couldn't even force himself to scream. His face twisting in agony, and finally even his eyes glowed that same burning silver, the light pouring out of his mouth widening into a steady beam.

Just as suddenly, the light coalesced into a glowing silvery bead, hovering in the air outside of his body. Obsidian understood as soon as he saw the glowing bead, and his eyes found Dong Tu's with the earnestness of a man bidding a desperate farewell. The light filling Obsidian's body went out—

And so did the light in his eyes.

Obsidian's eyes went dull and blank as the life left them, snuffed out like a candle in the wind.

The rest of time seemed to stop. An odd ringing filled Dong Tu's ears, blocking out any other sound. Black snow danced on the air in odd patterns like a wounded eagle trying to flap its wings, while she watched, stunned, as Obsidian's body went limp. He plunged into the abyss, disappearing in the clouds that blocked the endless depths from view...and all that was left behind was the silver bead, still suspended in the air above the gorge. The black snow around them exploded outward with a deafening thunderclap and then vanished without a trace, and the ringing faded from Dong Tu's ears as she reached for Obsidian's falling body, screaming his name in despair—far too late.

Phong....

Phong....

PHONG!

Luu Dong Trung kept his arm around Dong Tu's waist and flew them both over to the silvery bead that Obsidian had left behind. Once Dong Tu stopped screaming and struggling, she saw that it wasn't silver at all, but a gleaming black pearl. It hung suspended by its own energy, constantly spinning, putting out the same silver light that used to glow faintly behind the silver in Obsidian's eyes.

"The Storm Pearl!"

Multiple voices spoke at the same time, in the same thunderstruck tone.

Tuong Y Ve gasped.

"The Storm Pearl of the King of Poison!" He looked over at the long-haired young man still holding Dong Tu, floating above the ground, and couldn't believe his eyes. Wasn't that the same man he'd kidnapped just days before? The same weak, chi-less young man that he'd bullied on the banks of Thanh Liet Lake? Had the girl's bratty little brother, Luu Dong Trung, really just stolen the legendary Storm Pearl from their northern King of Poison in a single strike?!

But it was the truth. No one standing on those cliffs could deny it.

Luu Dong Trung—Tuyet Hoa Phi Vu—had just used his chi to tear the Storm Pearl clean out of Obsidian's body.

CHAPTER 15

Diabolical

Tuong Y Ve prepared to leap up and take the Pearl for himself, but was knocked back by a strike from Ly Minh Lam. Ly Minh Lam flew up to Luu Dong Trung and eased Dong Tu into his own arms, so that Luu Dong Trung was free to finish his mission. The pair had been friends since childhood, long before meeting at the caves around Tien Thuc Falls, and Ly Minh Lam wasn't at all surprised by Luu Dong Trung's impressive show of might.

An unseen wind blew through Luu Dong Trung's hair, and his eyes glowed with triumph as he studied the Storm Pearl.

"Dong Trung, how could you?" Dong Tu choked out. She still couldn't believe what she was seeing.

Luu Dong Trung reached cautiously yet calmly out to take the Storm Pearl, and the bead glowed silver in his hand. Both Ly Minh Lam and Luu Dong Trung stared fixedly at the Pearl, and its silver light reflected brightly in their eyes.

Ly Minh Lam, however, didn't try to take the Pearl from Luu Dong Trung, and instead turned his eyes on the other man with just as much fixed intent.

"The Storm Pearl will absorb all of your chi! Luu Dong Trung, don't!" Dong Tu shouted. She'd heard the stories of all the people who had died trying to swallow the Pearl before it had come to Obsidian, and she couldn't understand why Luu Dong Trung would want to steal the Storm Pearl at all, let alone risk his life for it: all it had ever brought was misery. Luu Dong Trung smirked, met Dong Tu's stunned gaze, and put the Storm Pearl in his mouth.

Luu Dong Trung seemed to transform before her eyes. The gentle man she'd considered her little brother melted away as his long hair continued to blow in the wind, and it was Tuyet Hoa Phi Vu that spread his arms open wide, as if absorbing the power put off by the Storm Pearl. His eyes closed—and then snapped back open, his glittering earrings shaking. He swallowed the Pearl down, and as it worked its way down his throat, his eyes turned the same unnatural silver that Obsidian's had been. The veins around his eyes turned that same liquid silver, and he let out an exultant cry.

His cry turned into a deafening shout of pain almost instantly as the Storm Pearl's dark, icy energy began to flood his body. The silver could be seen spreading through his veins on one bare shoulder, leaving his whole body striped like hundreds of gleaming snakes were ripping through him.

Luu Dong Trung screamed and writhed in pain, tearing his shirt open to watch the way the manifestation of that silvery power streaked his chest as well; he scratched and tore at his chest in agony until it was a mess of bloody claw marks, and the silver even worked its way through his hair, leaving strands upon strands of platinum interwoven with the rest. Cold smoke poured from his mouth, and white snow began to whirl around him in a vortex.

Ly Minh Lam and Dong Tu watched anxiously as the snowy vortex blocked Luu Dong Trung from view, and Tuyet Hoa Phi Vu's screaming continued to shatter the air above the rush of the wind. He'd used the Sunlight Strike to defeat Obsidian and steal the Storm Pearl, and that was enough to prove just how strong his chi really was—but the Storm Pearl's energy was powerful too, and extremely selective of who it chose to bond with. If it didn't like Tuyet Hoa Phi Vu, his own strength would be useless.

Obsidian had been able to control the Storm Pearl because when he was born, he had absorbed enormous amounts of sacred energy from what was called the Solar Radiance technique; Tuyet Hoa Phi Vu, on the other hand, carried a genuine fragment of the Sunlight Pearl itself. The Storm Pearl and the Sunlight Pearl were like yin and yang, two sides of a single, balanced coin, and the fighting styles derived from their power had also evolved into the same equal yet opposite mirrors of each other. So while the Storm

Pearl could still destroy Tuyet Hoa Phi Vu...aside from Obsidian, who *else* would be able to bond with it?

And was it simply a coincidence that the Storm Pearl's name—*phong vu,* which meant storm—was reflected in the names of the only two men who could hope to wield it?

From the center of the vortex, Tuyet Hoa Phi Vu's cries of pain turned into victorious laughter once more. The pillar of snow burst in all directions, finally exposing him, and they could see white snowflakes radiating out from his own body.

Tuong Y Ve sent an attack flying up at Luu Dong Trung from below, and Dong Trung narrowed his eyes and whipped his gaze down to Tuong Y Ve. Where his gaze went, so too did the snowflakes, and they pelted toward Tuong Y Ve like thousands of sharp, miniscule darts. Tuong Y Ve attempted to shield himself with his own chi, but the snowflakes broke through the barrier with ease and cut him to ribbons.

Tuong Y Ve stumbled back a few steps, looked back up at Luu Dong Trung, and bolted: this was no longer his fight.

Still holding Dong Tu safely in his arms, Ly Minh Lam finally brought them both back down to the ground. Luu Dong Trung remained in the air, testing the new abilities the Storm Pearl had given him; snowflakes danced and floated in the air all around him, giving new life to the meaning of his old name: *dancing snowflakes.*

Obsidian's black snow had been of no real use. But for Luu Dong Trung, for Tuyet Hoa Phi Vu, they became an endless wave of impossibly sharp, tiny blades; lethal flying darts he could control with nothing more than a glance, that could cut through anything they touched. Obsidian had used his own chi to calm the snow; meanwhile Tuyet Hoa Phi Vu was like a fish in water, swimming freely in its own habitat. He'd not only stolen the Storm Pearl, it had accepted him, and had given his already considerable powers a serious upgrade.

Dong Tu could barely speak, but still, she tried.

"Luu Dong Trung—how do you have chi? Ly Minh Lam, why—Dong Trung, why did you work with Liet Than to kill Obsidian?!"

Ly Minh Lam awarded Dong Tu an understanding, sympathetic look, and then called out to Luu Dong Trung as he continued to float and play in the air above them.

"Tuyet Hoa Phi Vu, guess who Dong Tu just called Liet Than! You should put more effort into your Public Relations, get your name out there. No one seems to know who Liet Than is!"

Only then did Luu Dong Trung finally come back down to earth—literally. He fixed his long hair, smoothing it back out; the silver that had stained his body was gone, leaving Tuyet Hoa Phi Vu just as beautiful as before, but some of his hair had retained its new platinum coloring. He leaned down to match Dong Tu's height and stared deeply into her eyes, and after a moment he squeezed her cheeks and offered her a rueful smile.

"Poor Dong Tu. After all this time, have you really not figured it out? How long have I been by your side? Am I *still* so invisible?"

Liet Than of the Monstrous Eighteen was extremely talented, but not well known. Only a precious few people knew his name, and most of the people who had heard of him were practically on their deathbeds, looking for someone who could send them peacefully to their rest.

Tuyet Hoa Phi Vu shook his head slowly.

"I don't care if the Whispered World doesn't know me, but how could you, who's been so close to me for so long, not have guessed?"

Tuyet Hoa Phi Vu had never claimed to be good at hiding his identity. He'd barely even tried. In fact, there had been a few times when he should have, *would* have been exposed... if Dong Tu had ever stopped chasing Obsidian's ghost long enough to notice.

"Dong Tu, didn't you think it was weird for Tuyet Hoa Phi Vu to have escaped from Switch so easily?" he asked, lifting an eyebrow. Dong Tu shook her head.

"I thought—didn't Ly Minh Lam, Liet Than, save you?"

The two men busted out laughing at the same time. If only Dong Tu knew what had really happened that night...

Half a year before, the night Tuyet Hoa Phi Vu had been kidnapped by Switch and brought back to that deserted hut, Stargazer had arrived, bringing wine for all three of them.

"You never share food, Stargazer," Switch pointed out as she gulped down the alcohol. "Why're you being so nice today?"

Stargazer didn't answer immediately. Instead she pulled out a mat, spread it on the floor, and sat down.

"I'm getting old. I'm trying not to drink as much. Switch, have you ever heard the name Liet Than?"

Tuyet Hoa Phi Vu shot Stargazer a warning look, but Stargazer shook her head.

"Tuyet Hoa Phi Vu, I don't like to interfere with the business of the Whispered World. But I know what you're planning. You're going to get yourself hurt—and I'm not talking about tonight."

Tuyet Hoa Phi Vu frowned, his face as pretty as the cup of wine he held. He stared at Stargazer without speaking, serious and yet questioning. Switch assumed from the ensuing silence that Stargazer was implying Tuyet Hoa Phi Vu was going to try and escape.

"You couldn't escape even if you wanted to. Don't think for a minute that I'm too drunk to catch you. I could catch you easily even when I *am* drunk," she warned. Eyes glazed from the drink she'd practically inhaled, Switch turned to Stargazer. "What's Liet Than? Is it pretty? Is it edible? I don't know, I don't care...why should I care?"

"Pretty? Oh yes. Can you eat him? You'd have to ask," Stargazer chuckled, throwing a mischievous glance at Tuyet Hoa Phi Vu. "Switch, you're letting your guard down dangerously low. You should know all the identities of the other Monstrous Eighteen at the very least. You're not the only one. This will be a costly lesson."

"Crazy old woman," Switch grumbled, reaching for Tuyet Hoa Phi Vu's arm to continue the fun. She paused. There was a kind of energy emanating from Tuyet Hoa Phi Vu, and it didn't feel female. Switch shouted, "Are you a man?!"

Tuyet Hoa Phi Vu blinked in surprise, but it was gone as quickly as it came. He gritted his teeth in frustration. Switch was ruining his plan, and Stargazer had already guessed it, *of course:* give anyone from the Monstrous Eighteen even the tiniest opening and they had a tendency to figure things out almost instantly. He had to deal with this, and quickly.

"Switch, I have business with Dong Tu, and you being around is extremely inconvenient. So what should I do with you, hmm? Should I kill you? Or should I leave you in some deserted place forever?" Tuyet Hoa Phi Vu said, serious as a heart attack. Switch burst into laughter.

"You? Do something to *me?* Have I drunk so much that I'm hearing things?" As soon as she finished the sentence, her whole body was lifted up into the air and thrown across the room by an invisible force. She hit a wooden column and plummeted to the floor, and proceeded to vomit up both blood *and* all the alcohol she had in her stomach. Tuyet Hoa Phi Vu lifted her up and pinned her against the wall by her neck, and Switch stared at him in pained confusion as he leaned in until his face was centimeters from her own.

"You want my face now? Switch, you've messed with the wrong man." Tuyet Hoa Phi Vu's voice was deep and chilling, and his expression was just as icily intense. Switch gathered her chi and grabbed the hand Tuyet Hoa Phi Vu was using to pin her by her neck. A shocked sound slipped past her lips: her chi was blistering, but Tuyet Hoa Phi Vu didn't move, his hand still soft and whole despite showing no signs of internal chi whatsoever. How could it be? Was there really someone alive who had the strength to hold one of the Monstrous Eighteen against their will, without using any chi at all?

As if he were reading Switch's mind, Tuyet Hoa Phi Vu smirked.

"Switch, the world is so much bigger than you know..."

The skin of Switch's face began to hiss. Smoke began to pour from the sides of her jaws, and with a pained screech, her face separated itself from her body without Tuyet Hoa

Phi Vu so much as batting an eyelash. She scratched and clawed at Tuyet Hoa Phi Vu's arm with all her might, until she faded into unconsciousness—and she still had no idea how she, one of the Monstrous Eighteen, could have her chi be sealed off by someone who seemed to have none at all.

Stargazer, meanwhile, sat calmly on her mat as if nothing had happened as Tuyet Hoa Phi Vu let Switch's unconscious body drop to the floor. He brushed his hand off on his shirt and lifted an eyebrow arrogantly at the old woman.

"Are you going to tell them who I am?"

Stargazer threw him an orange rather than answer, and Tuyet Hoa Phi Vu snatched it out of the air easily.

"Long time, no see, Liet Than. You're getting taller." Stargazer studied him with narrowed eyes, clearly displeased with what she saw. "You need to eat more. I thought you were a fishing rod when I saw you from a distance."

"Master—grandma—next time, could you please not meddle in my business?" Tuyet Hoa Phi Vu rested his leg on a nearby rock, slowly peeling the orange and eating it in sections. Stargazer shook her head, knowing her stubborn student had to be thinking of making mischief again.

"Liet Than, do you really want to steal the Storm Pearl this time?"

Tuyet Hoa Phi Vu nodded as if it were obvious. He'd mastered the history and inner workings of the Whispered World, read every book and scroll there was on the subject, and had brought his chi to its maximum potential. It was time to enter the Whispered World and hunt for treasures, and with his innate talent and the fragment he already carried, the Storm Pearl was the obvious choice of weapon *and* treasure. All he needed was to get close to Obsidian, so that he could kill the other man and take it for his own.

The next day Tuyet Hoa Phi Vu tossed Switch into her cave at Tien Thuc Falls, and searched out Ly Minh Lam—his long-time friend and ally in his endeavors in the Whispered World. The two of them walked along the waterfall and discussed the best ways for Tuyet Hoa Phi Vu to approach Dong Tu.

"Obsidian's been missing for years," Liet Than explained. "The last clue left is a girl named Dong Tu. I've been gathering information for a while, but now I want to blend in and learn more, which I can't do if Switch is out there causing trouble. I can't just leave all of the sudden without raising suspicion."

"You know, attacking Switch wasn't the best idea. She's one of the Monstrous Eighteen too, and people won't take kindly to it if the rest of the Whispered World finds out," Ly Minh Lam pointed out worriedly.

"I did take it a bit too far," Tuyet Hoa Phi Vu admitted. "If only she hadn't shown up...I wonder why so many members of the Eighteen are interested in that girl? Switch,

Stargazer, Obsidian...even Leatherback and Anole. I don't get it."

"And all you want from her is to get information on the Storm Pearl?"

"Mainly...but maybe more than that. I mean, if I can't take the Pearl by force..." Tuyet Hoa Phi Vu shook his head. "The Whispered World has always thought of Liet Than, of *me*, as weak. I give them an inch, and they take a mile. I'm just a joke to them. But Dong Tu...she *is* weak. She has the most basic knowledge of fighting, but she protected me with her life. She's a little thing, but she used every bit of her body to try and shield me. I don't need strength in a partner, I just want a sincere heart....Maybe that sweet little thing does interest me a little."

"Sweet little thing?" Ly Minh Lam repeated, looking up. Liet Than had enjoyed hanging around girls since they were children, but this was the first time in all their years of travelling together that Ly Minh Lam had heard him refer to a woman with so much warmth and admiration. He was beginning to see the situation more clearly. "It would seem Obsidian has *two* things you want."

The pair heard noises from above, and Ly Minh Lam and Liet Than looked up to see Bao Thuong, Dong Tu, and two other guards searching frantically for Tuyet Hoa Phi Vu at the top of the waterfall. Ly Minh Lam lifted an eyebrow, picked up a piece of gravel, and shot it up from where they stood hidden below. It hit Dong Tu in the temple, knocking her unconscious, and she fell limply into the water and right over the falls.

"Good luck to you with your treasures," Ly Minh Lam teased with a wink. Liet Than smiled to himself, and used nothing more than the power of his gaze to control Dong Tu's fall. Rather than falling to her death on the rocks at the bottom, she descended gently into his arms, as if being carried by clouds.

"Unlike the Storm Pearl, *that* treasure will take time," Ly Minh Lam said as Liet Than cradled Dong Tu in his arms. "May your patience and effort be rewarded."

CHAPTER 16

Liet Than

The cold waters of Tien Thuc Falls thundered down the mountainside, carried all the way across the land until they poured into Thanh Liet Lake. Not far from the place where Dong Tu had fallen into the falls herself was Thanh Liet Cave—where Liet Than had recently chosen to live, since his mission was complete. After seizing the Storm Pearl from Obsidian, he and Ly Minh Lam brought Dong Tu there.

Dong Tu sat, paralyzed, for three days and nights. She didn't know whether she was awake, or if she was dreaming; she refused food, refused water, and refused to speak to anyone. A shifting tide of numbness and emotion washed over her relentlessly, and she didn't know if she should be angry or full of sorrow. She couldn't believe the mistake that had catalyzed it all had only happened that spring.

The massacre of Tuyet Hoa Phi Vu's family was something that would haunt Dong Tu for the rest of her life. She'd tried to make up for the tragedy by offering him—still thought to be a woman, then—a place with her family, yet little had she known that bringing him into the family would cause a domino effect that brought problem after problem to their door. Because she hadn't known the most crucial piece of information: Tuyet Hoa Phi Vu was the true name of one of the Monstrous Eighteen's most infamous and powerful members.

Lam Liet Than, the Legendary God.

Or, as Dong Tu finally knew him, simply Liet Than—*Frigid*.

She'd compared him to an onion many times, when thinking about all of the layers kept hidden behind that beautiful, impassive face. But this...this was like finally peeling all the way down to the last layer and finding a chicken thigh underneath. How was she supposed to react to *this?* Had the world turned upside-down? And what kind of person did that make Tuyet Hoa Phi Vu, or Luu Dong Trung, or *Liet Than* in the end?

How could they possibly all be the same person?

Those weren't the only thoughts ceaselessly bombarding her. The other pressing question was of Obsidian—namely whether or not he was even *alive*. Rationally she acknowledged that Obsidian's life had been interwoven with the energy of the Storm Pearl, and that without it he likely couldn't survive. She'd seen Liet Than hit Obsidian with the Sunlight Strike, she'd seen him hit Obsidian with a force so powerful his mask had shattered into pieces. She'd seen the Storm Pearl torn from Obsidian's body, she'd seen him fall and disappear into the clouded darkness. And while she wished desperately to wipe every second of that from her memory, she couldn't.

She could, however, refuse to believe Obsidian was actually dead. And she did. Obsidian was alive until Dong Tu saw his corpse with her own eyes and felt it with her own hands. He was still an excellent martial artist, he would have found a way to survive that fall! They'd *just* been reunited, she couldn't let anything separate them again, and Dong Tu knew she had to find her way back to the gorge and find Obsidian.

The problem with searching for Obsidian was her second most pressing issue: she'd been kidnapped by Liet Than and Ly Minh Lam. If she wanted to escape, Dong Tu was going to have to find a weakness or an opening. But that was a difficult task. Despite living by his side for half a year, she still had no idea who Liet Than really was. She'd been in his presence even while attempting to search him out! And of the things Dong Tu did think she knew, how many of them were actually true?

Which persona was the real him? The fragile beauty, Tuyet Hoa Phi Vu? Or perhaps it was Luu Dong Trung, the wimpy little brother who had always demanded her affection. Or...or perhaps he truly was the wicked Lam Liet Than of the Monstrous Eighteen.

So Dong Tu sat, lost in the vortex of her thoughts, staring into the void like her mind had left her entirely. Liet Than visited her several times, but she never blinked, never spoke a word. She didn't even look at him. Dong Tu didn't offer him a single reaction. Any time he touched her it was like touching an empty, soulless vessel. What she *wanted* to do was leap at him. She wanted to bite, claw, tear, and shred him to pieces, enraged—but she found no strength with which to attack him. It was unlikely to come until her mind found a way to make sense of what had happened.

More than tear him to pieces, Dong Tu just wanted to believe that Liet Than was really her Luu Dong Trung, or even the unfortunate Tuyet Hoa Phi Vu. *Anything* but the evil man who'd just cruelly murdered her beloved Phong.

On the fourth day her mind began to clear, and the fires of hatred finally exploded into life in her chest. Dong Tu stood weakly and groped around Thanh Liet Cave, searching for Liet Than. She saw Ly Minh Lam focused on writing something in what had been turned into the study.

"...Exchange Dong Tu for your life. If you fight back, I will kill her," Liet Than dictated quietly as Ly Minh Lam quickly wrote it out. "How does that sound? Is that serious enough?"

"That's pretty evil, let's send it," Ly Minh Lam replied, and Liet Than nodded.

"To who? And to what address?" he asked in return. They'd been writing an ultimatum to Obsidian, and didn't seem to give a single thought to the fact that at that second, he was probably lying at the bottom of the gorge.

Ly Minh Lam considered Liet Than's question quietly, and perked up as an idea popped into his head.

"Send it to Ivy at Hoa Hon Palace. She's the closest." Ivy, the palace's owner, was to Obsidian what Luu Dong Trung had been to Dong Tu: a younger incidental sibling who was constantly, jealously pushing for more. Ly Minh Lam was sure that if she got the letter, she would definitely give it to Obsidian herself.

"No way, she's more likely to crumple it up and throw it away," Liet Than denied, scratching his chin. Ivy was stubborn and fearless, and properly getting her attention wouldn't happen with a letter.

"Just send it," Ly Minh Lam said. "Send another copy to Dao Que Chi."

"Then a copy for the Poison Legion's sects, and another one to the Valley of Life and Death, to announce that I, Liet Than, have slain their great King of Poison," Liet Than added.

Dong Tu stepped more fully into the room, and the two men clumsily hid the letter behind their backs like naughty children. Ly Minh Lam didn't miss the fact that Dong Tu's eyes were fixed on Liet Than like she wanted to skin him alive, and took that as his cue to see himself out. He excused himself quietly and went to send the letter.

The only two people left in the room, Dong Tu and Liet Than stood staring at each other in silence. Liet Than could see the barely-contained fire in her bloodshot eyes, and he hesitantly invited her to sit. His expression betrayed nothing, like it always did, but her visible fury made his hands shake as he poured her a cup of tea.

Dong Tu studied him in steely silence, still asking herself if she knew the person before her. Tuyet Hoa Phi Vu…Luu Dong Trung…Liet Than. A man with long, silky black hair, dressed neatly and nicely. Glittering silver phoenix eyes that looked outstanding thanks to his dark eyeliner. His nose was straight, and his lips were so full an attractive crease formed straight down the middle. Those same teardrop earrings framed his striking face. With the exception of the shining platinum strands that stuck out vividly from the rest of his hair, the man who stood before her, Liet Than, was no different from Tuyet Hoa Phi Vu.

"Who are you really, little brother? Did you lie to me from the very beginning, just to learn the Sunlight Strike and steal the Storm Pearl?" Dong Tu asked directly. The time for politely beating around the bush was long gone.

Liet Than watched her apprehensively, trying to make sure Dong Tu wasn't going to suddenly attack him and tear him apart with all the rage her trembling body was failing to control. Finally he drew an air of confidence back around him and pushed the teacup toward her.

"First of all, I'm way older than you. We need to change this whole 'little brother' thing." Because of his fresh, youthful face, people had always assumed he was much younger than his real age. Liet Than smoothed his hair, tugged his shirt straight, and took a steadying sip of his own tea.

Dong Tu scrutinized the man before her, and Liet Than tried hard not to shrink like a violet beneath her gaze. He was Lam Liet Than, the man who'd just defeated the King of Poison, wasn't he? Why couldn't he stop fidgeting and face her? What was he so afraid of?

She turned her head to stare at a blank space like she hadn't heard him, and Liet Than realized his words had no effect on her. Still, when he continued, it was unhurried.

"Second, it's true. I found you because I wanted the Storm Pearl." Liet Than had looked for Dong Tu because of the rumors of Obsidian, and he'd fully intended to use her to get the Pearl from the very beginning. "The Storm Pearl is one of the most precious and unique treasures in the Whispered World, and anyone who doesn't try to go after it isn't worthy of it! Obsidian…he's a hard man to track down. But you…all I had to do was find the Luu Dojo."

"And your forced wedding in Lac Do? Was that made up?"

Liet Than nodded. He'd taken inspiration from Dong Tu's own fatal wedding, and it was ridiculous to him that Dong Tu hadn't been the least bit skeptical about the similarity between the two events. How many girls were forced into marriages like that? What were the odds that two of them would actually meet each other?

"Was the massacre at Snowflake Tower made up too?"

Again Liet Than nodded.

"My parents and my two elder brothers are safe and sound, thank you for asking."

"Did Ly Minh Lam know everything?"

"Yes. Ly Minh Lam grew up with me, the two of us are closer than I am with my blood brothers," he affirmed, still nodding.

Dong Tu could remember the day they'd come upon the massacre, when Tuyet Hoa Phi Vu had cried his heart out, begging to come home with Dong Tu. Ly Minh Lam had covered his face with his hand, the mole beneath his eye just barely moving, and she realized what she'd taken to be an expression of sympathy was Ly Minh Lam hiding his laughter.

Dong Tu gripped the cup in her palm worryingly tight, her whole body shaking. For months Dong Tu had seen Liet Than as her brother, cunning but harmless. Who would have thought…?

Liet Than continued his story, interrupting Dong Tu's thoughts.

"When I came to the Luu Dojo, my first plan was to capture you and make an exchange for the Pearl." He stopped, remembering the moment they'd met. How his first impression of Dong Tu was to wonder how such an average little girl had managed to win *the* Obsidian's heart… how she'd mistaken him for a woman, and he'd played along, teasing her to amuse himself. He remembered the night when she'd voluntarily transferred her chi to him, despite her own chi being hundreds of times weaker than his own.

Liet Than remembered the drunken kiss that had sealed his decision to stay. There was something about Dong Tu that even he couldn't explain: it was as if they'd known each other in a previous life, as if she were someone he'd subconsciously been searching for—and once he'd met her, his soul had known her instantly, and he couldn't leave her.

Unable to put his thoughts into words, Liet Than let his eyes wander around the room, avoiding Dong Tu's gaze. He found his courage again after a moment, and looked directly into her eyes.

"I came to your dojo because I wanted the Storm Pearl, but I discovered the Luu family had their own precious pearl. Obsidian had the Storm Pearl, which he didn't want to use, and an incredible woman he didn't want to keep. Two precious treasures absolutely wasted in his possession." He could feel his face flush hotly. This wasn't the first time he'd revealed his feelings for her, but this was the first time he'd done so as *himself*, with the whole truth laid out for her to see. It made him indescribably anxious. He was Lam Liet Than, the Legendary God, one of the Monstrous Eighteen, the latest bearer of the Storm Pearl; yet it wasn't an overstatement to say that if Dong Tu changed her mind and decided to become his, he might die of happiness.

Unfortunately it seemed like Liet Than had plenty of time to live, as his words didn't even seem to reach Dong Tu's ears. He took a moment to work through his disappointment by pouring himself another cup of tea.

"...Third, I don't care about the Sunlight Strike. That was just chance. I learned it for your benefit, not mine. I didn't need it to steal the Pearl." He paused. "Fourth...I have never lied to you." And he was serious.

Dong Tu stared at him, speechless. How could he lie so boldly, so smoothly?

In truth, it wasn't a lie. Liet Than hadn't lied to anyone, he just hadn't corrected any of their own assumptions.

That didn't mean Dong Tu believed him.

"Everything you've told me since the day we met...how much of it was true? How many were lies? Why did you pretend you had no knowledge of martial arts?"

Liet Than chuckled, "Dong Tu, I sincerely only know just a little bit about traditional martial arts. I'm not pretending. As one of the Monstrous Eighteen, people from the Whispered World call me Frigid. Would you like to know why?"

―――

Tuyet Hoa Phi Vu's family was actually from Thanh Liet province. The magistrate had earned the love and respect of the people—but he was also the subject of much of their gossip. The most popular story told was aimed at his children: the idea that the magistrate had three young masters in his family, but while two of them were boys, one of them was better off a girl.

The magistrate's eldest sons, Tuyet Hoa Vo Thuong and Tuyet Hoa Vo Le, were sharp, strong, and efficient, like two priceless swords. They were admired for their rugged masculinity and fighting skills. But the youngest son, Tuyet Hoa Phi Vu, had been gifted with nothing but a flawless, angelic face. When he was young, the housemaids had loved to pamper him: they put crowns of flowers on his head, warmed his cheeks with blush, accented his pretty lips with rouge, and had dressed him up like a girl. Tuyet Hoa Phi Vu had loved playing with the maids, preferring it to spending time with other boys his age. Playing with the other boys bored him, and he had preferred to spend his days in the laps of the young ladies.

The magistrate wanted Tuyet Hoa Phi Vu to pay more attention to practicing martial arts so he could become famous. And even though he'd had his master, Stargazer, since birth, for the next thirteen years the magistrate invited many more martial arts masters to come and teach Tuyet Hoa Phi Vu their specialties.

He made exactly no progress.

In fact he seemed to regress the more his father pushed, and without fail, every other master left after a month. Like everyone else, they could feel no chi within him whatsoever, and every time they left, they shook their heads and told his father that his son's lack of chi meant he would never be able to learn martial arts like his brothers. Instead they suggested he be taught to play instruments, or write poems. Lovely, peaceful things.

Even Tuyet Hoa Vo Thuong and Tuyet Hoa Vo Le tried their best to teach their brother, but they too gave up on him in the end. The idea of Tuyet Hoa Phi Vu becoming a famous martial artist was abandoned. Towering stacks of martial arts books sat collecting dust in his room as he fed his love of jewelry, fashion, and even arranging flowers. What time wasn't spent on beautiful things was spent playing and joking with his maids. He was as beautiful and delicate as the young maidens, and the older he grew, the more splendid he became; by the time he was grown, his beauty and sense of style outshone every woman in the area.

Tuyet Hoa Phi Vu's father seemed to have surrendered himself to the fact that while he had three sons, two of them were masculine, and the other would always be—and would always *choose* to be—feminine.

But it didn't come without its own problems elsewhere. Tuyet Hoa Phi Vu had rarely spent time with other boys his age as a child, but when he had, he'd been the constant target of mocking and abuse from everyone save Ly Minh Lam. Gia Tu Kiet, the son of another official in the district, was one of the worst. Gia Tu Kiet would pull Tuyet Hoa Phi Vu's hair, jerk him around by his shirt, or throw mud and gravel at him, and every time Tuyet Hoa Phi Vu would end up hidden away, crying into his hands, vulnerable and unable to rely on anyone to protect him.

He'd told Dong Tu the story before, but he'd stopped there, giving Dong Tu enough to tap into that compassionate heart and make her feel for him. But that wasn't the end of the story, and he was finally going to finish it for her.

At thirteen, Tuyet Hoa Phi Vu had grown sick of the dull and dreary pace of Thanh Liet province. He itched to go and explore, to find excitement, like a bird with all its feathers finally grown in and prepared for flight. One day Gia Tu Kiet saw Tuyet Hoa Phi Vu wandering the garden, and he and a small group of children approached the lone boy. Gia Tu Kiet stuck a stick in his face, and Tuyet Hoa Phi Vu screamed: he detested being dirty, but he detested bugs, spiders, and any other insect-like creature with too many *legs* even more, and Gia Tu Kiet had just shoved one in his face on that stick.

The other kids burst into laughter, and while Ly Minh Lam tried to make them stop, he was powerless. Gia Tu Kiet wasn't going to be deterred. Tuyet Hoa Phi Vu made to run and Gia Tu Kiet grabbed the collar of his dress—and the bug fell into the open gap. It wasn't clear if it was intentional or not, but it didn't matter: Tuyet Hoa Phi Vu could feel the scratch of those skinny bug-legs scrabbling all over his body, trying to find a way out of the dress.

Tuyet Hoa Phi Vu broke.

He began screaming. Blood-curdling shrieks of pure terror rent the air, and he curled over, hands pressed to his mouth, stricken tears streaming down his cheeks—and wherever the scream sounded, a shockwave seemed to shake existence itself apart at the seams. His dress disintegrated. What happened to the bug, only God knew, but the odds were good that it too had become dust. The other children's clothes crumbled into dust, and their hair burst into powder that was blown away with the relentless waves. The Tuyet

Hoas' garden took heavy damage: the trees and bushes were stripped of their leaves, smaller plants disintegrated, and even their roof was blown off.

Everyone in the house came pouring outside. The magistrate, his sons, all of the servants, and Stargazer. They stopped, startled, when they saw the full extent of the damage: it looked like a bomb had gone off. And at the epicenter, left in nothing but his underwear, hair still neat, was Tuyet Hoa Phi Vu. It wasn't hard to see that he was the cause; the evidence all around left no question. His brothers seemed to unfreeze after a beat and came running over. They checked his pressure points, but still, they found no internal chi thrumming through his body. They checked his pulse, too, as Tuyet Hoa Phi Vu continued to quake there on his knees. They still felt no chi.

Mortified and terrified, all Tuyet Hoa Phi Vu wanted to do was to run. As soon as the desire formed into a coherent thought, a powerful, invisible force knocked his brothers aside, and he took off running. He ran right into the open arms of one of the closest maids, and began to sob loudly.

Stargazer smiled.

"I've been waiting for thirteen years," she said. "Thirteen years I have been waiting patiently, searching all of the Whispered World to see who and what the Frigid God is all about, and my patience has been rewarded."

She'd predicted her little student would become a genuine game-changer throughout the Whispered World, someone truly extraordinary, the day he'd been born. Throughout his childhood it had been assumed he had no chi at all, because even the most learned masters the magistrate had brought in had been unable to detect even the faintest sliver.

And they'd been so, *so* wrong.

Tuyet Hoa Phi Vu's chi was so powerful it couldn't be contained in his body. It was stored outside his body, to be drawn upon whenever Tuyet Hoa Phi Vu needed it, an enormous amount of energy that put all of his former teachers to shame. He hadn't bothered to learn from the innumerable tomes his father had forced on him because he couldn't do it; he hadn't bothered because their teachings were useless to him. None of the many techniques he'd studied could hold a candle to his own outstanding power, so why waste the time?

"This is the one that will shake the Whispered World to its foundations, the child reborn with a fragment of the Sunlight Pearl. He will grow to master an unbelievable force," Stargazer said, pleased and proud. She closed her eyes and breathed a sigh of relief. "My job is done. The rest is up to you, Tuyet Hoa Phi Vu."

As a child, Tuyet Hoa Phi Vu had never understood what Stargazer had meant by *job* when all she'd done for the last thirteen years had been eating, sleeping, and teaching him next to nothing; but she was clearly happy with witnessing the revelation of his powers, and wanted to return to roaming the world once more.

The Tuyet Hoa family continued to gape at the scene: it seemed they were unable to translate their astonishment into words. After that, Tuyet Hoa Phi Vu was allowed to do whatever he wanted. His father never mentioned learning martial arts again, and whenever he passed by, Gia Tu Kiet and the other children averted their gazes and kept their distance. A few years later he chose the name Lam Liet Than: because of his talent, he defeated his enemies without moving a muscle. His attacks were whipping and light like the winter wind, intangible as a cloud, clear and cold as Thanh Liet Lake. The only things that moved were his trademark teardrop earrings, which swung with the force of his strikes.

Lam Liet Than, the Legendary God.

As Dong Tu listened, all of the missing pieces finally fell into place. She thought back over the time she and Liet Than had spent together, and every instance took on a brand new light. The first time Switch had escaped from Tien Thuc Falls, Dong Tu had been sure she was attacking Ly Minh Lam. But in reality she'd aimed directly at Liet Than, who'd been standing in front of Ly Minh Lam! And the many thugs who'd come to the dojo to kidnap Dong Tu...she'd known it wasn't Ryujin or Le Minh who'd defeated them, but now she realized it had been Liet Than!

All of the evil people from the Whispered World wielding their swords and machetes, their spears and bows, they had all been disarmed and driven away by an unseen defender—or else all they'd seen was naïve little Luu Dong Trung, calmly sweeping the courtyard like nothing had happened.

"You thought it was Obsidian who'd been protecting you, but you were wrong. It was me," Liet Than confessed quietly. "If I hadn't chosen to stay with you, if you'd only had Obsidian to count on, you'd have been dead a long time ago."

That time in Thanh Liet Lake. If he hadn't leapt into the water and used his chi to create a wall of bubbles between Dong Tu and Tuong Y Ve, if he hadn't kissed her to distract her from the way he used his same power to knock Tuong Y Ve away beneath the water, Tuong Y Ve would have poisoned her.

On the deserted road on the outskirts of the district, it had been Liet Than who'd created the dust storm and chi-force barrier between she and Tuong Y Ve.

And that day by the lakeshore, before Obsidian had come flying across the lake, it was Liet Than's invisible chi that kept Tuong Y Ve's arms bound to his body. Not some reluctance to kill Dong Tu and Luu Dong Trung.

"Did you really never find it strange, Dong Tu? That the whole world seemed to revolve around you? You thought it was Obsidian, didn't you." Liet Than hadn't merely cooked for her, brought her water for washing, washed her feet, served her and catered to her every whim. He'd changed the *world* for her.

"Wherever you've gone, I've been beside you, making the world turn around you," Liet Than continued in a whisper. The words came from the very depth of his soul: he was her secret champion, her secret servant in the dark, always overshadowed by Obsidian. "But you never realized it was me, right?"

Dong Tu's heart was so filled up with memories of Obsidian and grandiose ideas of who he was, and what he did for her, that even though Liet Than had practically reshaped the universe to bring her the sun *and* the moon, she'd never even given him a second thought.

Snowflakes began to fall throughout the room. Unlike Obsidian, Liet Than's chi was external, which was why he'd been able to control the snow the Storm Pearl made, both at the gorge and right in that moment. Dong Tu followed his gaze and realized the snowflakes were dancing and swirling around her in the tenderest caress. They caught in her lashes, fell into her tea; sometimes they continued to swirl, sometimes they fell in a heavy shower, and sometimes they glided smoothly around with the grace of dragons and phoenixes.

It was a spectacular sight.

"Dong Tu...I could give you the world, however you wanted it. No matter how I have to do it. Just say the word."

The snow seemed to curl around Dong Tu like it wanted to persuade her, too. But Dong Tu shook her head.

"My world is just fine." She stood and turned away. It didn't spark her ire, his show, his confession. Instead a mirthless smile twisted her lips: she felt like a child who'd been teased by him one too many times. Liet Than, Luu Dong Trung—whoever he was, he'd lost her trust the moment he'd attacked Obsidian. "Apparently I owe the great Liet Than a favor, and I had no idea. How rude of me."

Liet Than watched as Dong Tu began to stride toward the exit, and called after her.

"Dong Tu...please consider it. I love you." She stopped, and Liet Than lowered his voice back down to a whisper. "What do you want, Dong Tu? I can give it to you. I can give you everything."

Dong Tu's eyes slid closed with a soft sigh. She turned her head and spoke quietly, sadly over her shoulder.

"The only thing my world is missing...is Obsidian."

After the long months spent with Luu Dong Trung at her side, the one thing she'd known for certain was that he was normally calm, easy-going, and forgiving. And of course he was: he'd been trying to win her heart.

But Liet Than was a different story.

As Dong Tu headed for the exit, she witnessed the anger of Lam Liet Than for the first time. The beautiful snowflakes that had fallen around her so gently launched themselves through the windscreen and the paper walls, their deadly-sharp edges leaving them in tatters. As Dong Tu made it out of the room the wall came crashing down in pieces, revealing Liet Than, watching her with uncontrolled fury. From a distance she could see bloody red streaks in his silver eyes, and the snowflakes tore into everything around her—

Even if not a single one of them touched her. Just enough destruction to cause fear, and show Dong Tu how angry he truly was.

Dong Tu had thought that she was close to Tuyet Hoa Phi Vu/Luu Dong Trung for a long time. She'd thought she understood him intimately. She'd considered him family. The revelation that he was Liet Than had sent her reeling, leaving her shocked and doubting even herself. But strangely...seeing Liet Than so undone by his anger, Dong Tu felt peace settle over her once more.

Liet Than was nothing more than the same spoiled child he'd always been. No matter how many identities he tried on, no matter how much he kept hidden, an onion was still an onion.

Dong Tu stood in the hallway for a long time. She didn't move, she didn't speak, she displayed no emotion at all. She refused to bend to his attempts to intimidate, to rush in and comfort him; not when he behaved like a baby throwing a fit because he'd asked for a gift he couldn't have. The more she tried to cater to his anger, the bigger his tantrum would become—and it was just that. A tantrum.

Dong Tu drew in a deep breath, and when she spoke, it was short and sharp.

"Luu Dong Trung, you underhandedly attacked Phong when he was trying to save your *life*." With that she turned and left, going to her room without a single look back at Liet Than. She heard him let out an indignant scream, and snowflakes whipped angrily through the hallway for a long time after that.

The next day, Liet Than had changed his attitude entirely. It seemed Dong Tu wasn't wrong: an onion was indeed an onion. Somewhere between the demonic Liet Than, the heavenly beauty that was Tuyet Hoa Phi Vu, and her little brother—tall and slender, with the pretty phoenix eyes the color of crystal clear water—was the man she'd known for half a year.

"Dong Tu, kiss me," Liet Than asked. It would be his last move: if Dong Tu had fallen for Obsidian because of the goodbye kiss they'd shared in the Valley of Life and Death, then Liet Than was determined to give her a farewell kiss to remember. "If you don't love me, fine. Just give me this one kiss. A true, final kiss. And if you still don't feel anything for me, I'll let you go find Obsidian. I'll even help you."

"You'll help me find Obsidian?" Dong Tu verified doubtfully. Liet Than nodded.

"Believe it or not, forcing people to do something they don't enjoy isn't my thing. I tried for over half a year to get you to fall in love with me, but it did no good, so I'll trade one real kiss for your freedom and Obsidian's safety. I promise to not kill him the next time I see him. And after this one kiss, if it still doesn't change your mind, I'll give up. I'll only keep one of Obsidian's precious treasures."

He didn't let a single second go to waste. As soon as he finished speaking he closed the distance between them, tipped her chin up, and kissed her. Annoyingly, Dong Tu shrunk back into herself instinctively.

This wasn't the first time they'd kissed, and Liet Than *was* extraordinary. He was beautiful, he smelled good, and he was so *tender* with Dong Tu; he'd practiced their farewell kiss hundreds of times in his imagination, enough that in the moment, he melted into it naturally. And since Dong Tu was already used to him being physically affectionate and close, and since she did adore Liet Than in at least one way, it was fair to say that kissing him wasn't unpleasant. As his soft lips moved against hers and his clean, sandalwood scent enveloped her—a feeling and a scent she knew so well—

Dong Tu finally felt the confused fog that had overtaken her mind fade away.

In recent months, every time Dong Tu tried to recall her kisses with Obsidian, the memory of her kissing Liet Than had always lingered in the wings. Enough that she'd wondered, sometimes, if her heart had changed without her realizing it. But now, with Liet Than kissing her so passionately, the feeling of him so real on her lips, she was able to make sense of it all. The memories of kissing Obsidian were cloudy because they'd happened so fast, in situations that were so intense and dangerous, the danger had overshadowed every other memory.

The kisses she shared with Liet Than were fresher in her mind, and she had been subconsciously using those memories to supplement the physical feelings she could no longer remember from kissing Obsidian. It had left the memories mingled, yes, and she couldn't remember the differences between their kisses, but one thing *had* become clear.

Liet Than's kiss was incredible. It disarmed her, it made her soft...it made her want to melt into the arms of the man before her. But the only arms she wanted to be in, the only lips she wanted to be kissing when she opened her eyes, were Obsidian's.

Obsidian, and *only* Obsidian.

Liet Than hung on as long as he could, but the longer he went without any reaction from Dong Tu, the more his heart sank, until he finally stopped.

"You really feel nothing for me," he murmured, his eyes full of sorrow.

"I do," Dong Tu corrected him. "But I love you like a sister loves her brother, and no amount of kissing is going to change that. Please stop this. It's not appropriate."

Liet Than studied Dong Tu intensely, his expression twisted with deep consideration and displeasure. Then he grabbed her shoulders, bent down, and kissed her one more time. He held her far tighter than he had before, almost painfully tight. Dong Tu felt his hands move behind her back, and Liet Than sent a palm strike through her. It did no damage to her—because the force instead slammed into Liet Than's body. His lips shook against hers, and it felt like a blistering fire spread from his lips to her own. She tried to push him away, but he only held her tighter, until the fire burning between them both melted into some kind of glowing halo around her body.

Finally Liet Than released Dong Tu and he collapsed to the floor, yelling in pain and clutching at his chest, rolling back and forth.

"It hurts—it really *hurts!* Oh, Dong Tu, Dong Tu—!"

Dong Tu's eyes widened in surprise, not sure if this was just another joke. But she realized quickly that as overly dramatic as it seemed, Liet Than was truly in pain—and it seemed that he had just used the Sunlight Strike to separate the piece of Sunlight Pearl he had within his own body and pass it to her. She dropped to her knees beside him, panicked. Losing the Pearl could cost him his life!

"Luu Dong Trung, are you okay?!"

Had Liet Than, the Frigid God, just sacrificed his life for Dong Tu?

CHAPTER 17

Sunlight Strike

Obsidian blinked, peering through his thick lashes into the dim light around him. He could make out a polished ebony ceiling, and the smoke from burning incense curled slowly into the air and dissipated before it reached the dark, rich wood. He tried to move, but his whole body felt impossibly heavy and strangely numb. He could open his eyes and blink, but he was unable to open his mouth; his ears rang, but he could hear nothing beyond that. What little use of his senses that Obsidian had were practically useless, and he felt as if he were slowly being crushed beneath the pressure and weight of the water at the bottom of the ocean.

A delicate hand brushed past his eyes, feeling his forehead. The wrist was adorned with a jade bracelet, though its image was blurry—familiar, yet also strange. The hand moved back down, once again passing gently by his eyes, this time holding needles in its fingers. He couldn't feel the hand touching his body, but from what little he could make out, it was clear the woman was performing acupuncture. Obsidian struggled, trying to move, but it felt like he was falling back into that black abyss, unable to move or scream.

What was going on? Where was he?

The second and third times Obsidian woke up were no different. Incense smoke, ebony ceiling, paralyzed and numb. He couldn't even tell where his hands, feet, or even head really were. The fourth time he woke, the hand and bracelet were back, once more performing acupuncture. The jade swung slightly, and every shape gave off faint colors like a kaleidoscope. He went back and forth between dreaming and waking many times, and it felt as if much time had passed; but eventually Obsidian woke and was able to *focus*.

The jade became clearer, and he realized he recognized the jewelry. That wasn't all: he could vaguely feel the warmth of the room, and the scent of heavy incense filled his nose. He knew that scent, agarwood; it was the favorite of another of the Legion, Ivy. Obsidian recognized the room, too, and realized he was in Hoa Hon Palace, where Cassia had to have been taking care of him. But why was he there? And why couldn't he feel his limbs?

A few days passed, and Obsidian gradually began to take in more of his surroundings. He was naked, soaking in an herbal bath. The water was black, and was filled with pieces of floating barks and herbs, and Obsidian realized he could twitch his lips and head. His hearing was also gradually beginning to return, and all Obsidian heard—for three days straight—was Ivy screaming and cursing Dong Tu and Liet Than with all her might. A few more days passed and his hearing sharpened: he was able to hear the considerably more gentle tones of Cassia and Ivy talking over each other. The sound irked him, and finally, after what felt like a century, he managed to open his mouth and speak.

"So noisy," he rasped, and both Ivy and Cassia leaned in closer immediately.

"Phong, you're awake! When did you wake up!?" they asked in unison. They leaned in even closer and Obsidian wanted to take a step back, but he was still fully immobile—which meant he was at the mercy of the two most annoying women of the Poison Legion *and* the Valley of Life and Death.

Cassia was as slender as ever, clad in white. Her expression was meek and sad, but it did nothing to diminish her overwhelming, ethereal beauty. Hoa Hon Palace was always as hot as a furnace, but despite her long, loose clothing, Cassia hadn't sweat a single drop. She tenderly tipped Obsidian's face up to where she could look in his eyes, the jade on her wrist swinging gently; she was a skilled and integral member of the Poison Legion, but she had the most angelic face.

Ivy, on the other hand, was exactly the opposite. Her appearance reflected her personality: no matter how he looked at her—front, back, from the side, from above, from below, whether he was waking or dreaming, Obsidian could only see Ivy as a true villainess. Round eyes, full, pouty lips, outfits that were so revealing they barely counted as clothes (and that were often encrusted with gemstones), and always, always drenched in purple. Dark, sensual, and dangerous.

"Phong, what did that Dong Tu do to you this time?" Ivy was demanding, over and over. "This time I'll have to kill her to make sure she'll never hurt you again!"

It didn't matter how many times she asked, however: Obsidian seemed to have used up his ability to speak for the day, and wouldn't argue with her. Luckily—or *unluckily*—the sounds of footsteps and fighting came echoing loudly down the hallway. It sounded like someone had just beaten the guards in the hallway, and was on their way to his room. Cassia sat on the edge of the tub and spread out her dress to help block Obsidian from view, and Ivy stomped furiously out of the room to stop the man who'd just been preparing to bust down the door.

"Tuong Y Ve!" Both women exclaimed his name simultaneously.

"You will call me the North King of Poison!" Tuong Y Ve corrected them. "Obsidian is dead. Have you forgotten your manners?"

Cassia bowed her head to avoid attracting any more of Tuong Y Ve's attention, and shifted her arm behind her to make certain Tuong Y Ve couldn't see Obsidian. Meanwhile Ivy formed a distraction, and began to argue the point of Obsidian's presumed death as she stepped even closer. If Obsidian had only disappeared, he wasn't confirmed dead, which meant Tuong Y Ve's claims of being the new King of Poison were unfounded.

"He lost the Storm Pearl! Do you really think he can live after that?!" Tuong Y Ve shouted. "The Storm Pearl's energy drains its host even in normal conditions. It was taken from him in one single strike, it's impossible for Obsidian to be alive!"

Tuong Y Ve wasn't entirely wrong. Normally, no matter how powerful a master was, if they had the Storm Pearl stolen from them it meant instant death. After Obsidian had fallen, Tuong Y Ve sent messages to every sect of the Poison Legion declaring himself the newest King of Poison. Members from all over had flocked to the gorge to find his body, and to see for themselves if Liet Than had indeed taken the Storm Pearl from Obsidian.

Luckily for Obsidian, the first people to find him were the people of Hoa Hon Palace, ruled by Ivy—who was extremely fond of Obsidian (to say the least). Hoa Hon Palace was closer to Thanh Liet Lake and Tien Thuc Falls than any other strongholds of the Poison Legion, giving them the advantages of speed and proximity. The people had searched relentlessly, day and night, and finally found a trail of blood that led to where Obsidian had holed up in a cave, gravely injured. He'd been breathing when they found him, but he had looked...almost soulless.

Ivy had ordered her men to bring him back to her palace, and hid him while she summoned Cassia to come and treat him. Both women had insisted on keeping both his whereabouts, and the fact that he had lived, a secret. Obsidian had been wounded, and had been robbed of the Storm Pearl: if Samsara, the leader of the Poison Legion, learned of it and knew he was alive, it would cause far more harm than good. At best, she'd imprison him. At worst? She'd have him executed immediately.

Thankfully it hadn't been difficult to conceal Obsidian because the Whispered World implicitly understood the ramifications of having the Storm Pearl ripped from one's body. Obsidian had swallowed the Storm Pearl at less than ten years old, and that had been more than thirteen years before; it wasn't like pulling a sapling from the ground, it was like tearing out an ancient tree whose roots had dug down *deep* into the earth. If it was uprooted completely, could the soil remain unchanged? With the Pearl uprooted, could Obsidian's soul? No, those of the Whispered World believed it was impossible for him to have survived.

Being the one who had brought about Obsidian's demise (or so he believed), Tuong Y Ve had naturally assumed he would be named the next King of Poison. And just with the coveted title in reach, Ivy had protested, saying Obsidian's body had to be found and his death proven before they could officially announce his successor. Tuong Y Ve had been furious when they agreed, and had gone straight to Hoa Hon Palace to deal with Ivy.

That was why Cassia had hurriedly spread out her dress to cover the medicine bath, and why Ivy was attempting to argue with Tuong Y Ve and push him out of the room: both women knew that if Tuong Y Ve saw Obsidian in the bath, still broken and paralyzed, he'd kill him in an instant.

Obsidian helplessly sank deeper into the herbal bath. Cassia's long, flowing dress covered his head, and the spider tattoo on her back seemed to be moving between her thin shoulder blades. Cassia was gorgeous, and split between two extremes: she had the front of a goddess, with a face as lovely and delicate as a fairy, pure as a white rabbit in need of protection—like a delicate flower adorned with morning dew. But behind her back, that exquisite, intricate spider had been worked into her supple skin, stretching across a back that was stronger than anyone would expect.

Cassia was no less intimidating than Obsidian himself.

Obsidian sank gradually lower. The herbal bath flooded his nose, rendering him unable to breathe as well as move. The water reflected the spider on Cassia's back, and seeped into her clothes from where the fabric fell into the bath itself; the white fabric was beginning to stick to her skin, and Tuong Y Ve and Ivy were *still* fighting about whether Obsidian was dead or not. It seemed he had survived the fight and the long, long fall to the bottom of the cliff, only to drown beneath Cassia's dress.

How ironic.

Obsidian quietly breathed out enough to make the water bubble. Cassia heard the sound, realized what he needed, and let her hand casually dangle behind her so she could carefully lift his chin and let him breathe.

Tuong Y Ve heard the bubbling, and turned his glare on Cassia.

"What's in the tank?" he asked suspiciously. Cassia let herself fall into the pool, her whole body right on top of Obsidian's—smushing him right back into the water.

"Tuong Y Ve, I am trying to take a bath! Please, get out! Show some respect!"

Ignoring her order for him to leave, Tuong Y Ve went around Ivy and slowly approached Cassia. She shifted her clothes to make sure he couldn't see anything beneath her, and thankfully the water was pitch black. Cassia wrapped her feet around Obsidian's neck and held him under the water, making sure the only thing Tuong Y Ve could see was her wet body and the way her now-soaking white dress clung to it.

"Tuong Y Ve! Cassia outranks you! How dare you be so rude?!" Ivy yelled.

It was true: they technically belonged to two different sects. The King of Poison belonged to the Poison Legion, while Cassia was from the Valley of Life and Death. But the Poison Legion served the Valley, so her being the second most important member in the Valley outranked the Four Kings. Even if Tuong Y Ve was promoted, he would still fall below Cassia. It was also clearly shown in the differences between their tattoos: Obsidian's was intense, but Cassia's was far more detailed and comprehensive with its symbolic imagery.

"Aren't you the woman Thanh Nhan promised to the northern king?" Tuong Y Ve growled, his eyes glued to the way Cassia's wet dress hugged every dip and curve of her body. "And now *I'm* the King of Poison in the north. Doesn't that make you mine?"

Cassia's eyes flashed and she lifted her chin imperiously, her gaze stern.

"I am Dao Que Chi, the Cassia of the Valley of Life and Death! Get out!" she commanded. The promise didn't take hold until Tuong Y Ve was officially the new king, and she was still an apothecarist for the *Poison Legion*. Alongside Thanh Nhan herself, Cassia mixed and developed the poisons that made the Legion so fearsome. Tuong Y Ve had no bearing on the power she truly wielded as the woman at Thanh Nhan's right hand. Tuong Y Ve took an awkward step back, and Ivy whipped a silk band around his neck and jerked. He fell, and smacked straight onto his back on the floor.

"Besides, Thanh Nhan gave Cassia to Phong, not to you!" Ivy then dragged him out of the room, getting Tuong Y Ve out of there before Obsidian drowned in earnest. Tuong Y Ve was sent away from the palace, and Ivy returned; she started chattering at Obsidian at once.

"Phong, you have to recover quickly. Without you in the Legion, Tuong Y Ve is ruining everything! Now everyone thinks you're dead!"

That was the ending Obsidian had dreamed of most. For the Whispered World to think him dead, and for the Storm Pearl to pass on to someone else. It would give him a one-in-a-thousand chance to live a normal life…

"It's terrible. With you gone, there's only three Kings of Poison left. The lack of stability is going to destroy us from the inside out," Ivy continued. She knew that was the life Obsidian wanted, but she couldn't let him just leave! The Poison Legion couldn't function the way it was.

But in Obsidian's opinion, geometrically speaking, a triangle was a more solid structure than a square anyway. Even with just three kings, the Poison Legion would be fine. Obsidian knew that wasn't an argument he was going to win, though, so instead he let out a soft grunt.

"I can't move," he rasped.

Having already changed her clothes, Cassia quietly explained, "Phong, when Liet Than took the Storm Pearl, it damaged your organs and your chi. Falling off that cliff added even more damage. Your body was badly wounded, it'll take you a while to recover."

Obsidian gritted his teeth.

"Liet Than..."

Ivy scowled.

"Phong, when you recover, we'll go kill Liet Than!"

Obsidian's chi had been decimated by the strike that rid him of the Pearl. His chi had almost been entirely wiped out, and many of his bones were broken in the fall. Cassia had soaked him in medicine for many, many days, performing acupuncture nearly continuously. Obsidian tried to gather his chi, only to notice that it seemed like someone else had used their own chi to help supplement his own—like a ceramic vase being shattered and repaired in the same blow.

It wasn't an energy that belonged to Cassia or Ivy.

"Phong...with the destructive nature of the Storm Pearl, you really shouldn't have survived. But the moment the Pearl was withdrawn, someone used...some kind of technique to heal your chi instantly. Do you know who it was?"

"Liet Than," Obsidian murmured. His tone was no longer angry, it was astonished.

"Liet Than?"

Ivy and Cassia's eyes both widened. Why would Liet Than attack *and* heal Obsidian?

"The Sunlight Strike," Obsidian realized. "Liet Than struck me with the Sunlight Strike to take the Pearl." At the time, Liet Than had been right beneath him. He could have used any attack he liked to kill Obsidian, but instead he'd chosen to use the Sunlight Strike.

Whatever Liet Than was up to, he was no simple man...

———

No simple man indeed!

Dong Tu worriedly listened to Liet Than's heartbeat, checked his breathing—she even used her own chi to examine his. His body had gone soft as vermicelli, but his lack of internal chi was the same as it always was. Just when Dong Tu was sure Liet Than was going to die, he opened his eyes with a smile.

"You're worried about me!" Liet Than pointed out triumphantly. Dong Tu pushed him away, and he rolled to the side and continued to roll dramatically for *way* too long. Once he'd gotten bored, he got up, wiped the sweat from his forehead, and pulled Dong Tu closer, using her own sleeve to wipe his face.

"Dong Tu, I've suffered a lot of pain because of you. You'll have to promise to remember me for the rest of your life."

Dong Tu, however, hadn't gotten past her own astonishment.

"Did you just give me your fragment of the Sunlight Pearl?!"

Liet Than nodded. His face genuinely had gone paler, his health fading, though she didn't know how far it would go. While kissing Dong Tu, he'd used the Sunlight Strike to separate the fragment from himself and give it to her instead. It meant Dong Tu would be able to withstand any poison—including the particularly lethal cocktail that suffused Obsidian's skin.

"Will you be okay without it?" Dong Tu went on, concerned, and pleased satisfaction returned to Liet Than's face.

"Are you afraid I'll die? Are you worried about me?"

Rather than sass back at him, Dong Tu silently bowed her head and clung tightly to Liet Than's hand. Obsidian held an irreplaceable spot in Dong Tu's heart, but Liet Than was there too. It wasn't in the way he wanted, but he was still there, and he wasn't replaceable, either.

Liet Than leaned over and pulled Dong Tu into a proper hug. He'd take what he could get, and being Dong Tu's brother wasn't so bad...he was disappointed, but even he couldn't have the whole world. Some things were simply untouchable.

"Do you really think I'd risk my life for you?" Liet Than hid his disappointment with his usual humor. "What, do you think I'm as stupid as Obsidian?"

"You're okay, thanks to the Sunlight Strike."

Liet Than studied Dong Tu lovingly. Thanks to her, Obsidian was alive, Dong Tu had her own fragment of the Sunlight Pearl, and he had the Storm Pearl. All because of the Sunlight Strike. That day in the Luu Dojo, what felt like an eternity before, Dong Tu had done what many a master could not: she had taught him something useful. She hadn't known what the technique could be used for; the nature of the move wasn't helpful in a usual fight, not when it was neither a killer nor a cure. But he'd learned nonetheless.

Liet Than had chuckled silently to himself while reading through the technique. Use of the Sunlight Strike required profound levels of chi to achieve its full potential. Only those on the level of the Monstrous Eighteen at the very least could even hope to learn it properly, evidently; even the powerful Ryujin had misunderstood its complexities.

The reason it hadn't made any sense upon first glance was because one had to understand how the Pearls had come into being in the first place, and how they'd been used in the beginning, when they'd both been whole. The Sunlight and Storm Pearls had been created using the combined might of a couple that had ruled the Whispered World three centuries before. They had been called the Queen of the Sun and the

King of the Moon, the creators of the Lunisolar Scriptures, and the Sunlight Strike was among the many powerful moves they had developed. The reason for its existence was simple: both Pearls worked by binding themselves to the person who carried them, and once swallowed, it was almost impossible to separate the carrier from their Pearl. The Sunlight Pearl was far more benign in nature, so it was possible for its carrier to survive the separation.

But the Storm Pearl was different.

The Storm Pearl was cold, strong, and malignant, and so the pair had developed the Sunlight Strike so that both Pearls could be utilized and shared safely.

The Sunlight Strike had four steps, and when used by someone with the proper level of skill, they followed a certain pattern:

First the Pearls were safely expelled from the body. The Storm Pearl couldn't just be taken by force or else it would do irreparable damage, but the Sunlight Strike could separate the energies while minimizing any damage to the body.

Second, no matter how skillful the separation was, the Sunlight Strike would inevitably cause internal damage. It was just the nature of the move. So the second step was to heal the wounds to the muscles, blood vessels, and internal organs.

Third was to heal the damage to the bearer's chi. The longer the person carried their Pearl, the more damage would be done to them.

The last step was to help restore the deficit of internal chi caused by the removal of the Pearl.

If those four steps were performed correctly, the users of the Pearls could swap, swallow, and repeat without losing their life; but it required so much energy to perform the full set that only those over a certain level of knowledge and power could use it safely and effectively. Liet Than had used all four steps successfully, separating his fragment of the Sunlight Pearl so that he could pass it along to Dong Tu. He'd only rolled around for the sake of being dramatic, since using the strike to remove the Sunlight Pearl itself was as easy as swallowing the fragment and spitting it back out again.

And he *had* chosen to use the Sunlight Strike to retrieve the Storm Pearl, rather than using any other skill that would have torn Obsidian to pieces. He'd chosen to save Obsidian's life at the expense of his own chi. The difference was that when he'd stolen the Pearl, Liet Than had only used the first three steps of the Sunlight Strike. He'd omitted the fourth and left Obsidian to fall, knowing that Obsidian wouldn't die, and that his injuries would have been inevitable no matter what.

"Having done that much, I don't regret letting him fall over the cliff," Liet Than pointed out. He'd been in the midst of a battle with his romantic rival, and had helped him more than Obsidian could have guessed. Letting him fall had just been Liet Than's way of putting Obsidian in his place. The younger man could crawl out on his own! Besides, Obsidian was one of the Monstrous Eighteen; as long as he wasn't killed or entirely disabled, he'd recover his own chi eventually.

"You weren't trying to kill Phong in the first place?" Dong Tu asked.

Kill.

It wasn't that Liet Than hadn't wanted to. In his mind he wanted to take Obsidian out, the sooner the better, the more tragic the better. He'd wanted to kill Obsidian since the night Dong Tu had gotten drunk and mistaken him for the other man...but when the universe had practically handed him to Liet Than on a silver platter, he'd hesitated.

"All because of you, Dong Tu," Liet Than continued, not answering Dong Tu's question. Parodying Dong Tu's accusations from before, he teased, "All this time, I've only stayed by your side to secretly learn the Sunlight Strike!"

Dong Tu laughed wetly, and tears brimmed right at the edges of her lashes. She tugged Liet Than into a tight, overjoyed embrace, and Liet Than reluctantly hugged her back—just so that she would lean her head on his shoulder when she inevitably began to cry out loud. He really was happy for Dong Tu, in his heart...but it was a heart that had been broken to pieces.

Suddenly Liet Than's own eyes filled with tears, and the tears began to roll steadily down his cheeks. He began to cry just as loudly, if not louder, his broad shoulders shaking; he couldn't kill Obsidian, and he couldn't have Dong Tu, and it was a pain he almost couldn't take.

"Dong Tu, am I not enough for you?" Liet Than sobbed, secretly hoping Dong Tu wouldn't answer. Dong Tu hugged him tightly, caressing his hair as she comforted him.

"Oh, my dear...there is no little brother in this world better than you."

CHAPTER 18

Dancing Snowflakes

Summer passed into autumn. The ground was gilded with golden leaves, while bare branches rustled and swayed against steely blue skies. Autumn brought cool relief after the sweltering heat of summer to everywhere except Hoa Hon Palace. It was as oppressively hot as always, constantly filled with curling columns of incense smoke, and sweat dripped down Obsidian's face drop by drop as he sat and soaked in the medicine bath. Ivy sat beside him, quietly reading a scroll to herself.

"...'Exchange your life for Dong Tu's. If you fight back, I will kill her,'" Ivy recited softly. Cassia leaned forward, frowning curiously.

"What is that?"

"A challenge letter from Liet Than," Ivy replied darkly. She was unlikely to ever forgive the other man. Or Dong Tu, for that matter. Obsidian perked up seriously.

"When did it come?"

"Probably about two months ago," Ivy told him, her expression shifting into a displeased pout at the way Obsidian's attention had instantly shifted. Liet Than had sent the letter at least two months before, but Ivy hadn't bothered to open it. It was no surprise that despite her superb fighting skills, Ivy's reputation within the Whispered World was...not good: if someone sent a letter rather than showing up in person to challenge her, they would end up waiting in vain for her on the day of their duel, their letter still unopened.

Obsidian reached for the letter, and strained everything he had trying to stand up. He instead stumbled out of the tub and onto the floor, demanding, "Give it to me! I have to go!"

Cassia and Ivy rolled their eyes as they watched, but as he struggled to get his feet under him their faces lit up.

"Oh, your chi has begun to recover!"

They both began to chatter happily about his progress, and two months after the proposed date and time for the duel, Hoa Hon Palace finally replied to the letter.

Liet Than hurled the responding letter at the ceiling after he read it, and it exploded into pieces by itself.

The day has finally come.

Just as he'd expected, Obsidian had survived. But the dadao Obsidian carried when he arrived at Thanh Liet Cave for their exchange made Liet Than do a double-take: it wasn't a weapon he had known the other man could use. Long, flared, and curved, the single-edged sword was new, and it was not the kind of blade a man carried into battle unless he came for *blood*. The dadao was almost as tall as Obsidian himself, and the pure fury in Obsidian's every step made it clear that while he'd come in peace as agreed, if things went sideways and Dong Tu got hurt? He'd raze Thanh Liet Cave to the ground and take Liet Than's pretty head as a trophy in retribution.

It was enough to make Liet Than wonder if Obsidian had come with his own deadly tricks up his sleeve.

"Liet Than, are you sure fighting Obsidian is a good idea? You don't have the Sunlight Pearl shard anymore," Dong Tu said, her voice heavy with concern. She didn't want the two of them to fight, no matter who might win: on one side would be Obsidian, and on the other, her beloved brother Luu Dong Trung.

Liet Than nonchalantly waved off her concern.

"Do you really think the King of Poison could even get one hit in now?" he asked, smirking. Liet Than would have been more cautious had Obsidian still carried the Storm Pearl; but Obsidian was recovering from injuries that would have killed anyone else, and Liet Than was now the bearer of the Storm Pearl. Everyone knew who was going to win that fight.

"Obsidian's biggest advantage is still his own skin," Dong Tu pointed out. Liet Than looked up and eyed her skeptically.

"Do you really think I don't have a piece of the Sunlight Pearl anymore?"

Dong Tu blinked in confusion. He'd already given her a fragment of the Sunlight Pearl! Did he have another?

Ugh, why do these two have to fight each other?! Dong Tu thought frustratedly.

The day of the duel had finally come, with all parties finally in the know, and several unexpected additions also showed up: as it turned out, not only had Obsidian come to Thanh Liet Cave for the fight over Dong Tu, but Tuong Y Ve, Ivy, and Cassia had too.

"Aren't I popular," Liet Than laughed amusedly. "And why has everyone decided to come for a visit, if I may ask?"

"Dong Tu!"

"I came for the Storm Pearl!"

Obsidian and Tuong Y Ve's answers came at once, their words overlapping. Obsidian's answer was expected, but Tuong Y Ve's was a surprise: the last time he'd fought Obsidian, he hadn't bothered to bring poisonous weapons when he'd assumed he'd be dealing with someone they had no effect on, and had been forced to retreat from Liet Than. This time he was determined to use every weapon and poisonous advantage in his arsenal to fight Liet Than and repay his insult.

Tuong Y Ve turned and glared at Obsidian.

"What perfect timing. After I take the Storm Pearl, I'm going to finish you off!" Tuong Y Ve threatened, but the only response he got from Obsidian was a smirk: Obsidian's eyes were fixed on Dong Tu, standing there beside Liet Than, and he would not be distracted.

From across the cave, Liet Than narrowed his eyes at the sight of Obsidian's pale face. He realized Obsidian's injuries from being robbed of the Storm Pearl hadn't healed, yet there Obsidian stood, prepared to fight both Liet Than and Tuong Y Ve. Once again ready to gamble with his own life in the process. Liet Than wondered if Obsidian had charged out to save Dong Tu the moment he could stand, or if, despite his injuries, he was actually capable of defeating *the* Lam Liet Than at his most powerful.

That imposing sword did give Liet Than pause, but he still had doubts. In top form, healthy and in possession of the Storm Pearl, Obsidian might have been on par with him. But not like this. Not when he had just recovered from a long paralysis, and was taking his first wobbly steps back out into the Whispered World like a newborn foal. Had he always been this reckless with his own life? This wasn't even the first time Obsidian had sacrificed himself to protect Dong Tu in three months!

"These two are disgusting," Liet Than muttered jealously to himself. "I've been stuck in this sappy love story for half a year and I'm not even the hero. *Tragic.*"

Hero or not, it wasn't in Liet Than's nature to be commanded and dominated by others. He pretended to be weak and inferior as a joke to tease clueless people, and considered it shameful to call himself Lam Liet Than when he wasn't acting majestically enough to fit the part. Liet Than flicked his long hair imperiously, his sparkling earrings swinging, and turned to Tuong Y Ve in a manner that bordered on flirtatious.

"Tuong Y Ve! I know we've confronted each other a few times in the past, but you unfortunately only had the chance to meet Luu Dong Trung, not Liet Than. Consider this our official introduction!" He turned and inclined his head politely to Obsidian.

"Phong, if you wouldn't mind, I'd like to start this little duel first!"

Liet Than flew toward Tuong Y Ve like lightning the moment the words left his mouth. Tuong Y Ve kicked at him, but it was immediately parried by a swirling shield of Liet Than's ice-white snowflakes. The snowflakes continued to act as extensions of Liet Than's body, forming icy, impenetrable currents to defend from Tuong Y Ve's palm strikes; his hair blew fetchingly in the wind as they surrounded him and formed two giant white wings that reflected the sunlight. They made him look like a giant white bird hovering in the air.

With the combined powers of his own chi and the Storm Pearl, every move Lam Liet Than made became surreal and mesmerizing.

Meanwhile Tuong Y Ve countered by releasing poison after poison into the air: the Poison Legion utilized countless forms and variations, and Tuong Y Ve was releasing both toxic vapors and poisonous powders. They managed to penetrate Liet Than's wall of chi, but strangely Liet Than remained as unbothered as a turtle sunning itself on a log. He still smoothed his hair just as calmly, still kept his chin up arrogantly, and his lips did not lose their ever-present smirk.

The more Tuong Y Ve attacked, the closer he came to losing the fight, and the more aggressive Liet Than became. It all came to a head when Liet Than stalked forward, seized Tuong Y Ve by the throat, and lifted him into the air with one bare hand.

The longer Dong Tu watched, the more relentlessly her concern for Liet Than twisted in her stomach. Hadn't he already given her his shard of the Sunlight Pearl? Shouldn't touching Tuong Y Ve be lethal?

But Liet Than didn't flinch. He channeled his exasperation at Obsidian into fighting Tuong Y Ve, his eyes gleaming with violent fury; on a normal day, he was either calm or mischievous, but when he fought his expressions turned ice cold and eerily, imposingly demonic.

Slowly choking, Tuong Y Ve waved his hand in surrender.

"I—I surrender—!" he forced out. "The Storm Pearl is yours!"

The wicked gleam in Liet Than's eyes subsided almost instantly, and his murderous smirk turned to one of triumph.

"Of course it is. You should have known that before you came here. From now on the Storm Pearl is *mine, only* mine, *forever* mine! Forever!" He released Tuong Y Ve, who stumbled backwards, coughing and gasping for air. Despite his win, Liet Than was still frustrated, and he glanced at Obsidian as he turned to the others. "Who else wants to try me? Or is it your turn now, Obsidian?"

Obsidian calmly opened his hand in front of his face.

"Liet Than, return Dong Tu to me."

Liet Than could sense that not even Obsidian's *hand* had recovered from his internal injuries, his chi still weak—and his other hand, the one clutching the handle of his dadao, was trembling. Liet Than merely blinked, and a sweeping wave of energy washed over Obsidian. Obsidian gathered as much of his own chi as he could to resist it, and it was in that moment that Liet Than understood just how little Obsidian had been able to recover, yet. He looked like a man ready to fight, but he didn't even have a tenth of his usual power.

Even if Liet Than won, if he fought Obsidian in that condition he'd be humiliating himself. Obsidian might have wanted to risk his life for Dong Tu's, but he could have at least considered his rival's honor!

Liet Than's anger finally broke, giving way to sympathy. He and Obsidian had as many similarities as they had differences, and their greatest common thread was how deeply they both loved their small, fiercely protective Dong Tu. Standing there, across from Obsidian, a man fully prepared to die...Liet Than knew the rumors were all true. For this *one* girl, Obsidian would risk it all.

Where they *differed* was in their want of power.

Liet Than wanted Dong Tu *and* the Storm Pearl. He wanted everything; Obsidian only wanted Dong Tu. And while Liet Than *wanted* everything...he knew he couldn't have it. He couldn't have both, and it was because of the agony of his heartbreak that he suddenly understood Obsidian's anxiety.

He couldn't see Obsidian as a rival anymore. Not when he felt an oddly brotherly sympathy for him. Hiding his thoughts, Liet Than smiled.

"Phong...you should go. You won't be able to beat me today," he said softly. Obsidian didn't budge, his hand clenching more tightly around the handle of his sword.

"Liet Than, return Dong Tu to me," he charged, his voice unchanged. Liet Than opened his mouth just a little, like he was going to speak, and then darted toward Dong Tu. He wrapped her up from behind and held her like that, front to back.

"But Phong, who keeps your Dong Tu?" Liet Than asked disapprovingly, mischief in his gaze. A flash of surprise shot across Obsidian's tense face, and Liet Than began to walk he and Dong Tu slowly across the cave. He kept Dong Tu tight to his body, and snow began to swirl around them once more, forming another pair of wings behind Liet Than. The wings stretched out wide, and then curled forward around Dong Tu and Liet Than protectively.

Liet Than squeezed Dong Tu close to him, and bent to whisper in her ear.

"My dear sister, Dong Tu...are you sure you want Obsidian? I have the Storm Pearl now, not him. I'm the great Lam Liet Than. Do you really want to leave me for Obsidian?"

Dong Tu nodded, her eyes meeting Obsidian's on the other side of the snowy wings.

Liet Than managed to hold her tighter, and lowered his head enough to kiss her neck.

"Dong Tu, I'm asking you one last time. Don't make a decision you'll regret."

Again she nodded, her eyes still fixed on Obsidian's figure across the space.

Liet Than opened his heart one last time, desperately searching for a miracle, and when he spoke again his voice was thick with tears.

"Dong Tu, if we were in another world, and you and I had met each other first, would you love me the way you love Obsidian?"

Dong Tu didn't answer. She blinked a hazy mist out of her eyes.

"If we were in another world, and you and I had met each other first, would you love me, or Obsidian?" Liet Than tried again. He didn't move to release her; he couldn't force himself to let her go. All the regret in the world was wrapped up in that single word: *if.*

Luu Dong Tu, I am the snow. Will you keep winter?

Dong Tu was jarred back to reality then, and threw a sharp look at Liet Than.

"Stop fooling around, let me go," she snapped. Liet Than blinked, then pouted. He kissed her on the cheek one last time before loosening his grip, and Dong Tu ran straight for Obsidian.

In that second Liet Than shed his wicked, mischievous air and let his true feelings show: he was a heartbroken young man who'd just lost his first love. It was only evident for a moment, and then Liet Than pulled himself together, his expression smoothing back out into his usual aloof nothingness. The only remnant was a tear sliding down his left cheek, which formed into a snowflake and flew behind Dong Tu as she moved further and further away from him.

The closer Dong Tu came, the more Obsidian began to relax. The wrinkles above his eyebrows gradually smoothed back out, and the acidic expression that seeing Liet Than holding Dong Tu so tightly had caused was fading. The death grip he had on the handle of the dadao began to loosen, and it was a miracle that he could hear her heart pounding above the sound of his own. He could sense her aura more and more clearly the closer she came.

It was not the same as it had been just two months before.

The only person who could hide their chi properly was Liet Than. The only person who could hide the aura of the Sunlight Pearl itself was Liet Than. Dong Tu most certainly could not, and Obsidian could feel the warmth of its energy emanating from her body as she ran toward him. His face didn't change, but the murderous energy disappeared, and those thick-lashed eyes crinkled with a smile.

Liet Than snapped his fingers, and a stream of snowflakes began to trail Dong Tu. They shot straight at Obsidian, and he didn't bother to defend himself: instead he let his sword fall to the ground with a loud clatter and walked through the snow to meet her, letting the river of snowflakes rip at his clothes and gloves as a single tear escaped down his cheek.

They both seemed *radiant*, beaming happily at each other without breaking their gazes, and as soon as Dong Tu came close enough she leapt into his arms. Obsidian caught her, wrapped her up, and lifted her off her feet with the force of his hug. He reached hesitantly for her face, his fingers trembling as the rips in his gloves left bare skin to brush against bare skin. After years of separation, they could finally feel the warmth of the other's skin without fear.

Chest to chest, their hearts seeming to beat as one, Dong Tu and Obsidian wrapped their arms around each other and their lips touched. It was the first time Dong Tu had truly kissed Obsidian and been able to feel just how sweet his kiss was.

Snowflakes continued to flutter and fly all around them, and unbeknownst to the ecstatic couple, some were formed from Liet Than's own tears as he watched them reunite.

Opposite Liet Than, another beauty was shedding silent tears. Keeping her face down, Cassia wiped her cheeks and turned to Tuong Y Ve.

"Congratulations, King of Poison. It's time to return to the Legion and carry out your ceremony!"

"What do you mean?" Tuong Y Ve asked, surprised.

"Obsidian is dead. You killed him. Who else but you will succeed him?"

"Is Obsidian not standing right there, alive?!" Ivy interjected, not understanding, and Cassia gave her a pinch. Tuong Y Ve, however, had understood. He made a grand gesture.

"I, King of Poison in the north, hope that you two will protect this secret." Tuong Y Ve then sighed with relief: he had lost the battle, but won the war. The title of Poison King would be his. Cassia smiled.

"I'll carry it to my grave."

"Obsidian's been as good as dead since the day he drank all those poisons in exchange for Dong Tu's antidotes," Ivy agreed, finally understanding what was going on, and then proceeded to pout. The three of them turned to leave, but Cassia tossed one more sad glance over her shoulder.

"Farewell, Phong," she murmured softly.

On the opposite side, Liet Than also turned away.

"Farewell, Dong Tu," he murmured.

"Liet Than!" Dong Tu called loudly, stopping him. "Without your fragment of the Sunlight Pearl, will you be all right?" She hadn't forgotten that he'd just breathed and soaked in all of those toxins from his fight with Tuong Y Ve, and besides that, how was he supposed to resist the Storm Pearl's consuming energy without it?

A half-hearted smile twisted Liet Than's lips.

"Don't worry. It was just a fragment, and it's not the only one in the world." Liet Than paused and turned to face Dong Tu more fully, and his expression was sincere when he looked her in the eye—even if it was also laced with sadness.

"Be happy, sister."

And, like a snowflake dissolving in the sun, Liet Than jumped into the air and vanished.

Cold wind swept the last of the dry, brittle leaves off of a tiled roof. It belonged to the home of the magistrate of the Thanh Liet district, and a sign beside the entrance was engraved with the family name: Tuyet Hoa. The magistrate, Mr. Tuyet Hoa, poured himself a cup of tea and sat sipping it where he could look out over the courtyard. His two eldest sons were practicing martial arts in the pleasantly chilly weather, and seven beautiful women dressed all in white stood waiting in two rows, bows in hand and arrows on the strings.

Inside the house, Bach Duong lifted his cup of tea and nodded at Mr. Tuyet Hoa with a pleasant, "Cheers."

"I wonder...what wind has brought you to my humble house today, Mr. Bach?" The old man asked. He assumed that Bach Duong, the son of a great general, wouldn't pay a visit just to say hello and have a cup of tea—but that really was all Bach Duong had on his mind. His beautiful eyes widened and he nodded as he set his tea down.

"Quite a while ago, I had the chance to meet Miss Tuyet Hoa. I was passing by and wanted to give my regards. I do apologize, I meant to visit sooner, but I was mistakenly informed that your residence was in Lac Do, and didn't realize you were here instead until recently."

Mr. Tuyet Hoa was startled at the mention of 'Miss Tuyet Hoa' and the notion that Bach Duong had been 'mistakenly informed.' He choked on his tea, which came pouring out of his nose, and deftly covered his mouth so that Bach Duong wouldn't see his friendliness become anger. It couldn't be anyone but that brat, Tuyet Hoa Phi Vu!

Bach Duong didn't seem to notice the other man choking, and leisurely continued.

"Actually, I was very happy to learn that your family doesn't live in Lac Do. Almost a year ago, a massacre occurred at a restaurant called Snowflake Tower. I went there at once, worrying your family might be involved, but fortunately it was just a coincidence."

"W-what—why was there a massacre?" Mr. Tuyet Hoa stammered. Bach Duong calmly prepared to explain the affairs of the Whispered World to a man he assumed had no knowledge of it.

"It had been a battle for a fragment of a treasure called the Sunlight Pearl."

"S-Sunlight Pearl?" Mr. Tuyet Hoa repeated, and hoped the way his hands began to tremble would go unnoticed.

"Yes, the Sunlight Pearl. There are two magic pearls that the people of the Whispered World are always seeking: the Storm Pearl and the Sunlight Pearl. The Sunlight Pearl was shattered into many fragments a long time ago, but every single shard is invaluable, and almost impossible to find. Someone put an open invitation out into the Whispered World, offering a fragment of the Pearl in exchange for knowledge of a secret martial arts technique, and a battle broke out between everyone who came. Very few of them survived," Bach Duong elaborated, innocently unaware of how much meaning the other man really gleaned from his words.

"So you were there? Did you see anyone with the fragment?" Mr. Tuyet Hoa asked, purposely keeping his tone mild and curious.

"Well, everyone came because they thought it was the Storm Pearl. It turned out some man brought a fragment of the Sunlight Pearl there, a dispute arose, and that man was killed. It all went to pieces after that, and the fragment fell into the hands of two masked men," Bach Duong replied, his gaze having shifted off to one side as he remembered. Both men had been tall and slender. One had worn his hair long, and the other wore his short, but just long enough to cover most of his eyes. It had been impossible to make out their features behind their masks.

While everyone else was focused on killing each other, the two men calmly flew over to the corpse of the man who'd brought the fragment of the Sunlight Pearl. The others surrounded the pair when they finally noticed, but they had been protected by some mysterious, invisible circle of energy that no one could touch. The long-haired man had retrieved the fragment, and lifted the mask just enough to slip it into his mouth.

After that, the two of them escaped out the door and flew away.

Bach Duong had chased after them; the long-haired man had seemed familiar, but Bach Duong couldn't remember why. It had ended up as quite a lovely spectacle, with three people running through the treetops on such a bright, moonlit night.

The short-haired man had eventually started to turn and fight Bach Duong, but the long-haired man had taken his hand and turned him back in the direction they'd been running. The short-haired man tried again, stopping on a tree with apparent impatience. The long-haired man gripped his shoulder again, and he and Bach Duong had glared at each other. Beneath the moonlight and the clouds that floated across its ivory face, Bach Duong still couldn't recognize the other man, but he knew in his bones that they had met before.

Bach Duong took the bow off his shoulder and fired an arrow at them, but the arrow didn't even reach the two men: the long-haired man waved his hand, and the arrow dissolved into dust and blew away with the wind. Once again the short-haired man tried to fight back, gathering his chi into a ball of wind, but the long-haired man made a gesture that stopped him.

"Let's go. That one's getting drunk at the inn, I want to see how she is," he'd softly said, and the other man tossed the ball of wind half-heartedly away from him. They both vanished, and as the partially-formed attack swept by him, Bach Duong realized it was time to stop his pursuit.

"The man with the long hair must be one of the Monstrous Eighteen. His chi was extraordinary. I hope he's not from one of the darker places in the Whispered World....At least the Sunlight Pearl's nature is not harmful for humans, so it should be okay," Bach Duong finished. Mr. Tuyet Hoa pretended to take a sip of tea, lifting his cup to give him a moment to collect his thoughts. He knew who the two masked men were from the description alone: they would be Tuyet Hoa Phi Vu and Ly Minh Lam.

Strange, he thought. *Tuyet Hoa Phi Vu already has a fragment of the Sunlight Pearl. Why would he need another? What is he up to?*

It was possible that all Tuyet Hoa Phi Vu wanted was to spend his life collecting treasure, but with *that* son, Mr. Tuyet Hoa just never knew.

"Sir," Bach Duong began, interrupting the older man's thoughts. "Where is Miss Tuyet Hoa right now?"

Mr. Tuyet Hoa shook his head with a sigh, unsure of how to explain. He too had been wondering where his stubborn youngest son had wandered off to for a long, long time. Their family should have been content with two sons.

The sky was still blue outside, but wind began to blow as if a storm was rolling in. It was still early winter, and yet suddenly thousands of crisp white snowflakes filled the air, fluttering and swirling as if in a dance. They sparkled in the lingering sunlight like thousands of hovering crystals, and everyone in the courtyard looked up in awe.

"The first snow is always so beautiful..."

"Mr. Bach, perhaps you should stay with us for a few days," Mr. Tuyet Hoa offered, and Bach Duong nodded politely.

"That would be wonderful! Thank you for your hospitality!"

Mr. Tuyet Hoa had his servants prepare a meal and bring out a chess set. His family's daily life was peaceful; he and Bach Duong played chess, drank tea, and discussed all sorts of things—and most importantly, they left the affairs of the Whispered World outside.

That first snow showered all the gardens of the Tuyet Hoa residence. Thousands upon thousands of snowflakes, a sight so splendid it could move even the hardest heart. And no one in the house, not even Mr. Tuyet Hoa and Bach Duong, knew that the Whispered World now had a new master, whose every footstep was accompanied by sparkling white snowflakes.

A beautiful master, calling himself *Tuyet Hoa Phi Vu Dong Trung Lam Liet Than*—

Dancing snowflakes in the middle of a frigid winter.

(THE END)

AUTHOR'S NOTE

As much as we tried, not every nuance translates between English and Vietnamese. Vietnamese is a complex language in which a single word can have multiple meanings, depending on changes in spoken tone and pronunciation. Many of the characters' names and titles were carefully chosen in order to create a colorful wordplay that added both depth and levity in the original Vietnamese version of this series. This includes Liet Than's many names, and the speculation surrounding their meanings that becomes so integral to *Frigid's* plot.

With that in mind, we'd love to provide some background on Liet Than's title.

His official title is Lam Liet Than. Used within the full title, the word 'liet' means fearsome, legendary, majestic, epic, or savage. 'Liet', however, is phonetically spelled the same as the words used for paralysis, stiff...and erectile dysfunction. When those in the Whispered World call him Liet Than instead of using his full title, they are absolutely making a joke.

The word 'liet' also has another meaning. When used in the name Thanh Liet Lake, it means frigid, freezing cold, a clear cup of wine, and crystal clear water—all of which were used to describe Tuyet Hoa Phi Vu throughout the book.

Liet Than starts off his career in the Whispered World by calling himself Lam Liet Than, the Legendary/Majestic/Fearsome God. However, because of the way he fights—which doesn't involve martial arts—the Whispered World began to mock him, referring to him as Liet Than, the Paralyzed/Stiff/Crippled God. The humiliation is what drives him to find the legendary Storm Pearl, to build the aesthetic techniques he eventually masters and reclaim his reputation.

But by the time he masters his signature techniques, his confidence and state of mind have also grown, and he finds he doesn't mind the mockery anymore. Because of his love for Luu Dong Tu (which means 'the girl who keeps winter'), he not only decides to embrace the joke, but to keep the memory of her name (winter) in his title, choosing to let 'liet' stand for 'frigid winter.'

Printed in Great Britain
by Amazon